Judge Jackie Martin's job is to impose order on the most chaotic families in New York City. So how is she blindsided when the man she loves walks out on her?

Jackie Martin is a woman whose intelligence and ambition have earned her a coveted position as a judge on the Manhattan Family Court—and left her lonely at age 39. When she meets Lou Greenberg, Jackie thinks she's finally found someone who will accept her exactly as she is. But when Lou's own issues, including an unresolved yearning for his ex-wife, make him bolt without explanation, Jackie must finally put herself under the same microscope as the people she judges. When their worlds collide in Jackie's courtroom, she learns that sometimes love's greatest gift is opening you up to love others.

Praise for Both Are True

"In this moving novel, Gentin examines what it means to start over at a time in life when most people seem to have it 'figured out.' As Jackie and Lou try to move on without each other, they are forced to reexamine all their choices— with surprising consequences."—*Nicola Kraus, bestselling co-author of The Nanny Diaries*

"Gentin's flowing, provocative, and descriptive style will draw you in to this fascinating sneak peek behind the scenes of life as a New York City Family Court judge. A unique take on the age-old question of whether a career woman can balance her professional life and find peace in her personal life."—*Lainey Cameron, Award-winning author of The Exit Strategy*

"A thought-provoking legal drama, *Both Are True* asks hard questions and wholly engages the reader."—*Sally Koslow, author of Another Side of Paradise*

"Poignant and funny, *Both Are True* is simultaneously a compassionate tribute to the complexity of family life in New York City and an intimate portrait of one unlikely couple—a love story you'll think about long after you turn the last page." *—Elyssa Friedland, author of Last Summer At The Golden Hotel*

"Reyna Marder Gentin writes compelling women's fiction with just the right blend of romance. *Both Are True* is the moving story of two lovers at a crossroads, and if you're anything like me, you'll be rooting on these perfectly flawed characters. Gentin captures the subtle nuances of relationships and what it means to open ourselves to others. Fans of legal thrillers will appreciate the courtroom drama, a testament to Gentin's years practicing law, and I, for one, appreciated the quick wit throughout. I'm a fan. Brava, Reyna!"*--Rochelle Weinstein, bestselling author of This Is Not How It Ends.*

"Gentin deftly weaves a story of a complicated relationship with fascinating legal insight, exploring themes of parenting, love, and all the difficulties and nuances involved with both."*—Susie Orman Schnall, author of We Came Here to Shine*

"The youngest judge on the bench must decide: love vs. love of the law. A compelling page-turner by Reyna Marder Gentin. *Both Are True* is way too good to be legal! Enjoyed this book from start to finish."*—Marilyn Simon Rothstein, award-winning author of Lift and Separate*

"Reyna Marder Gentin brings her steady literary hand and legal background to this heartfelt story of second chances, being human, and (not) having it all. A compelling drama laced with loves lost and loves found, *Both Are True* is women's fiction ripe for book club discussion."*—Jennifer Klepper, USA Today bestselling author of Unbroken Threads*

BOTH ARE TRUE

Reyna Marder Gentin

Moonshine Cove Publishing, LLC
Abbeville, South Carolina U.S.A.
First Moonshine Cove Edition June 2021

ISBN: 9781952439100

Library of Congress LCCN: 2021909530

Cover Design by Rachel Thompson and interior design by Moonshine Cove staff

In the fall of 2014, Reyna left her practice as a criminal appellate attorney with a nonprofit public defender's office where she'd worked for many years. It was time to try something new. What began as a lark when a friend asked

Reyna to join her in a writing class at The Writing Institute at Sarah Lawrence College has turned into her passion.

Reyna's first novel, a romantic legal thriller entitled *Unreasonable Doubts,* was published by She Writes Press in 2018 and was named a finalist in the Women's Fiction Writers Association Star Award for debut fiction. William Landay, bestselling author of *Defending Jacob,* called the novel "an intriguing blend of romance and legal suspense from a new writer to watch."

In 2021, Reyna took a foray into children's literature. TouchPoint Press published her middle grade novel *My Name Is Layla*, which features a dyslexic protagonist and is a story about resilience and empathy. *My Name Is Layla* is for young readers -- and for all readers -- who are inspired by the idea of a kinder world. School Library Journal said "Layla's struggles at school and home are authentically depicted and readers who face their own challenges will relate."

With *Both Are True,* Reyna has returned to contemporary fiction, the law, and New York City. If you love these three as much as she does, this novel is for you.

Reyna is married to Pierre Gentin, whom she's known since her high school days on Long Island. Their two children, Ariella and Micah, are the light of their lives.

.

reynamardergentin.com

Other Works

Unreasonable Doubts, She Writes Press, 2018

My Name Is Layla, TouchPoint Press, 2021

Short stories: *The Duck*, The Blue Nib, Issue 40, 2020

Saving Grace, The Write Launch, Issue 33, 2020

A Journey Down the Aisle, The Write Launch, Issue 14, 2018

Complicity, The Write Launch, Issue 9, 2017

A Reckoning, The Westchester Review, Volume 9, 2017

Acknowledgments

Thank you to Gene Robinson and everyone at Moonshine Cove Publishing for giving me the opportunity to share Jackie and Lou's story. Thank you Rachel Thompson for the beautiful artwork for the cover of the book. A big shout out to Ann-Marie Nieves at GetRed Pr for her tremendous work, as well as to Suzy Leopold for her friendship and dedication to so many authors.

I began working on *Both Are True* in a wonderful workshop at The Writing Institute at Sarah Lawrence College in the summers of 2018 and 2019. The class, "Five Days, 10,000 words" was a grueling and exhilarating experience led by fellow Moonshine Cove author Steve Lewis. The premise was simple: get something on the page. Don't edit, and don't judge yourself. Come to class and get support and critique from your fellow writing warriors. I want to thank Steve and my classmates for their encouragement and guidance: Sheila Berenson, Lynn Edelson, Michelle Gewanter, Vladimir Klimenko, Nan Mutnick, Elise Pollack, Dvora Rabino, and Jessica Rao. An extra special thanks to Dvora, who, long after the workshop was over, generously read the manuscript as I continued to work on it and made invaluable comments with kindness.

Much appreciation also goes to yet another teacher and workshop at The Writing Institute, Marcia Bradley's advanced novel class. Although it's always a bit frightening to subject oneself to the discerning focus of other writers, nothing improves a novel more than honest critique. Thank you to Marcia and all of the women in the workshop, whose opinions I value tremendously: Julie Goodale, Ellen Hopkins, Lori McLaughlin, Jennifer Tulchin, and Andrea Weinstein.

One of the great surprises and pleasures of writing has been becoming a part of a community, learning to give to and receive support from people whose work I admire but whom I may never have met in person. I want to thank these women for allowing me, on some level, to join their ranks, and for their generosity in reading and recommending *Both Are True:* Lainey Cameron, Elyssa Friedland, Jennifer Klepper, Sally Koslow, Nicola Kraus, Marilyn Simon Rothstein, Susie Schnall, and Rochelle Weinstein.

Thank you, as always, to my brother-in-law Stevie Friedgood, for his endless patience in working with my website and all things technological.

I want to thank everyone I've worked with over the years in Family Court, both at the beginning of my legal career in the Juvenile Rights Division of The Legal Aid Society, and now as a volunteer in the Pace Family Court Legal Program. These experiences were and remain formative for me, and played an important role in developing Jackie's character and understanding what she faced in her position as a Family Court judge.

Thank you to my family and friends for sticking with me for all of the ups and downs of writing this book and the two that preceded it. It's not a pretty process, and your support means the world to me.

And to Pierre, because no love could be more true.

For Pierre, Ariella, and Micah. Nothing in life is simple, except my love for the three of you.

BOTH ARE TRUE

You can't hurry love.

—The Supremes, 1966

September

Jackie

Jackie looked expectantly at the coffee maker but the carafe was empty. Why was Lou still in bed? Today was too important to skip her morning caffeine or upend her routine.

She took down her favorite mug from the cabinet. The room was spotless and she smiled, only vaguely aware that her intense pleasure at the sight of an orderly kitchen might be considered extreme. Shades of her mother, who'd been known to clear the dinner plates from the table while the family was still eating.

Lou had erased all evidence of his evening with his poker buddies—recycled the too many bottles of Budweiser, emptied the ashtrays filled with cigar butts, and disposed of the remains of a meatball hero with the trash. He'd even remembered to fill the diffuser so any lingering odors were masked in the sweet scent of cinnamon and cloves. She appreciated Lou's consideration. A new relationship was a delicate dance and Jackie could be a challenging partner. She was still shocked that six months earlier she'd overcome her usual mistrust and invited Lou to move in after dating only a short time.

Jackie didn't begrudge Lou his weekly card game. She knew that working remotely as he did could be isolating. She was glad he had friends and felt comfortable inviting them over. Jackie wanted Lou to feel that her apartment was his too, even if she was still getting used to the idea. She wondered what Lou had in common with these men who toiled away at conventional jobs, saddled with mortgages and saving for their children's inevitable orthodontia. She supposed they were decent enough guys; they just weren't the sort Jackie would have picked for Lou as companions.

Truth be told, she was a tiny bit jealous of Lou's social life. She'd been so focused on her legal career that she'd let her own friendships slide. Jackie had plenty of colleagues in her new position—the other judges, the law secretaries, the court officers, and the myriad court personnel. But work "friendships" were fraught, especially within the power hierarchy of the court system. Jackie knew she had a lot to learn about the internal politics and whom she could trust. These days, other than Lou, she confided only in her sister, Mindy.

As she contemplated the coffee grinder, an alien appliance that Lou had contributed to her kitchen, he sauntered in. He came behind Jackie and put his arms around her waist, the cotton of his blue and red striped boxers brushing against her linen skirt.

"Good morning," he murmured. His breath was warm in her ear and his stubble tickled her cheek. She leaned back into his arms and rested her head on his chest.

"Not sure," Jackie answered. "No coffee."

"You know, you could learn how to make coffee," Lou said, squeezing her tighter. "What did you do before me?"

"I snuck by the doorman wearing sunglasses and a jacket over my pajamas and went to Starbucks, praying I wouldn't see anyone I knew."

Jackie pulled away from Lou and turned to face him.

"I'm nervous. Do you remember what's happening today?" she asked.

"Remember? You haven't stopped talking about it for weeks. You'd think Judge Judy herself was about to emerge from the television to evaluate your job performance."

"Very funny." But because he'd been listening, she softened. She pressed herself close to him and breathed him in. "You smell like cigars and you don't even smoke."

"At least I won't die of lung cancer. Although my old man went from stomach cancer, and it's all the same. I'm already doomed."

"Don't say that. Promise me you'll get old and cranky and maudlin and incontinent with me."

"It's going to be fine today," he said and kissed her on the forehead as he headed for the shower. "You look nice."

"Doesn't much matter what I wear under the robe."

But in some ways it did matter. At 39, Jackie was the youngest judge on the bench in Manhattan Family Court. She'd been appointed by the Mayor to finish out the remaining term of a judge who'd been elevated to the Appellate Division. In some ways, she was a puzzling choice for the position. She brought no personal experience as either a spouse or a parent to the job. And Jackie was low on family law credentials—she'd never practiced in the field—she was capable, confident, and an experienced attorney with a hard-won reputation for integrity. It was an open secret that she'd gotten the interim appointment as a reward for her loyal service on the Mayor's private legal team and her active participation in Democratic party politics. The learning curve was steep, but Jackie was a model student, always had been. She was determined to turn her temporary position into a regular ten-year gig when this appointment ran out in another six months. Maybe even use the job as a springboard to a higher court as her predecessor had.

Apart from her age, Jackie was blessed with a baby face and stood only five feet tall. "Small but mighty," her father liked to say. If she didn't wear a robe and sit high above them, she might've been confused for one of the children over whom she presided. When she dressed, Jackie imbued herself with authority as best she could. She wore nothing less than three-inch heels and donned carefully tailored suits or dresses in muted tones of taupe or heather gray. She wore her horn-rimmed glasses rather than her contacts, pulled back her long brown hair and fastened it severely with a clip at the nape of her neck, and carefully applied her makeup. Anything she could do to buck herself up and boost her standing in front of the unruly litigants in her courtroom. And although Jackie knew it wasn't rational to worry about today's review—*she'd done well so far, what could go wrong?*—she couldn't help it. If she didn't pass with flying colors, she'd be subject to continued scrutiny and that left her vulnerable.

"I'm leaving," Jackie yelled from the hallway outside the bathroom door. But Lou was in the shower, washing off the cigar stink, and he didn't respond.

It's okay, she thought. I can face this day without him.

At 8:00 a.m. on an abnormally hot mid-September morning, the avenue was already bloated and sticky, the people striding purposefully but the neighborhood lethargic. Jackie stepped out the front door and scanned left and right, on the lookout for people she'd made unhappy in court. As though they'd know where she lived and stake out her home. It was paranoia, but it was hard to shake.

It was only four blocks from her apartment to the subway at 72nd Street and Broadway. The proximity to public transportation had been a selling point when she'd purchased the place, but, recently, Jackie felt too much in the center of the action.

Lou, in contrast, had an exuberance for New York and all that the city had to offer that was boundless. She winced slightly as she passed the historic Beacon Theater, remembering how Lou had tried to cajole her into seeing Jerry Seinfeld perform on the spur of the moment earlier in the week.

"It's not my type of humor," she'd said.

"Then your humor needs an upgrade."

"I have a busy day in court tomorrow. I need to get my sleep."

"You need to lighten up a little." But he'd pulled her ponytail gently when he said it and smiled.

"It's okay. Go without me. I don't mind."

"I don't want to go without you." She'd disappointed him, but she hadn't been able to see any way out. Besides, she couldn't just do as she pleased. She had responsibilities.

Jackie shook her head to clear the memory–she had to focus on today. She'd been informed by the Supervising Judge that a representative of the judicial panel would be in her courtroom to assess how she conducted herself and she was determined to wow the evaluator. Or at least to have an unremarkable day.

She descended the long staircase down to the subway and waited on the packed platform. Men and women in suits, hot and grumpy, teenage girls in too-short skirts and revealing shirts, teenage boys in shorts, long and droopy, exposing their butt cracks. A woman with a backpack jostled Jackie as she pushed toward the front and crossed the yellow safety line with her two young girls ahead of her. Determined to get on the next subway train to arrive.

"There's always another one," Jackie said.

The woman turned and glared. "Maybe we have somewhere we have to be."

"We all have somewhere we have to be," Jackie said, trying to sound reasonable.

Jackie wondered what it was about this job that made her feel like she had to interfere in everyone's lives, all the time.

The woman shook her head and moved her children forward, so close to the edge that Jackie could see the girls' hair move in the air stirred by the approaching Number 3. She watched as they got on the train, squeezing themselves into the last available space so the doors could close as they left Jackie behind on the platform. Although it pained her to waste time, Jackie hated the jammed subway cars in the morning. She often let two or three trains go so she could commute in a civilized way. As much as she relished living in Manhattan, where everything rushed forward or backward, she hated being pressed against her fellow New Yorkers in a subway car. The touch and smell, especially on a warm day, was too much humanity for her. She needed some distance.

When Jackie got to the courthouse, she stopped to buy what would usually be her second round of coffee. She patronized the same guy every morning—Roger—mostly because he made her coffee exactly the way she liked it. But also because she respected him. A married man, Roger took his responsibilities seriously, worked hard, and took care of his wife and children. It was a welcome contrast to many of the men who turned up, or failed to turn up, in Jackie's courtroom.

"Good morning, Roger. The usual."

"Morning, Judge. Must have been hot down there, hey?"

"Why? Is my makeup running?"

"No. It's already 80 degrees out here. Has to be boiling underground." Roger took the two dollars Jackie handed him and gave her back fifty cents. She pondered, as she did each time they conducted this transaction, whether Roger would be insulted or grateful if she told him to keep the change. But she was afraid to rock the boat and quickly dropped the two quarters into her suit pocket.

"How's the family?" Jackie always made a point of asking. She liked the moments of normalcy Roger provided before she entered her courtroom where every day was a shit show.

"Everyone is fine, Judge, thanks for asking."

"Happy to hear it. Okay—wish me luck!" She said that each day too, believing somehow that Roger's words would protect her.

"Good luck, Judge!" A ritual.

What he really wished for her she had no idea, but maybe it was better that way.

Jackie kept her courtroom as orderly as possible to combat the deluge of her docket. Her law secretary, Angela, was the best in the business. In her late 50s, she'd been working at the courthouse for nearly 25 years and was customarily designated to the newest judge to show him or her the ropes. Angela was totally conversant in the law, unfailingly well prepared, and had a keen eye for recognizing which cases could potentially throw a new judge for a loop. Rumor had it that she was also the unofficial eyes and ears of the Supervising Judge. Jackie, so inexperienced, relied on Angela to run interference, while praying that she wouldn't tattle on her when she made the inevitable rookie mistakes.

"Angela, we have company this morning," Jackie said, tilting her head toward the attractive but officious-looking young woman with an iPad sitting in the back row in a stylish navy suit.

"Yes, Judge. Estella Lopez," Angela said *sotto voce.*

"Welcome, Ms. Lopez," Jackie said from the bench, covering the microphone with her hand and projecting her voice to reach the back of the courtroom. "I hope you won't need to take too many notes. I'm banking on a quiet day." Lopez nodded, but looked decidedly like she'd prefer some fireworks.

"What's on tap, Angela?" Jackie perused the docket sheet, but she was never good with names. The list was a long litany of abandonment, abuse, domestic violence, drugs, neglect, juvenile delinquency. Only once in a while did Jackie preside over something happy, an adoption or a family reunification. In the short time she'd been in the job, she'd come to recognize that although she did her best to discern the underlying dynamics of each situation, to be decisive and fair, much of the time she had little idea what was really going on. And even less ability to fix the problems. It was a state of affairs that would make any control freak's skin crawl.

"All continued hearings on cases you've already seen," Angela said. "Only one new matter, Clark. A neglect. Here's the petition." She pulled it up on Jackie's monitor.

The charges named only the mother, Darlene Clark. The fathers were often missing in action, as though these troubled families had sprung from a vast maternal pool without any male input. Jackie had calculated the percentage of her docket that involved single moms

17

and it was staggering, although the cause and effect wasn't clear. Were the children neglected or turning to crime because they had no male role models, or did the fathers abandon ship when the situation at home became unsalvageable? Either way, the mothers were often left holding the diaper bag.

This mom, Darlene Clark, was accused of neglecting her two daughters, ages seven and five. According to the Department of Social Services, Clark had failed to ensure the girls' attendance at school, not taken them for routine medical care and inoculations, and not fed them sufficiently. The allegations were serious but didn't rise, yet, to the level of abuse. Maybe with intensive court-ordered support and education, Ms. Clark could turn this around. Jackie hoped so.

She disposed of the first few cases quickly. When her chief court officer, Mike, called the Clark case, Jackie looked up from her computer screen. She motioned to Angela, who was immediately by her side.

"What are those kids doing in here?" Most of the children who appeared before Jackie were of the teenage juvenile delinquent variety, boys and girls 14 or 15 years old who would've faced real time in a real prison if they'd been a year or two older and prosecuted as adults. Jackie hardly ever saw the children who were the subjects of the neglect or abuse cases. They were either already in protective custody, or, if it was safe for them to remain living at home while the case proceeded, they were waiting in the daycare on the second floor while the mothers appeared in court. There was no reason to drag them here. Yet here they were, two girls carefully dressed for the occasion in matching denim shorts and purple t-shirts. They looked underweight, but not alarmingly so. Jackie watched as Mike gently led them away from their mother and seated them in the back. He handed them each two chocolate kisses from the glass jar Angela kept on her desk.

"Potential in-court removal. Imminent risk of harm," Angela said, leaning over to speak in Jackie's ear.

"Excuse me?" Jackie had seen a lot during her brief time on the bench, but this was something new.

"I spoke to the caseworker from Child Protective Services after the petition was filed this morning. She said that when the school nurse called in the neglect, the agency tried to evaluate the children and assess the situation. The caseworker went to the home on three separate occasions. Each time the mother claimed the kids weren't home and wouldn't let her in to look for them."

"So, what are the kids doing here?" Jackie asked.

"Sometimes, instead of involving the police right away when the parent is uncooperative, the caseworker gives the mother a final chance and directs her to bring the children to court. The mother gets scared and usually complies. Depending on what the caseworker finds when she sees the kids, she has the authority to remove them into protective custody. Here, in the courtroom," Angela said. "You'll still have to determine if the removal is indicated down the line. This is a temporary, emergency measure."

"You're telling me it's possible that we're going to ambush this mother and take her children from her right in front of Ms. Lopez from the Judicial Review Panel?" Jackie swallowed hard, willing herself to stay calm.

"Afraid so, Judge."

"This can't be happening..."

As she spoke, the caseworker, flanked by two additional court officers who appeared out of nowhere, escorted the Clark children from the courtroom in stunned silence. Darlene Clark, who may not have completely understood the legal ramifications of what was happening, understood enough. She let out an ear-splitting wail, a blaring distress signal emanating from the deepest core of her being.

That keening—so unnatural and otherworldly—sent Jackie back to her parents' house on Long Island . . .

She's ten years old and it's springtime. On top of a bush that abuts the front porch, a robin has built a nest. The eggs are blue. She understands why the color is called robin's egg blue, because it has an intensity of identity and a purity she's never seen anywhere else. Before and after school Jackie checks on the nest, watches the mother sitting protectively on the eggs. A couple of weeks pass and miraculously the tiny baby birds hatch. Now both mother and father go back and forth to the nest, sustaining the young with worms. Jackie loves the birds like they are the pets her mother has never allowed.

One afternoon, Jackie is inside playing the piano. Over the sound of her oft-practiced but never perfected Fur Elise, she hears the most piercing, grief-filled sound. That keening. When she races to the window, a hawk is inches from the nest. The mother bird is inconsolable. It's a sound that Jackie never would have thought the bird capable of making, a howling so profound. Jackie bangs on the window and flails her arms, shouting at the hawk, "Drop the baby bird, drop him!" The hawk flies away, baby bird in its mouth, while the robin's death knell continues. In another moment, the mother bird quiets and turns back to the nest. Jackie imagines her finding the strength to comfort the babies that are left after a loss that is unfathomable. The father, attentive when times were good, is nowhere to be seen.

And now this woman in her courtroom was making that same sound. "Please, Ms. Clark," Jackie said, in her most soothing voice. "The caseworker is speaking with the girls. She hasn't made any recommendations yet; they may go home with you today. And if the agency determines that first we need to get some services in place to help you care for your children, then we'll work toward bringing them home as soon as possible."

Jackie didn't think Ms. Clark had heard much of her little speech, as she continued to sob. But something about Jackie's voice must have reached her. She quieted and stared straight at the judge. In that moment, the women recognized each other from the encounter in the subway that morning.

"You bitch!" Ms. Clark yelled. "You had it in for me the whole time because I got on that train ahead of you."

"You need to watch your language, Ms. Clark." Raised voices and cursing were part of the territory. She could handle this, even with Ms. Lopez tapping furiously in the back of the courtroom.

"Don't you fucking tell me what to do!" Ms. Clark cried. She stood and leaned over the table in the well of the courtroom, her shoulders and chin forward and eyes blazing. "You're not going to get away with taking my children from me." Her voice got louder, and Mike walked toward her as he quietly spoke into his walkie-talkie and summoned back-up.

"Please sit down, Ms. Clark, so we can finish what we need to take care of here." Jackie raised her voice more than she intended. When Ms. Clark continued to yell obscenities, Jackie felt she had no choice. "If you don't cooperate and sit down, I'll have to hold you in contempt of court." She'd never threatened a litigant with contempt, had never even seen the holding pens she knew were down at the end of the hallway.

"I'm not gonna sit down. You think because you're way up there, you control everything. I'll show you who's in charge!" Ms. Clark managed to come around the table and take a step or two toward the bench before Mike and another officer moved in behind her and swiftly cuffed her as Jackie watched, aghast. Her view was partially blocked by the burly back of a third officer who had stepped protectively in front of her as Ms. Clark was led toward the side door of the courtroom.

"Get into your robing room, Judge," Mike called out, motioning with his chin toward the door behind Jackie.

"I'm not going anywhere. Let's sort this out," Jackie said, her voice shaking.

"I'm not asking you, Judge. I'm ordering you. Get out of the courtroom," Mike yelled.

Feeling paralyzed, Jackie was startled when Angela grabbed her arm and nearly propelled her through the door to the robing room, closing it behind them. They said nothing for a few moments, as shocked as the Clark children must have been when they were taken away from their mother moments before. A knock on the door broke the silence. Assuming it was Mike, Jackie called, "Come in."

Estella Lopez stood in the doorway. Her iPad was now ominously packed away, signaling that at least this phase of her review of the interim judge was closed. "I didn't want to leave without speaking with you, but, honestly, I don't even know what to say." Her voice was strident, her face pale.

How about, *I'm so sorry you had to go through that,* Jackie thought.

"Look, I'm not making excuses for that woman, but she was distraught and angry. You took her children from her. Can you imagine what that feels like?" Ms. Lopez said.

"I understand distraught and angry, Ms. Lopez. I see that here every day in more permutations than I would have imagined existed before I started this job. But what was just below the surface was disrespect and rage, bordering on violence. And I won't abide that in my courtroom."

Ms. Lopez appeared unmoved. "You're supposed to have a judicial temperament that rises above the chaos. Instead, you fomented it by threatening to hold her in contempt."

Angela sat quietly at the table, her hands in her lap, the picture of contrition. "I'm sorry, Judge. I should have warned you how out of control things can get. Her anger wasn't aimed at you, personally."

"And if a stray bullet hits me when I wasn't the target, am I any less dead?" Jackie found Angela's tone disturbing, as if her law secretary thought she would have handled the situation better than she had. But she didn't have time now to worry about Angela. She needed to salvage the situation with the evaluator. If it wasn't already too late. "Ms. Lopez, do you have a moment to sit down with us?"

"I'd prefer to stand."

"Fair enough. I know you're busy." Jackie wondered how long it would take Lopez to relay what had transpired to the Supervising Judge. She had to put it in a better light.

"I find being a judge humbling. There are days when I put on this robe and I think to myself, who am I, a total stranger, to get in the middle of a family in crisis and tell people what to do or how to behave?"

Jackie rose from her chair and took a conciliatory step closer to Ms. Lopez.

"I'm so sorry that Ms. Clark's case spiraled out of control and I very much hope that we'll be able to get her children home as soon as possible. But I can't let a litigant's show of emotion dictate how I make decisions. Family court is intense and unpredictable, and I have to stay objective and maintain authority. I hope you can try to look at today's proceeding with that in mind. Thank you for hearing me out. Now, please excuse me. I have to finish the calendar."

Jackie walked past Ms. Lopez and sat down behind the bench.

"Call the next case, Mike."

She hoped no one could hear the tremor in her voice.

At the end of the interminably long day, Jackie left the courthouse, passing Roger's coffee cart as he met her gaze.

"Rough day, Judge?"

"No, Roger, just the usual," Jackie said. His morning "good luck" hadn't done the trick. Irrational as it was, she knew she'd buy her coffee from someone else the next day.

Unable to face taking the subway, Jackie hailed a taxi. She unlocked the door to her apartment and sensed emptiness.

"Lou?" she said. "Lou?" she said, louder.

Then she saw the note on the kitchen table, held in place by a bottle of Bud, now sweating in the heat.

Lou

Lou glanced at his watch, knowing full well it would read six on the dot. He woke at the same time every day, an internal clock so precise and unrelenting that he couldn't turn it off to sleep in on weekends or vacations. It was his one compulsive trait; otherwise, he considered himself very laid back. Nothing like Jackie, who put the "A" in "Type A" personality.

Truthfully, Lou liked to wake up early even when he didn't have anywhere particular he needed to be. Although he worked remotely and spent most of the day in Jackie's apartment, the only time Lou really felt at home there was in the early morning. He'd grind the beans and put on the coffee, collect *The New York Times* from the doorman in the lobby, and then chill until Jackie's phone alarm blared at 7:00. After so many years living on her own, this apartment was Jackie's space. Lou felt like a guest, albeit mostly a welcome one.

Today Lou didn't jump out of bed as usual. He felt uncertain, a creeping anxiety that started as a tingling in the soles of his feet and moved stealthily up to his chest, an unpleasant sensation passing through his shorts on the way. He could pinpoint exactly when the feeling had started: right after his second shot of whisky and the third hand in last night's card game.

"Are you going to marry this woman or what, Lou?" Rob had asked, apropos of nothing. He leaned back in his chair, a cigar clamped in his teeth.

"No idea," Lou had responded.

It was true. They had something good going, but these were early days. Lou found Jackie attractive, intelligent, and fiercely uptight. She was also independent and her legal career was her priority. Jackie said she had no interest in getting married—that she'd already seen too much misery in Family Court and too many women left in the lurch by men always on the lookout for the next thrill. She was guarded, to put it mildly. Lou had gamely accepted the challenge of making Jackie relax and enjoy herself, figuring he'd see if she was capable of really opening up to the possibility of love down the line.

Frankly, Lou was a little bit relieved that Jackie wasn't anxious to tie the knot. He wasn't jumping into marriage headfirst again. His divorce from Tara had been legally uncontested but emotionally debilitating. They'd had no real assets to divide and had come to an amicable out-of-court visitation schedule for Lou with his stepdaughter, Bryn. Tara had always worked outside the home and Lou had willingly and lovingly taken care of Bryn for years from when she was a little girl until she was eleven and he and Tara separated.

The visitation agreement provided for Lou to spend one weekday afternoon and every other weekend with Bryn. It had worked well for quite a while. But when Bryn turned thirteen, she'd started begging off. Homework, afterschool activities, and commitments with her friends pulling her in different directions. She'd come late or leave early, always with some excuse. The last time they'd planned to meet, Lou waited for an hour outside Bryn's middle school at dismissal time and found out later that she'd gone to a friend's without telling him. He'd received a one-word text, "sorry."

Lou had been distraught and Tara was sympathetic, but she said she couldn't force Bryn to spend time with him. "She barely hangs out with me either. She's a teenager now."

By the time the divorce was final and Lou had met Jackie, Bryn had stopped getting together with him entirely. Lou spoke with his lawyer to explore whether there was any legal action he could take to enforce the visitation schedule. The guy's advice was hard to hear but unequivocal. "Let it go, Lou. You have to respect her decisions. If you push too hard, this will be irreversible. Hopefully she'll come around when she gets older." So, Lou swallowed his pain, texted

Bryn periodically, and sent her spending money via Venmo. He missed her terribly.

With all that recent heartbreak, this arrangement with Jackie was working fine. Why complicate things?

It was what Rob said next that had thrown him.

"It seems to me like you've got a good gig going here. She's got you hidden away in this fancy apartment, cooking and cleaning for her, and my guess is you're paying the rent in sexual favors, am I right?" Pete snorted and Martin guffawed. Rob blew his cigar smoke in Lou's face, which made the other guys laugh even harder.

"Shut up, you assholes," Lou said. "You're just jealous that your wives can come up with a thousand things they'd rather do than get naked with you. And lower your voices. Jackie's sleeping." She rarely stayed awake past 10, intent on getting her nine hours of shut eye.

"Just calling it like I see it," Rob said.

Lou understood how it must look to these guys. Jackie had a significant job out in the public eye. She left each morning for work like she was going out to conquer the world. What did Lou do all day until she came home?

He wasn't unemployed. He was underemployed, underpaid, and unfulfilled. Lou's main source of income came from his work as a bookkeeper for a number of online companies, a begrudging use of the accounting degree that his father had forced him into and for which he still resented him even though he was long dead. Lou's clients would never make him rich, but they kept his head above water. His ability to piece various jobs together and to work remotely had been critical in the years he'd been taking care of Bryn and for that he was grateful.

What Lou regretted was that he'd failed to follow his true passion. He dreamed of being a writer and, to his credit, he'd made a start as a freelance columnist. Lou wrote a popular column for one of his accounting clients, an Internet magazine called "*The Balabusta's Bible.*" In Yiddish, Balabusta roughly translated to an accomplished housewife who ran a tight ship. Lou always thought of that old perfume commercial—the one about the woman who could bring home the bacon, fry it up in a pan, and never (never never never) let you forget you're a man. His readers were mainly Jewish professional women who raised highly successful and well-behaved children, kept a beautiful home within their budgets, cooked delicious and healthy meals (sometimes minus the bacon), and still managed to turn it on for their husbands between the sheets. In private, he called the magazine the "Ball-buster's Bible."

Lou's weekly contribution was a 500-word personal essay that ran under the heading, "A Straight Man's Voice in a Woman's World." He'd insisted on the inclusion of the word "straight" so there'd be no confusion when he got the job after he and Tara split, during the dog days of the divorce proceedings when he was lonely and desperate to get back in the game, on the prowl for anyone who would give him a tumble.

The column turned out to be quite the aphrodisiac. Lou wrote about topics that women, both married and single, Jewish and non-Jewish, found appealing: the difficulties of dividing mutual friends with your ex, the stress of caring for aging parents and the mixture of grief and relief following their deaths, the despondency of being single and the perils of falling in love. Occasionally, Lou wrote a column about cooking, another one of his hobbies, and once in a blue moon he wrote a flat-out funny piece about current events or politics. Women found him sensitive and sexy. They wanted to be his friend and his lover. In his writing, Lou could create what he believed every woman wanted, a man who understood her, but still turned her on.

Lou's piece ran on the *Balabusta* on Thursdays. On Fridays it appeared in about forty other Internet magazines in syndication, gathering a small but devoted audience of women with an urban sensibility and a certain neediness hiding beneath their success. Lou, or the persona he'd invented, was a household name among this demographic. As well-known as he was, the gig didn't pay any better than his accounting jobs. Lou's patchwork salary had covered his share of the rent on the tiny overpriced roach-infested apartment in Upper Manhattan he'd taken when he and Tara had first split, complete with a roommate named Greg who played Fortnite until the wee hours and often forgot to shower. Now that he lived with Jackie, he used his earnings to help with the expenses in her apartment. But Rob was on to something. Jackie had refused money for the co-op maintenance fees because Lou was often strapped for cash.

"What's the difference?" she'd asked when he proposed contributing more. "I own my home. I was paying that money before, and I'd be paying if you were here or not. Now I have you to come home to at night. That's worth a lot to me." Lou knew she'd meant it. The unrelenting chaos of Jackie's job often left her completely fried by the end of the day. She was happy to come home to dinner and a clean apartment, and to a man who listened to her talk about the stress of her day but also knew when the time for talking had passed.

His employment hodgepodge wasn't exactly an ordinary 9 to 5 within the panoply of professions that guys like Rob, Martin and Pete understood. That was part of the reason he hung out with them. They made him feel regular, one of them. The headline of his column notwithstanding, men usually thought Lou was gay. His friends, like Rob and Pete and Martin, didn't think he was gay. Quite the contrary, they thought he was a kept man, waiting at home to service Jackie on demand in return for a place to lay his head. Even though it wasn't true, instead of making him feel lucky or desired, it made him feel unmanly. Lou hated himself for thinking this way, but the guys had made him feel small.

So, he stayed in bed, his eyes closed, until Jackie awoke. He waited until he heard her get out of the shower, and he watched her surreptitiously as she dressed. Only when he heard her put her coffee mug down noisily on the counter did he come out so that she wouldn't worry that there was something wrong.

"Promise me you'll get old and cranky and maudlin and incontinent with me," she'd said. Lou couldn't promise so he complimented her outfit and practically ran her over as he catapulted himself into the shower. He stayed under the steaming water long past the time when the cigar smell had been replaced with the clean scent of Ivory soap. When he heard Jackie say goodbye and lock the front door, he emerged.

Lou stood on the bath mat and examined himself in the full-length mirror and for a moment, he felt revived. At 43, he still had his hair—on his head and elsewhere—thick and black and curly. He was the picture of health; his weight stayed steady at 166 pounds, solid on his 5 foot 10 frame. With his lack of disposable cash for dining out, he'd continued his routine of cooking dinner most nights as he had for Tara and Bryn. He favored a Mediterranean diet, fish and olive oil, vegetables and fruits, fava beans and couscous, cumin and zaatar. Lou stuck to two shots of whiskey a week at most; he bought the beer for his poker buddies. He did sit-ups and push-ups, planks and wall-sits. His core was defined and hard. When he and Tara were first married, he'd urge little Bryn to punch him in the gut, a game she seemed to find infinitely delightful at age six but that had worn thin by the time he moved out.

As he gazed at himself in the mirror, he kept returning to his eyes. As comfortable and pleasant as his life now appeared, he wasn't satisfied. He'd gone from Tara's home almost directly to Jackie's without striking out on his own. He hadn't taken any real time to be by himself, to figure out his priorities or how he wanted to live.

Most critically, although Lou's column was going well, he dreamed of being a real writer. Maybe not the kind of literature he'd read in college. But not what he was writing now: thinly veiled erotica or emotional confessions for over-achieving middle-aged women who yearned to connect to a man who understood them better than their husbands. Lou had *aspirations* for God's sake. His talent was being sucked out of him, slowly and steadily, and channeled into pop-psychological drivel. The women who read his column worshipped him, pouring out their desires and adulation in coded comments online: "You get me in my soul," and "I wish you were here in my kitchen, stirring my pot with that big wooden spoon." It was flattering, but it wasn't what he craved. Lou wanted to write something he could be proud of, maybe a mystery or a political thriller. Something he could hold out to the world and say, "I did this."

As Lou let the towel drop from around his waist to the floor, he had an epiphany. As long as he was Jackie's house-husband, he would never push himself past his comfort zone and be the writer he yearned to be. He would never be the man he wanted to be either. It wasn't Jackie's fault. He'd been on the rebound and he'd let her fall for a fictional character, the guy in the column. Sensitive and thoughtful, as accomplished in the kitchen as in the bedroom, always there *just for her*. He had poured himself into the role of taking care of Jackie just as he had taken care of Tara and Bryn. Now it was time for Lou to be himself, whoever that turned out to be. For that, as much as he might regret it, he would need to leave Jackie behind.

Lou dressed quickly and then pulled down his suitcase from the closet at the end of the hallway. Later he would gather other belongings, the stack of *New Yorker* magazines he hadn't gotten to yet, his cast iron skillet, his coffee grinder. For now, he threw his clothes in a bag.

When he was finished packing, Lou sat down at the kitchen table. He hadn't eaten breakfast. He felt a grumbling in his stomach and contemplated making an omelet. He could almost smell the finely minced shallots and shitake mushrooms as they simmered in the butter, awaiting the eggs. But it didn't seem right to eat alone, at best a guest and at worst an intruder in the apartment that would not be his residence any longer. He took a piece of paper from the drawer Jackie kept neatly filled with home office supplies.

Jackie,

I know this is cowardly. You deserve so much better.

But I have to go.

--Lou

He folded the note over once and put it under a bottle of Bud he took from the fridge.

Jackie

"'You deserve so much better. But I have to go.' That's the note he left? The great writer?"

Mindy looked dumbfounded as she slid the piece of paper back across the kitchen table. Her apartment, just a few blocks from Jackie's, might have been on another planet. With three young children and a workaholic husband, her place was a perpetual mess. Tonight, the dirty dishes were on the table long past dinner, the girls' books and toys were strewn all over the living room, and Sam's wrinkled shirt and suit from the day before were draped over a kitchen chair while he continued to toil away at the office. The disarray made Jackie anxious and she already regretted that she'd raced over. Her need for a sympathetic ear after she found the note had been a moment of weakness and a miscalculation.

"Remind me how we could have grown up in the same family?"

"You mean because I can eat off your kitchen floor and you can barely find mine?" Mindy made a futile dab with her napkin at a splotch of ketchup on the table and succeeded in smearing it onto the sleeve of her white shirt.

"Yes. I mean, no. Those are just the outward signs. You thrive in this chaos–it doesn't rattle you. I need things under control. Nothing makes me happier than making a list and crossing each item off when I've completed it." Jackie envisioned circling the entry "find lasting love," as still to-do, and she suppressed a sniffle.

"Jackie, this chaos, as you so kindly put it, is a family. Anyway, your question is a no-brainer. Your issues are all Mom and Dad's doing."

"Who said I have issues? You and I are just different. Besides, it's too easy to blame our parents for anything that hasn't worked out. They didn't tell Lou to leave."

But, as usual with Mindy, Jackie knew there was probably a grain of truth in her comment. Before she could ask her sister to explain her theory, Mindy's oldest daughter, Nicole, eleven going on nineteen, breezed in, iPhone in one hand and iPad in the other.

"What're you doing here, Aunt Jackie?" This social media addiction was typical of the kids Jackie saw in her courtroom. Even the ones who ostensibly had no money for expensive devices. Nicole had inherited the gift of the gab from her mother. She always had a provocative comment at the ready and, also like her mother, Nicole plucked a truly profound observation out of the blue once in a while.

Jackie wasn't offended by the unintentional but unmistakably incredulous tone of her niece's question. She loved the girls and tried to be an attentive aunt, but she didn't spend a lot of time hanging out with them. Jackie was "always working," according to Mindy, and Mindy "always had stuff to do for the kids," according to Jackie. When they could steal time together, the sisters usually preferred to score some last-minute theater tickets or grab a late dinner, just the two of them.

"I'm not sure why I'm here, if you want to know the truth," Jackie said. She took a bite of the apple cake that Mindy had put in front of her, the taste conjuring their mother better than any photograph ever could. The home cooking also made her think of Lou and she put down her fork. Jackie watched Nicole retreat to her bedroom.

"You're here because the man you thought might finally be the one—or at least the one for a long time—up and left you for apparently no reason whatsoever," Mindy said. Her back to Jackie, she wrapped what was left of the lasagna in aluminum foil and crammed it into the Subzero.

Jackie ignored Mindy's latest pronouncement and drew her back to her earlier one. "What did you mean before about Mom and Dad?"

Mindy stopped her half-hearted attempt to clean up and sat down at the table. She looked so earnest that Jackie was afraid she might try to hold her hand which, under the circumstances, might have put Jackie over an edge.

"Nothing you don't know. You were always the golden child, the overachiever, the rule follower. They expected big things from you. You're a judge, for God's sake!"

"So? Is that a bad thing? I make them proud."

"Of course you do. But it's more complicated than that. You associated their love with being perfect—you were showered with praise when you colored within the lines when you were little or brought home the highest scores on your tests when you were older. They put you on a pedestal and no one else could ever live up to your standards. They made you a star, but they also made you untouchable and lonely. They didn't expect much from me so I got to be happy instead."

Jackie remembered how when they were kids their father sometimes joked that Jackie got the brains and Mindy got the beauty. In reality, her little sister often cut to the heart of things in a startling way. But this analysis was too much to take in on the night Lou had walked out the door.

"Maybe this break-up has less to do with my issues, as you so kindly put it, and more to do with Lou himself," Jackie tried.

She hoped this would nip in the bud what she knew was coming next: Mindy's list of all of Jackie's flaws that would drive a man away. She'd heard some version of the litany of her shortcomings from her sister each time a seemingly good catch walked out or was booted out the door. Controlling, tough, inflexible, neurotic, too honest, unforgiving, too much like Mom. Jackie knew she could be difficult. She thought she'd found in Lou someone who appreciated her, who saw past the rigid exterior into her heart. How sad to have been wrong.

When she'd met him six months earlier, Jackie was a newly minted Family Court judge with a swagger in her step and every intention of living up to the confidence she believed the State of New York had placed in her. She arrived at the Manhattan courthouse each day an hour before the calendar was called and put on a freshly-pressed robe. She presided over the morning's cases until precisely noon when she recessed and insisted that her staff take a lunch break. Although she was immensely reliant upon both Angela, her law secretary, and Mike, her chief court officer, she didn't socialize with her staff. Instead, each day Jackie brought a brown bag lunch of a tuna fish sandwich on a whole wheat bialy with sliced tomato and ate by herself in her robing room. When the weather permitted, she ventured out to sit on the steps of the State Supreme Court building in Foley Square, several hundred feet and a world away from the Family Court.

It was there that she first saw Lou.

Although she'd played the scene over in her mind dozens of times, Jackie couldn't remember what had initially drawn her attention to him. Perhaps it was mere happenstance. Whatever it was, between bites of her sandwich, Jackie watched as Lou, solid and athletic-looking in unpressed khakis and an unstructured sports jacket, approached a street vendor selling flowers in front of the courthouse. The flower man, an older Latino guy with graying hair and a melancholy smile, sat every day on a low green folding chair next to the bouquets, rubbing his knees when business was slow. Jackie had often watched people choose arrangements with tiny American flags to celebrate the swearing in of a new United States citizen, or tulips or daffodils to add a touch of festivity to an otherwise drab wedding ceremony in front of the City Clerk.

Lou wasn't like the other customers. He looked both determined and lost at the same time. His chest puffed out while his shoulders sagged. The push and pull of the contrasting emotions was riveting. Jackie put down her sandwich to concentrate.

Lou surveyed the offerings and stepped toward a bucket of red roses. How cliché, Jackie thought. She'd hoped he'd drift to her favorite, the gladiola, a delicate lavender color that called to her. But when he purchased a single red rose and stuck his whole nose into the flower and breathed it in like a hummingbird, she understood that he knew what he was doing. His certitude was sexy. As she relaxed into Lou's choice, her mood changed again when he scanned the crowd, weak and pathetic, a small child who'd been separated from his mother at the beach.

Jackie wrapped up the rest of her sandwich. She shoved it back into the paper bag and got up to leave. She refused to waste any more of her energy observing this man she couldn't instantly understand. She began to walk down the courthouse stairs. Lou was suddenly in front of her, rose extended.

"This is for you," he said.

Jackie was so stunned, for once she had nothing to say. She stood a moment and then she took the rose.

"I promised myself that I would give a flower to the loveliest woman I encountered when I left the courthouse. To celebrate," Lou said. When he smiled, his eyebrows rose along with the corners of his mouth, as if all his facial muscles were connected in a way that was different from other people. It gave him a look of joy and surprise that Jackie found puzzling but irresistible.

"What are you celebrating?" She stuck her nose in the flower and breathed deeply, as Lou had moments before. She didn't achieve his abandon, but the scent would always be with her.

"I'm free," Lou said. "My divorce is final. I just picked up the order from the clerk's office. I'm ready to begin again."

Jackie had extricated herself from enough unworkable relationships to understand the euphoria Lou felt at that moment. She also remembered the feeling that followed—almost immediately or weeks or months later—loneliness so powerful and overwhelming that the initial moment of exhilaration was obliterated. But on the steps of the courthouse, Lou's optimism was intoxicating and she succumbed.

"Would you sit with me a little while?" Lou asked. Jackie looked at her watch.

"I have ten minutes." She didn't want to sound off-putting, but she wasn't prepared to be late for court.

"Perfect," Lou said. Jackie had no idea what was perfect, yet she nodded in agreement.

They sat down on the steps. Although they exchanged nothing more than their first names and some pleasantries, Jackie felt her heart bend toward Lou that day. Then she stood up from the stairs and went back to work.

That night, Jackie called Mindy, who did not mince words in her reaction to the story. "You're telling me that a handsome, newly-available man gave you a single red rose during your lunch hour, and you didn't tell him your last name or ask him his?" If Mindy were a cartoon character, she would've slapped her forehead with her open palm in frustration.

"Yes," Jackie said. "I told you, it wasn't like that. Somehow, it felt like we already knew each other. Like saying our last names would be too formal or superfluous." It sounded absurd. Yet it was true.

"Well, how are you and this Lou person supposed to find each other again?" Mindy asked.

"Maybe we aren't meant to."

When the phone rang early the next day, Jackie had the fleeting and illogical thought that it was the mystery man from the courthouse steps, so it was especially jarring when she heard Mindy's voice.

"Go look at your computer!"

"Mindy, I'm getting ready for work. I can't hang around the house all day."

"I'm going to ignore that inane remark and its implications because this is too important. Shut up for a second and go to '*The Balabusta's Bible*,'" Mindy said, spelling out the Yiddish in case Jackie couldn't.

"Oh, come on, you know I don't read that stuff." Jackie wasn't the demographic. She stuck with the *Wall Street Journal*.

"Pull it up, you fool. About halfway down the first screen—'A Straight Man's Voice in A Woman's World.'"

And there, under the title, "On Meeting Someone the Day Your Divorce Becomes Final: The Ultimate Rebound, or Kismet?" was a picture of Lou. Before Jackie had a moment to digest that she was 'the someone,' Mindy shrieked into the phone.

"I can't believe that Lou Greenberg is your mystery man! I'm his biggest fan! He's such a great guy. Sensitive and romantic and intuitive—"

"Be quiet, and let me read," Jackie said.

As you, my regular readers know, I try to tackle relationship issues and emotional questions in a way that I hope is thought-provoking for accomplished women like yourselves. Today's column is more personal, and I write it from a place of deep gratitude. Yesterday, my morning started as it has every day for the past nine years. I awoke as a married man. Although I don't know each of you, my readers, I think it's fairly safe to say that for you, like me, some of the days of my marriage were fulfilling and happy. Other days were filled with strife and sadness. When the bad days came to vastly outnumber the good, my wife and I decided to call it quits. I truly believe we remain the good people we were when we married. We just are no longer good together.

Yesterday our legal ties were officially severed. As a symbol of the beauty of new beginnings, I bought a single red rose and gave it to the loveliest woman I could find on the courthouse steps. She took my breath away, and apparently my faculties as well, as I forgot to ask her last name or tell her mine. Now I'm nearly paralyzed with fear that the woman that fate or luck or coincidence or a tuna sandwich brought to me will elude me. And I may miss out on my destiny.

"You've got to contact him!" Mindy yelled into the phone.

"And what exactly would I say? My little sister who's not even Jewish reads your cheesy column and she recognized you from the story I told her about the bizarre experience I had during my lunch hour yesterday?"

Jackie was formulating an apology when Mindy responded. "Yes! That's great. Honest and vulnerable. Tell him I read his column and was thunderstruck to learn that he was your mystery man. He'll love that. All guys are closet narcissists. He'll be wildly flattered and all the more into you. And in New York, Jackie, everyone's a little Jewish."

It was Jackie's turn to be silent. Mindy was way more intelligent than their father understood.

Now, with the benefit of 20-20 hindsight and the words of the farewell note lingering between them, Mindy claimed she'd been circumspect about Lou and his intentions from the beginning. She insisted she'd warned Jackie that Lou was a man too wrapped up in himself, low on ambition and cash, maybe even a bit of a con. In truth, Mindy, ever the romantic, had egged Jackie on.

"Aunt Jackie, do you want to see my Snapchat? It's about Uncle Lou breaking up with you. Don't worry. It disappears after thirty seconds." Nicole smiled her sweetest inscrutable grin and then withdrew to her room.

"I don't know, Mindy. I guess it wasn't meant to be." Jackie sighed.

"Did you just sigh? You never sigh. You know, it isn't normal for someone to pack up and go like that, with no warning. Don't you want to understand what happened? You have to speak to Lou. I don't know how you could've missed the signs that he was restless, or unhappy. Or unfaithful."

Jackie didn't know either. Lou had seemed devoted to her. Just a few weeks earlier, she'd finished up hearing a difficult abuse matter with allegations that were so disturbing she'd had bad dreams for several days. Lou had comforted her in the middle of the night, brought her chamomile tea and reminded her that she was doing her best to sort out the situation and protect the children. When Jackie came home from work the day the case was finally over, she opened the apartment door and Lou raced toward the foyer.

"Wait, wait," he'd said, guiding her to the small bench by the door. "Let me help you with your shoes."

"I can take off my own shoes, silly." She'd playfully shoved him over and pulled off her heels. "Oh, that's so much better. It smells outrageously good in here. What did you make for dinner?"

"Close your eyes."

Lou led Jackie to the living room.

"Okay. Open," he said, squeezing her hand.

The room was sparkling with tiny white lights Lou had strung from her bookcases and around to the fireplace.

"Oh Lou, it's beautiful. Magical. Christmas in August!"

"I wanted to take you to Tavern on the Green to celebrate the trial being over. But I'm short on cash this week, so I made dinner. And decorated a little."

How could a man who would think to transport her beloved Central Park to her living room simply walk out the front door? She'd believed Lou was committed to her, and that this might finally be the relationship she could throw herself into whole-heartedly and for the long term. She loved Lou's touch and she loved the way he chopped onions. She loved the whole enchilada. *But had she ever really told him how she felt?*

"Jackie?" Mindy's voice brought her back.

"Yes?

"You can change, you know. You can learn to trust, let down your defenses. Maybe even break some rules. And if you do, maybe it'll

41

be Lou, or maybe it'll be someone else, but *you'll* be a different person. You won't be left on the sidelines of love."

Lou

The ancient elevator descended slowly from the eighth floor in no rush to get where it was going. Lou jabbed at the down button three or four times. He knew it was futile, but he was antsy to leave. That initial adrenalin rush that he'd felt when he'd written the note and the certainty that leaving was the right thing to do was already beginning to fade. If he didn't go now, his doubts would take over and he'd end up staying. As appealing as that was on some level, Lou forced himself to focus on the clarity he'd felt when he woke up. His immediate departure may have been triggered by his poker buddies, but the feeling that he was trapped, however comfortably and even lovingly, had percolated for months. Lou pressed the down button again.

On the fourth floor, the doors creaked open and old Mrs. Dranger got on. Her squeaky little Havanese, Adolfo, immediately lifted his leg and peed a few drops on Lou's suitcase.

"Oh, for Christ's sake," Lou muttered, dabbing at the wet spot with a Kleenex he pulled out of his pocket. If he planned on ever seeing this biddy or her pooch again, Lou might have made a scene, demanded that she reimburse him for the cleaning of his luggage. As it was, he merely pushed his way out of the elevator ahead of her.

"Good morning, Mr. Greenberg. I've got your *New York Times* here. You forgot to pick it up this morning," Dennis said. He was perky to a fault and Lou was tempted to ask him if he had dreamed of being a doorman when he was a boy. The crisp uniform, the air conditioning, the intimacy born of dealing with the small details of the lives of the residents of the building. Lou liked to think that people realized their dreams, whatever they might be. He felt he was now on the verge of realizing his own.

"Thanks, Dennis. I won't be reading the newspaper today. And do me a favor," he said, reaching into his pocket and pulling out the set of keys that Jackie had presented to him the day he moved in. "Please give these to Judge Martin."

"Sure thing, Sir." Dennis asked no further questions, discretion being the number one job requirement in his line of work. Lou knew that when some other man merited a set of keys to Jackie's apartment and her heart, Dennis's lips would be sealed.

The day was unbearably hot and humid to boot. Lou carried his suitcase with one hand, carefully avoiding the patch of wetness, his gym bag slung over his other shoulder. He was seized with the realization that he was free to go anywhere. He had on his person pretty much everything he owned. On day one of his new life as a single man and aspiring novelist, he felt certain that he needed to situate himself physically in a new place. It simply could not be Cafe Zaz on the corner, as if nothing had changed. Lou strolled, pondering. He'd made it a couple of blocks north when he looked up to see the Broadway Diner looming ahead of him.

He stowed his bags in the vestibule near the front where he could keep an eye on them and sat down in the first booth. He opened the sticky laminated menu and studied his options. The choices ranged from the classic hot open-faced turkey sandwich with gravy to spaghetti Bolognese to lamb shish to blueberry pie a la mode. He wondered, not for the first time, how any single eating establishment could offer such a wide variety of foods of every ethnicity. He recalled the time as a child when, against his mother's advice, he'd foolishly ordered the most esoteric item on the menu at the Starlight Diner. Sole picatta. He'd spent the rest of the evening on the toilet.

Lou looked up to find a middle-aged man with an exceptionally blond crew-cut standing before him. His name tag read "Sheldon" and his order pad was at the ready.

"What can I get you?" He wasn't chewing gum, but Lou could still sense the wad cracking menacingly.

Lou ran his finger up and down the columns of the menu and asked a couple of clarifying questions; Sheldon had no answers and Lou couldn't commit. He needed the comfort of Cafe Zaz. And today, more than ever, he needed the soothing balm of sweet Mia, twenty years-old and waitressing at the cafe to help pay her tuition at Hunter. Lou pictured how she would lean into him to take his order, close enough for him to smell her inexpensive but delicate eau de toilette. An innocent flirtation that Lou considered one of the small pleasures of being alive. He slid out of the booth, retrieved his belongings, and walked out the door.

Ensconced back at his regular table at the Zaz, Lou had opened his laptop when Mia approached. His usual order, toasted corn muffin with butter and a cappuccino, was on her tray.

"Thanks, but not today, Mia. Please bring me a toasted bran muffin with strawberry jam and a cup of Earl Gray tea. I'll pay for that stuff," he added, not wanting her to get charged for it. At least his meal would be different. He flashed his most charming smile.

"Whatever you say, Mr. G."

When Mia brought his order, she bent over him for a moment and looked at his computer screen, where he had written in all caps, "CHAPTER ONE."

"Whatcha working on, Mr. G? That doesn't look like your regular column."

Right. Lou was brought back to reality. He was on deadline. Although his new novel would now be first in his heart, he was in no position financially to give up the *Balabusta*. Besides, he wanted to share his aspirations with his readers, to be sustained by their encouragement. And he knew Jackie would continue to read. It was a spineless way to face her and he was ashamed, but it was somehow all he could muster.

"Keep the tea coming, Mia. I have a manifesto to write."

Two hours, six cups of tea, four trips to the can and a grilled cheese sandwich later, the column was done. Lou called Mia over to his table.

"Please sit down for a minute, love. I want to try something out on you. Don't worry, it's quiet in here."

Mia perched herself on the chair opposite Lou. They'd been through this routine a dozen times over the last six months. Lou didn't fool himself into thinking that young, hip Mia with the nose ring and blue streak in her hair cared about what he offered up for consumption to women like Jackie's sister, Mindy. But today, he believed it would be different. He wanted Mia to understand. He wanted them all to understand. To forgive.

When the Universe Is Talking, You Need To Listen

For as long as I've been writing this column, I've tried to be a man you could trust, a friend whose good counsel you could rely on. I wanted, above all else, for you to feel that I'd always put you first. I tried to be accessible and honest, even vulnerable, sharing with you my crises and my triumphs, both large and small. Through humor, straight talk, or pillow talk, I hope I've helped you to believe that there are men out in the world who will understand, respect, and admire you as I've tried to understand, respect and admire you.

This column has been more successful than I ever could have dreamed, reaching tens of thousands of readers each week. It's time for me to build on this good fortune and expand my horizons. While I will continue to write "Straight Man," I'm going to pursue another dream—a personal and professional goal that I've neglected until now. I believe that my aspiration to write in a different genre, and to produce something solid and lasting, will only make me more grateful for the time I have to spend here with you. I will remain a partner in this unique relationship that we share.

This new journey will take time and focus, as well as an enormous emotional investment on my part. I want to throw my whole self into this adventure and I feel that I can only do that unencumbered by other personal commitments. It's for this reason that, as of just this morning, with a heavy but hopeful heart, I have broken it off with the wonderful woman from the courthouse steps. I hope you will not judge me harshly.

The universe is talking to me, and I need to pay attention.

When he finished reading, Lou savored the far-away look on Mia's pretty face. He waited for her to speak, not wanting to break the spell, his finger poised above the send button.

"So, where're you going, Mr. G? Is that why you have your bags? Did your girlfriend throw you out?" Lou thought he sensed a note of real concern in Mia's voice and decided to settle for that.

Her question, though not the lofty reaction he was hoping for, in fact was right on point. No, Jackie hadn't tossed him. In a few hours, she'd return from her long and undoubtedly stressful day at work and find him gone and that made him sad. He didn't want to cause Jackie pain. But it had taken him years to extricate from Tara, long after the relationship wasn't working for either of them. Lou didn't feel like he had that kind of time now. It was better this way.

And no, he had no idea where he would sleep. His modest fame and reputation as a sensitive guy ensured that he could name any number of women, both married and single, who might be amenable to a one-night stand—maybe even Mia among them, who knew? That seemed both crass and fundamentally the wrong way to go. He hadn't left Jackie to be with other women. He'd left because he needed to be an elevated version of himself. His transformation into Lou Greenberg, crime novelist, or something along those lines, couldn't begin under Jackie's roof, nor could it start with a cheap fling in exchange for a place on someone's couch.

Lou sent the column into cyberspace. He put his laptop back into his gym bag with his socks and paid the bill, leaving Mia a $10 tip on top of the $15 dollar check. He would've liked to give her more, but he was suddenly conscious of the fact that he'd now be responsible for his own rent again. Feeling like their conversation had reached an end for the day, Lou waited for Mia to take a cigarette break and snuck out the back door.

It was close to 6:00 in the evening, yet the heat was unrelenting. There was no point in trying to walk anywhere lugging all his worldly possessions. Lou planted himself on a bench in Riverside Park, hopeful that a solution to the immediate issue of homelessness would occur to him. He wasn't destitute. A limited stay in a cheap hotel was an option. But the prospect of spending the night like a tourist in his own city, and a budget one at that, was overwhelmingly depressing.

Lou took out his cell and scrolled down his contact list. Although he preferred the company of women, he had guy friends. Thinking of his buddies, he wondered if and where the poker game would continue now that Jackie's apartment was out of the question. He thought about calling Rob or Pete, but then he remembered their ribbing him. He wouldn't give them the satisfaction of thinking that Jackie had simply tired of his services.

"Excuse me, man." Lou snapped out of his reverie as a young bald guy wearing spandex shorts and a Def Leppard t-shirt leaned his bike up against the bench. He sat down, legs spread, and shifted Lou's suitcase six inches to the left.

Lou picked up his phone and hit the speed dial for his ex-wife.

Jackie

"Maybe you should stay here tonight." Mindy yelled over the whir of the dustbuster as she charged around her living room sucking up the cheerios her youngest had spilled on the beige wall-to-wall carpeting.

"That's sweet of you. I just want to go home and crawl into bed. Work's been crazy. I have to get some sleep."

Mindy's offer was genuine and kind, but the thought of staying over was more alarming to Jackie than comforting. Jackie was struck, as always, at the gulf between the paths she and Mindy had chosen. Jackie's happy place had been the law firm; now she was staking her claim in the courthouse. Her sister's life—husband, children, PTA, church—was a disparate world that Jackie thought she'd never inhabit. Maybe she wasn't cut out for marriage or motherhood. Even after she met Lou, Jackie didn't feel a yearning for a more traditional arrangement, notwithstanding her mother's not-so-subtle hints that she hoped the relationship was moving in that direction. Jackie had believed that she and Lou had a bond, and now he'd broken that bond with a few mundane words: "I have to go." It made no sense.

"What's happening at work?" Mindy asked.

Jackie paused before answering. How could she tell Mindy that she'd sat helplessly while a mother's little girls were wrenched away from her by Child Protective Services, ostensibly for their own welfare, but also a tiny bit because the woman had pushed ahead of Jackie on the subway?

"Just a lot on the docket," Jackie said. "I mostly put out fires. I make a lot of quick decisions, and I'm not used to operating like that. Even when I have time to think more, it's less about helping and more about imposing order and trying not to have the families implode."

Mindy stopped the dust-buster and considered Jackie's predicament. "Sounds like being a new judge is kind of like being a new mom. They send you home from the hospital, but the baby doesn't come with an instruction manual. How're you supposed to know what to do?"

Jackie smiled. "I guess it is sort of like that. My law secretary is very experienced and efficient, but sometimes I feel like she's looking over my shoulder. Like she's waiting for me to screw up."

When Jackie tired of watching Mindy trying and failing to create some semblance of order in her kitchen, she pushed away from the table and slipped her feet back into her heels. She gave Mindy a quick hug and poked her head into the girls' room. Jackie kissed each of her nieces on the forehead, grateful that they would be fed and bathed and sleeping in their own beds.

When she got home it was close to 9 p.m. Maurice had replaced Dennis, and it was he who welcomed the Judge home. He handed her the keys that Lou had left earlier in the day.

"Did he say anything?" Jackie asked, momentarily forgetting the change of shift. She immediately regretted how pathetic her question sounded. She didn't wait for an answer and hurried to the elevator.

Lou's note was on the kitchen table where Jackie had left it. She'd envisioned it gone, the table set with a white cloth and candles, steam rising from Lou's vegetable couscous. She sat down at her place and kicked off her navy pumps, the sound of the shoes hitting the wooden floors with a lonely thump. Jackie stared out past where Lou should've been sitting opposite her, to the window facing the avenue. The corners of the double-paned glass were caked with dirt, but they did the job and the apartment was nearly silent, even with the cars and pedestrians streaming by at all hours of the day and night. The quiet had been the perfect backdrop for Lou's energy and high spirits, the antidote to Jackie's inhibitions. And now he had taken his *joie de vivre* away.

Jackie picked up the note and ran her fingers over the words. What did he mean, she deserved better? Did he mean that she deserved to be told face-to-face why the relationship was over? Certainly, that was true. No one should be left like this, abandoned like the old couch that had stood at the curb in front of her apartment building for weeks until rats made it their home and Jackie called the Department of Health. And it seemed so out of character for Lou. He was so sure of himself, so strong—he didn't need to skulk away like a small child. Or did Lou mean that Jackie deserved to be loved by and to love a better man?

Reading the words over again, Jackie noticed for the first time that Lou had written on her new stationary, the notepad that read across the top, "From the Desk of Judge Jackie Martin." The audacity! As though she'd walked out on herself. Jackie put the note in the garbage disposal, turned on the tap, and ground it into oblivion.

It was when she lay down in the darkness that the full weight of Lou's absence hit her. Jackie was no fool. She knew that the man Lou pretended to be on the *Balabusta* was too good to be true. But the real Lou had made up for his normal human shortfalls with laughter and an openness to love that stood in stark contrast to Jackie's withholding nature. He had made her feel the possibility.

Jackie reached for her phone. She wouldn't call him, couldn't trust her voice not to betray fury or devastation. He'd left her a note. Certainly, a text was a proper response. She stared at the blank screen of her cell until her eyes stopped leaking tears. Then she typed.

"Lou?"

When he didn't respond after an hour, she knew that he wouldn't. She put the phone face-down on his pillow and turned away.

Mindy was right; Jackie needed to change. She would try to become someone who could love and be loved without reservation. *But how would she do it? And if she failed?*

The next morning, Jackie joined the line in front of "Java Juan's" in the middle of the block.

"Can I please have a small coffee with milk and one Splenda? And I'll also take a bottled water." Jackie concentrated on taking $3.50 out of her wallet so she wouldn't be humiliated if Juan refused to take her on as a new customer out of some unspoken rules of conduct among coffee carts. Although she thought she sensed a fraction of a second of hesitation, Juan handed over her beverages with a curt nod. There would be no chit chat like she had with Roger, no wishes of encouragement. Jackie put the two quarters back in her wallet and handed four dollars to Juan.

"Keep the change."

Back on the bench, Jackie struggled to lift the fog in her head. She'd slept fitfully, waking and reaching for Lou only to remember that he wasn't there.

"Don't you think it's a little strange that someone with no kids has a job like yours?" Mindy had asked Jackie over coffee several months after she started. "I mean, you can't possibly relate to the stresses of parenthood."

It was a question Jackie had asked herself, but in the reverse. How could a person who had children, a person who actually *understood*, possibly do this job? There were times when Jackie believed that only someone with a stunted sense of compassion and nerves of steel could succeed. Jackie had a fleeting image of Mindy in her yellow terry bathrobe, sitting on her bench in the courtroom, and she almost laughed out loud. No, Jackie was much better off as an observer of the folly and pitfalls of parenting than as a participant. Someone had to keep things in order.

"Judge, this was delivered this morning." Angela handed her a manila envelope, the old-fashioned kind that closed with a red string. It was a holdover of the intra-court communication system that was now almost entirely replaced by email.

"What is it?"

"I don't know. It's addressed to you." Angela looked away and Jackie understood that her law secretary had opened the envelope and closed it again after she read whatever was inside. Angela was deferential, but, as Jackie's mother would have said, she had a finger in every pot.

Jackie pulled the single piece of paper out of the envelope and noted the embossed header of the Supervising Judge of the Manhattan Family Court. She was pretty sure she wasn't being invited to tea.

"Dear Judge Martin,

I am writing to let you know that after consultation with the Judicial Panel, I'm planning to have Ms. Estella Lopez conduct several more unannounced visits to your courtroom over the next six months of your interim appointment. This is not a disciplinary action. Rather, I seek to ensure that your conduct in the courtroom meets our high standards and the trust that has been placed in you as we determine whether to recommend to the Mayor that you be appointed to a full ten-year term. Additionally, I'm permitting Ms. Lopez to communicate with you and your staff as she sees fit if she has questions. I thank you in advance for your cooperation and look forward to working with you for many years to come.

Sincerely,

Jane Spinelli, Supervising Judge"

All because Jackie had refused to cower. And now her own staff would be asked to report on her. Who could she trust? For a second, Lou was with her, drenched in sweat from an early morning run, bucking her up as she left for work and reminding her to take her lunch. And then he was gone. She would have to face whatever came her way alone.

"Call the calendar, Mike. We're wasting time."

Lou

The front door of the tidy brick house in New Rochelle had been painted red when they'd moved in. Tara had insisted they repaint it black. "Red attracts the evil eye," she'd declared. Sometimes she said stuff like that. Lou had found it endearing when they were first married and maddening later on.

Maybe because he'd never owned much himself, Lou had a thing about "maintaining property values." He was an especially big proponent of curb appeal and was pleased to see that Tara had kept the grass trimmed and the flower bed planted; the lawn looked robust. The yard had been one of his responsibilities and he'd taken it seriously. When he was a kid, his father used to say, "in the garden, it's just you and God." Lou wasn't a religious man like his dad. Still, that had stuck with him. Looking at the yard he knew that, when he'd left suburbia for the concrete jungle, God had stayed with Tara and Bryn.

They'd managed the modest down payment with the money Tara had saved working as a supervisor at Banana Republic and with some help from her parents. Lou had contributed mostly his enthusiasm for home ownership. Now, standing outside what had once been the marital residence—a term that the lawyers threw around so much that it had lost all meaning—Lou felt a wave of sadness wash over him. He and Tara had been happy in the house at first. Later, the mortgage payments and mounting everyday expenses for Bryn had put tremendous financial strain on them. Tara liked working outside the home and appreciated that Lou had arranged his accounting gigs around the household and childcare responsibilities. But in the last few years of their marriage, they'd fought constantly about money. The house especially had become more of a burden than a blessing.

Lou hesitated for a second before ringing the doorbell. It was so early, but here he was with all his stuff. What choice did he have? At least he'd had the decency to call ahead. He'd spent the night at Grand Central Station, slumped on a bench opposite track 104 on the lower level within spitting distance of the NYPD outpost, his luggage propped behind him like a poor excuse for a pillow. It was the closest to vagrancy he'd ever come. Each time Lou dozed he dreamt of Jackie's smooth sheets and her soft skin.

When Tara answered the door, her appearance was so altered that Lou thought for a split second that he was at the wrong house. She'd cut off her long black hair into a stylish bob. And she'd lost the plumpness that she'd hated but that Lou thought softened her. The new look suited her. Lou was so taken aback, he failed to speak. Tara, on the other hand, had no trouble articulating her thoughts.

"What the fuck, Lou? This can't be happening. We made a clean break, remember?" Lou still hadn't said a word, but Tara continued, "And keep your voice down. Bryn has a biology test this afternoon. I'm letting her skip her morning classes to study." Tara was wearing pajamas, but not the sexy kind she wore when they were first married. These were more like the ones she wore when things went south— every inch of her body covered in flannel, like armor. Although she hadn't let him into the house yet, Lou felt a little relieved that she wasn't wearing lingerie for another man.

"I was good at biology in school. Maybe I could help her study."

Tara rolled her eyes, but she opened the door wider and Lou shoved his suitcase through. They stood awkwardly in the tiny foyer.

"You can't stay here, you know that, right?" Tara was flustered. She flitted from the fireplace to the couch to the bookcase to the staircase.

"What do you mean? You told me I could crash. I called, remember?" Lou knew he had no right to sound indignant. But for God's sake, he'd been walking around with this dog-piss-splattered suitcase since the day before. He was exhausted.

"I mean, you can sleep on the couch for a few days, but you can't move back in. Give a minute's thought to Bryn for once." It was a low blow and totally unwarranted, yet Lou's bluster deflated.

"Please, Tara, sit down. I promise I'm not moving back in. I just need a place to stay until I get myself together. I've already made some big decisions. I'm unattached. And I'm finally going to write something serious, a novel." It was the first time Lou had said either out loud. If Tara heard the film of fear that covered his words, she didn't acknowledge it. Lou remembered that they hadn't been emotionally in tune with each other for years. Now would be a strange time to start.

"Coffee?" Tara was already moving to the kitchen. Lou supposed she needed a caffeine hit as badly as he did.

"Yes, thanks. That would be great." He followed her, making a conscious effort not to ogle her newly svelte figure from behind. The living room looked eerily the same as when he had moved out. The kitchen was different. At first Lou couldn't pinpoint why; then it hit him. When Bryn was a little girl, she loved to paint and draw. The walls of the kitchen had been covered in her artwork. And not stuck up with masking tape either. Lou had encouraged Bryn to sign and date her pieces, and then he'd matted them on construction paper, carefully choosing the background colors to bring out some element in her work. And now they were all gone, the walls bare.

Lou felt a flutter in his stomach. He realized he needed both coffee and something to eat. If he helped himself, Tara would freak. So, he sat at the table and looked longingly in the direction of the refrigerator. Along with the garden, Lou had been in charge of the grocery shopping and the cooking. He wondered what was in the fridge now that he was gone. A moment later, Tara put a mug of some too-sweet hot beverage in front of him—Hazelnut Vanilla? — and plopped down a bowl of clementines that had been on the counter. It would have to do. He grabbed two before she could change her mind.

"You won't recognize Bryn." Tara fixed him with one of her hallmark full-on stares, a look Lou had felt should be used sparingly but with which Tara graced even total strangers.

Lou felt the sting of Tara's words. He wanted to scream that it wasn't his fault that he hadn't seen Bryn in six months, that it was Tara who'd gone along with Bryn's unilateral decision to give up the visits. But he didn't want to go on the attack when Tara had been generous about giving him a place to stay. And Lou was hopeful that he'd get a chance to spend some time with Bryn here, on her turf.

"I'm sure she's changing. She's not a little girl anymore."

"I don't mean just physically, although there's that too. I mean she's *changed*." Tara got up from the table and refilled her coffee cup, emptying the pot without asking Lou if he wanted more. He didn't.

"Well, I would hope she's changed. She's growing up. And now she's in high school. That's a whole new world—everyone becomes a different person in high school."

Tara sat down at the table opposite Lou. He thought she might say more about Bryn. Instead she started flipping through those newsprint flyers that come unwanted with the mail, the ones advertising gutter cleaning and driveway repaving and leaf removal. Bryn had been such an easy, fun-loving child. Lou hated to think of her as a defiant or moody teen. Was that what Tara meant?

"Why did you let Bryn cut her morning classes today?" Lou had an irrational glimmer of hope that maybe Tara had told Bryn he was coming and she'd asked to stay home to see him. Bryn's withdrawal, even if a normal teenage assertion of autonomy, had been extraordinarily painful for Lou. So much so that he'd relegated the feelings Bryn evoked to a locked closet that he dared not open. He hadn't even told Jackie or the guys about her. Now he yearned so to see her that it was hard for him to sit in the kitchen knowing that she was down the hall in her bedroom.

"I told you, she has to study for a biology test. Is your memory going?" Tara's father had early onset dementia. She was constantly on the lookout for symptoms in herself and others.

"No. I mean, it sounds like there's more to that story. You're not the type of mom that lets your kid skip school. At least you didn't used to be."

Lou was pushing it. He knew that one wrong move could send him packing, especially since he hadn't actually unpacked yet. But something seemed off. Tara's shoulders sagged slightly.

"The truth is I'm letting her sleep off whatever messed her up last night. Bryn went into downtown Yonkers with some girl who has her driver's license and she came back wasted. Don't give me that look. I wouldn't have let her go if I'd known, but I didn't. She didn't tell me her plans and she left before I got home from work."

"Who exactly was she with? Some girl driving has to be in the eleventh grade at least."

"I don't know who she hangs out with."

"What do you mean you don't know who she hangs out with?" Lou tried to control the exasperation that was coming through, but he failed. "We know all of Brynny's friends. There's Natey and Alex and Becca and that kid—you know, the one with the stutter . . ."

"Lou, those were Bryn's friends when she was younger. You know those kids because of carpool and playdates. You said it yourself. She's in high school now."

"I know those kids because I drove the carpool and made the playdates. Is this going to be my fault?" Lou couldn't believe what he was hearing. Tara had encouraged Bryn to maintain her relationship with Lou after they split but had eventually given up. Now whatever was going on was being laid at the feet of the absentee "dad." It took all Lou's self-restraint not to get up and walk out the door, again. But he had nowhere to go.

Tara got up and paced the length of the small kitchen. "I'm not saying it's your fault. I'm saying it's hard. Don't judge me." Tara cleared their coffee cups to the sink.

"Why did you walk out on her?" she asked.

"Now whose memory is faulty? I didn't walk out on Bryn. I never would have done that."

"I'm not talking about Bryn. I meant, why did you leave your girlfriend?"

Lou was struck by both the bluntness of the question and Tara's unwillingness to say Jackie's name. Then he remembered that he hadn't spoken to Tara about Jackie or much else since the divorce. She didn't know Jackie's name. Tara had reduced Jackie to a trope, another woman that Lou had dumped.

"I needed to start over."

Tara sat down in the chair opposite Lou. Her sudden stillness and concentration was unnerving. She spoke so quietly that he strained to hear her.

"You were always about the new beginnings."

Lou stretched out as best he could on the couch. He thought it might be hard to nap with the sun streaming in the picture window, but he had barely slept the night before. He was out as soon as he got horizontal, only distantly aware of Tara laying a soft blanket over him.

He dreamed he was in the playground of his elementary school. Younger versions of Pete and Martin and Rob were taunting him on the dodgeball court. They called him "wuss" and "loser," threw the ball close to his head.

He woke to find Bryn shoving him hard in the shoulder, the words coming out of her mouth too fast and furious for him to understand.

"Bryn—" He propped himself up on his elbows and tried to shake the wooziness from his head. But she was gone.

59

Tara stood in the doorway to the kitchen. While he slept, she'd dressed for her late shift at work. A cream-colored skirt and a red silk-blend top, the Banana Republic outfit *du jour*. Lou rubbed his shoulder and looked down at his feet. He was afraid to be lured into another one of Tara's probing stares.

"How did you expect her to react, seeing you there?"

"I didn't think it through."

"Well, that's a shocker." Tara picked up her purse and grabbed her keys from the key rack Lou had installed next to the front door when they moved in. "Bryn will be home from school around 3 and I get home at 7:30. I don't think it's a good idea for you to be here for dinner. I think that would be too much."

"For you or for Bryn?"

"For all of us." She left, closing the black front door quietly behind her, but letting the screen door slam shut.

Jackie

Waiting for Mike to call the calendar the next morning, Jackie's thoughts drifted to the beginning of her relationship with Lou. Maybe if she sifted through her memories of how they'd gotten together, she'd figure out how they'd fallen apart. Her initial anger at Lou was morphing into regret; if only she'd let down her guard and shown Lou how she felt about him, he wouldn't have bolted.

"Don't wallow in the past," Mindy had warned her. "It's not productive."

"I'm not wallowing. I'm trying to understand."

Mindy's opening gambit had been on the money. Lou was unabashedly flattered when Jackie tracked him down the day after his column about her appeared online. Following her sister's instructions to the letter, Jackie had emailed him at the address listed in his bio on the *Balabusta* website and asked him to send his contact info if he was interested in talking.

"You're in the driver's seat that way," Mindy, Queen of Hearts, counseled. "If he responds to your email, then you can decide whether you want to pursue it further."

He'd answered her almost immediately, sent his cell phone number and said he hoped to hear from her. She called him from her robing room during a recess between cases. There was a low but definite hum in the background, not at all the quiet writing atmosphere that Jackie had imagined. It sounded like Lou worked in a flea market.

"Wow. It's amazing that you found me."

"It wasn't that hard. My sister is a devotee."

"But not you?" Lou asked. He was cheeky, but the rose incident had already made that clear.

"You'll have to work a little harder to impress me." Jackie wasn't bad at flirting. It was when things got beyond the banter that she faltered.

They'd chatted for a few more minutes until Angela signaled to Jackie that her next case was ready. Then they quickly arranged to meet at noon on Sunday at the entrance to Strawberry Fields in Central Park. Jackie figured that would be public and safe. If Lou turned out to be a nut job, she'd go home disappointed but none the worse for wear.

Walking to their rendezvous point a couple of days later, Jackie stuck to the paved pathways, cursing herself for wearing heels in the park. She'd remembered how petite she'd felt standing next to Lou on the courthouse steps, and she thought she'd even things up a bit. Once she'd committed to nice shoes, she put on a floral dress too. Maybe he was planning to take her for lunch at the Boathouse.

She scanned the tourists in the spot where they'd made up to meet. Lou came up behind her and put his hand lightly on her back.

"Hey! Thanks for showing up." He was wearing a tee-shirt, cargo shorts, and running shoes. Jackie's vision of an elegant spring repast overlooking the water faded.

She extended her hand to shake his and immediately felt silly. Lou rescued the moment by taking her small hand in both of his large ones and giving her a quick peck on the cheek.

"This is crazy. I don't even know you," Jackie said. She reflexively took a small step away from him.

"It's okay. Your sister knows me. Besides, don't call it crazy. Say spontaneous." Lou smiled that wide grin again with the attached eyebrows and Jackie relaxed a little.

"No one has ever described me as spontaneous."

"Maybe it's time to start." Lou had guided her over to the lake where a line of row boats for rent waited to whisk lovers along the water. He was about to speak with the sullen teenager in the rental booth when Jackie called out to him. "I don't do boats."

"As a matter of principle?" Lou smiled, but his brow furrowed, and he looked happy and confused at the same time. The man's face was an ever-changing canvas of conflicting emotions.

"I can't swim. I don't go on any body of water where swimming could even be a remote possibility. I'm okay with a bath, for example. Although I prefer to shower." Jackie was a little embarrassed, but she'd made this speech before. It was easier to own up to her phobias than overcome them.

"How can you not know how to swim? Didn't your parents ever send you to summer camp?"

"Look, let's do something else. Let's go to the zoo." Jackie was getting irritated. If the point was to be together, get acquainted, what difference did it make what activity they chose?

But Lou was not to be deterred. "Look at the water, Jackie. There's zero possibility you could tip out of the boat. I promise you. I'll take care of you."

Strange as it was, something about Lou inspired confidence. He paid for an hour and stepped into the rowboat, turning around and holding out his hands for Jackie.

"I'm not sure—"

"The lake is like a mirror. The only way you're falling in is if I push you." Jackie had a fleeting vision of Lou becoming so annoying that she pushed *him* in, but she took hold of his hands.

For the first fifteen minutes, she sat opposite Lou at the far end of the boat. Hands clenched onto the rim of the bench, feet planted as firmly as possible in her idiotic sandals, Jackie stared straight ahead and silently prayed that her 100 pounds would somehow balance out Lou's more solid weight. But they went along without incident. Lou rowed smoothly and assuredly, taking care not to splash Jackie with even one drop of water, and eventually, she allowed herself to relax enough to focus on his arms. Lou was tanned and hairy but, thankfully, tattoo-free. A relief after what she saw everyday in her courtroom, teenagers and their parents covered in snakes and anchors and spiderwebs. Lou was strong and toned. Jackie found herself imagining what it would be like to be held by him.

"Want to row for a while? I'm getting tired."

"No!"

"I'm kidding. This is great. Isn't it beautiful? I love how peaceful it is out here and how you can still see all the activity in the park." Lou's voice was as dependable as his rowing, and Jackie wanted to hear more.

"Have you taken a lot of women out on the lake?" She regretted the "do you come here often" question as soon as she asked. But Lou was unfazed.

"No. You're the second. I took my ex-wife a couple of times."

"Does she know how to swim?"

"Yes, but she wouldn't row because it might mess up her manicure." Jackie couldn't tell if Lou was appreciative or critical of his ex's touch of femininity. She looked down at her own nails, which were clean, short, and unpolished.

"How long were you married?" She already knew the answer from his column, but it was the most innocuous question she could think of to keep the conversation going.

"We separated after eight years. The divorce took another year. But we probably hung on longer than we should have. Have you ever been married?"

"Me? No. I dated someone all through law school. When we graduated, he moved to California. I wasn't prepared to follow him there or to leave New York and my family. After that, I put all of my energy into my career. There've been other guys, but no one serious."

Jackie let go of the bench for a second to smooth her dress over her legs. The tiny red rose pattern reminded her of the flower vendor and the way she'd happened upon Lou several days earlier. How crazy life was that such a random meeting had landed her here. And how unbelievable that this man put her at ease.

"Sounds to me like you haven't met the right person. Unless it's the idea of marriage itself that bothers you?"

"I guess it's probably a little bit of both."

Jackie often thought about why she was alone as she neared forty. People assumed she must have had a traumatic experience in a past relationship, or parents who had gone through an acrimonious divorce or abandoned her. But it wasn't true. Jackie's parents would celebrate 45 years soon. And Mindy and Sam were totally devoted to each other and the girls, a shining example of love and stability. Was it that it was all too much to live up to?

"Why did you get divorced?" Jackie asked. So much for innocuous questions.

"It wasn't working anymore."

"Do you have children together?"

"No."

"Why not?" Jackie realized she might have gone too far, and she wasn't surprised when he didn't answer. Lou looked out over the lake at the other boats, away from her.

"We felt what we had was enough." After a moment, his gaze fixed on the opposite shore, he added, "You ask a lot of questions."

"It's an occupational hazard. I spend all day trying to figure out what makes the families in my courtroom tick. Tolstoy was right. 'All happy families are alike; each unhappy family is unhappy in its own way.' Anyway, as a journalist you must be in the same boat." They both smiled at her unintended witticism, and he looked at her again. She was relieved.

"I'm not a journalist, Jackie. I don't report or investigate. I write a relationship column for a women's internet magazine."

"People love your column. My sister loves your column. You have groupies."

"I have readers, and I give my all to them. But I'm not a journalist. I write, but I'm not a writer."

Lou rowed in silence for a while, and Jackie was at a rare loss for words. She'd become accustomed to asking difficult questions of litigants and attorneys, people who were required to answer her because she was in a position of authority. Lou's cryptic responses were endearing. They showed a willingness to engage with her coupled with a level of self-protection that Jackie admired. He made her feel less in charge, more of an equal. It was refreshing.

They continued to travel in the boat unscathed. Jackie was comfortable enough to awkwardly raise herself up a few inches from the furthest bench and shift over to one a little closer to Lou. She thought he might row around the lake one more time now that she was almost able to enjoy it. Instead, Lou expertly guided the boat into the assigned spot and jumped out onto the shore. He reached out his hand.

"You did it!" he said. Lou pulled her into a celebratory hug. She hugged back.

They said goodbye and Jackie walked home from the park, a smile playing on her lips despite the ache in her feet from her shoes. She caught herself humming. They'd made plans for dinner during the week, her choice of restaurant. She pictured the cozy Italian place on Columbus Avenue with the exposed brick walls and dim lights she'd been to once, years before. She was almost home when her cell rang.

"Hey, Min."

"So, how'd it go? I could barely sit still—is he as great in real life as he is online?" Jackie could feel Mindy's excitement. She was happy not to disappoint her.

"He's great. I mean, he seems great. He convinced me to go in a boat."

"That really is something!"

"I know. He could've just accepted that I was too afraid to go on the boat, but he persisted. It felt good to be pushed beyond my comfort zone. I know that sounds weird. I can't explain it."

"What else?"

"What else do you want to know?"

"What did you learn about him?" Jackie thought Mindy would've made a good investigative reporter.

Jackie replayed the conversation in her head. "He runs outdoors in any kind of weather. He's Jewish but he doesn't go to temple. He grew up in Mt. Vernon, an only child, and both his parents have passed away." Jackie wasn't sure she knew much more. They'd only spent an hour together.

"He's written about all of that in his column. What did he tell you about the ex-wife? He's freakishly private about his love life."

"You sure have a way of breaking a spell, little sister."

"The guy's been divorced for four days. It would be weird if the subject of his ex didn't come up."

Jackie could hear Mindy eating. Sounded like salad. Her habit of chewing while she talked on the phone was unbearable. She'd explained to Jackie that she barely had time to breathe with the girls around. She ate whenever the opportunity arose, which was most often when she chatted with Jackie.

"We talked about her a little."

"Name?" Mindy asked. She crunched on what sounded like a cucumber.

"Tara. Tara . . ." Jackie tried to remember what Lou had said her last name was, although Mindy's interest in the ex was a killjoy. "Tara Donohue. They lived in New Rochelle. When they separated, Lou moved to upper Manhattan. She was in some sort of retail job. That's it. That's all I know. And she likes to paint her fingernails." Jackie turned the corner onto her block and was assaulted with the smells of trash waiting for Monday collection, a blaring siren, and something squishy under her right foot. A sudden gratitude for New York City filled her.

"Okay, that should suffice," Mindy said. The chewing was now accompanied by the sound of Mindy tapping on her laptop.

"You know, I'm not in competition with his ex, Mindy."

"I don't think you have anything to worry about. She has no social media presence. Must be either a loser or a recluse."

"Hey! I have no social media presence."

"Well, that's different. You're a judge. You make people angry. You don't want your personal information floating around out there. And not for nothing, you should google yourself. There's still plenty about you online from before you got this job. As I always remind Nicole, once you put something on the internet, it can never be taken back."

Mindy went silent for a minute. Then she triumphantly exclaimed, "I found her." Jackie felt her shoulders tense. She was afraid to hear what Mindy had discovered.

"It's not much and it's out of date. She won 'employee of the month' as the manager of the Eastchester Banana Republic a few years ago. She's pretty. A little plump, but nice shiny long black hair. Keratin, I think. I wish I had hair like that. I'm emailing you the photo."

"Please don't email me anything. I'm home, Mindy. I'll talk to you later." Jackie said. But it was too late. Mindy had already hit "send." Jackie studied Tara's photo. She committed her face to memory and deleted the email.

Mike's deep voice pierced through Jackie's fog like a dagger.

"Matter of Clark."

Jackie thought maybe she'd misheard, although no one projected or enunciated better than Mike when he called the calendar. She scanned the docket sheet, first quickly and then more methodically, to find out if Darlene Clark's case was on again, so soon. It was.

Today, Jackie would determine whether her initial removal of the Clark children was warranted. If not, Jackie wouldn't hesitate to return the girls to their mother. More likely, though, there was much work to be done. The matter was on for a status hearing. Jackie would hear from the court-appointed law guardian who had now had the opportunity to interview the children regarding their wishes. Understandably, the kids always wanted to go home, regardless of the circumstances. She'd get a report from the overworked and poorly trained agency caseworker on the specifics of the neglect allegations and how the children were faring in the temporary foster care placement. Finally, the mother's attorney would argue for reunification and stipulate that Ms. Clark would attend any parenting class, substance abuse program, anger management training or anything else Jackie pulled out of her hat as a condition of getting her kids back. Sometimes there was a quick fix. More often than not, the court's supervision dragged on for months or years. Jackie would be a part of Ms. Clark's life, and visa versa, for the foreseeable future.

The attorney for the Department of Social Services, accompanied by a young caseworker from the foster care agency, took their places at the Petitioner's table on the right-hand side of the courtroom. Mike paused, looked around, and then sauntered out the back door. Jackie could hear him call out in his booming voice for the Respondent, Darlene Clark. After a moment, he returned alone.

"Judge, this is the third call this morning with no appearance from the Respondent, Darlene Clark. Do you want to hear the case now, without her, or try again after the lunch break?"

Although she knew it was only temporary, Jackie felt a surge of relief that Ms. Clark was a no-show. She wasn't sure she had the emotional bandwidth for another confrontation.

"No, let's do it now. Maybe counsel can shed some light on the situation."

Jackie worked well with Mike. She liked that he was deferential but still kept her on task. And she was always moved by a man in uniform. Mike carried a gun and was assigned to protect her; that earned him a lot of credibility. Besides, he'd been a *bona fide* cop for fifteen years, until he was sidelined by an injury. Mike said he missed being on the job, especially working with a partner.

"It was something to know you had a guy's back and he had yours," Mike had explained one day, pleased that Jackie had taken an interest. "A good partner is like a spouse, that level of commitment. Or, at least, that's what I imagine." Jackie trusted Mike to have her back.

"Okay, folks, let's get this party started," Mike said.

Jackie looked over at the DSS attorney, who gazed steadily at a file on the table and avoided eye contact. The attorney and caseworker stated their appearances for the record.

"Ms. Parker, do you know why Ms. Clark isn't present in court?" Jackie looked at her computer monitor to give the attorney some space.

Ms. Parker barely raised her head. "No, your Honor. No one has been able to reach Ms. Clark since she was released after you held her in contempt of court."

"Okay," Jackie said. If this was the sort of situation in which the new Jackie was supposed to be less controlling, she couldn't see how. She struggled to keep the edge out of her voice at the superfluous reference to the fireworks of the last court appearance. "Perhaps you can tell us something about the condition of the children. And you can give us an idea of the initial plan for the family and let the court know the specifics of visitation and whatever initial parenting programming the agency has set up."

"Well, your Honor, I'm not sure I can tell you much of anything," the attorney mumbled.

"Mike, can you please adjust Ms. Parker's microphone. I'm having some trouble hearing her." Jackie paused while Mike fiddled with the sound apparatus. He shot Jackie a look that she took as confirmation that the mic wasn't the problem.

"Okay, Ms. Parker. Let's try that again. Did you have something more to say about Ms. Clark?"

"Yes, your honor." Ms. Parker took a deep breath and finally looked Jackie in the eye. "Ms. Clark has not been in touch with the agency since she left the courthouse yesterday. In the afternoon she removed the children from the foster care placement and absconded with them. We haven't seen her or the girls."

Jackie felt a sudden throbbing in her head and wondered if a jump in blood pressure could cause that sensation in a matter of seconds. What would it be like to have a stroke right here, on the bench? She felt confident that Mike would catch her if she keeled over, but she didn't want to test the proposition.

She kept her anger in check, remembering Estella Lopez's disapproval when she lost her judicial cool. Internally, she fumed. How dare Ms. Clark defy her order and kidnap these children? This show of so-called maternal devotion from the same woman who hadn't bothered to get her girls vaccinated or send them to school. It wasn't logical, although Jackie understood that love could overcome reason. Still, the situation as it stood was unacceptable.

"When were you planning to inform the court of the status of this case, Ms. Parker? You should have asked to be put back on my calendar as an emergency matter as soon as you had the information. Do you understand that you, the agency, and ultimately the court are all on the line here, not to mention the safety of these two little girls? Why would you wait a whole day to alert me?"

Exasperated, Jackie stared at Ms. Parker until she sensed Angela at her elbow. She bent toward Jackie and whispered. "Judge, perhaps you could ask the caseworker directly. She may know more." Jackie nodded, embarrassed but grateful for the save. She blamed Lou for her frazzled state and her inability to take charge of the situation. She wondered if Angela would report her moment of incompetence to Ms. Lopez. She turned to the agency caseworker as Ms. Parker looked back down at the desk.

"Who were the children placed with?"

"The girls were placed with Darlene Clark's sister, Your Honor."

The default policy of all the agencies, kinship foster care was one of those ideas that was simultaneously obviously right and obviously wrong. A child removed from a parent was usually most comfortable when placed with a relative and the relative was presumed to have the most interest in taking good care of the child. On the other hand, poverty, substance abuse, mental illness and general dysfunction ran through families. The grandmother or aunt often shared many of the same issues as the parent who couldn't care properly for the child. And it was extremely difficult to monitor or restrict a parent's access to her child when a close relative was the caretaker.

Jackie watched the caseworker squirm and took pity on her. She envisioned Mindy, distraught, spiriting her daughters away from a court-ordered placement with Jackie. Jackie knew she'd hand the children over to her sister without reservation no matter the circumstances. They were *hers,* after all.

"Ok, listen. I'm not assigning blame here. It is, however, intolerable that this is how this situation panned out. Ms. Clark is unbalanced. There's no indication she'd do physical harm to her children, but we need to fix this. Your lapse means that she's on the run with these kids. They won't be in school and potentially they still won't get whatever medical care they may need. I'm issuing a warrant for Darlene Clark's arrest. I'll give a head's up to the appropriate precincts. Angela?"

Her law secretary was immediately by her side.

"Please find out the precincts that cover where Ms. Clark lives and where her sister lives. Also please ask the case worker for the addresses of any other relatives the agency considered for placement."

"Yes, Judge."

How many times would she have to lock up Ms. Clark before this case was resolved? Jackie massaged her temples as she gratefully watched Mike clear the courtroom for a break. Their eyes met and lingered an extra beat. Jackie was touched at what she perceived as his concern and a little startled at the intimacy. Was it part of Mike's job to look out for more than Jackie's physical safety? She escaped into her robing room and sat alone, sipping a diet Coke through a straw.

"You okay, Judge?" Mike poked his head in her doorway. Jackie was always surprised at how quiet on his feet he was for such a big guy.

"Yes. Thanks. Just another day in the trenches."

"Judge, can I give you a little friendly advice?" Mike took another step into the room and closed the door behind himself. "Keep your eyes open around Angela. She's a great lawyer—super smart. She knows more than most of the judges in the courthouse. But she's been stuck in this role for years. Like, always a bridesmaid, never a bride. She's gunning for more."

Jackie smiled. She thought Mike was being a little over dramatic, but she recognized that he had her best interests at heart.

"Thanks, Mike. I appreciate the warning. It's all good."

"Okay, Judge. Thought you should know." Mike went back into the courtroom, pulling the door firmly shut behind himself.

Jackie closed her eyes. A glass of wine would help. Too bad she had a whole afternoon's work ahead of her.

Darlene Clark and her children were missing and Lou had left her.

This was not the way things were supposed to be.

Lou

It was past noon when Tara and Bryn left the house. Lou lay on the couch with his eyes closed and tried to doze, but there was no way. The crisp September sun streamed in the bay window bathing the room in light and besides, he was totally wired. It was a state of agitation that he rarely experienced and it made him uncomfortable. It made him feel not himself.

Lou gave up and stared at the ceiling until his eyes focused on a brown ring with jagged edges. Evidence of a leak that he'd meant to repair a couple of years earlier when that was his responsibility. Now it no longer was. What else had deteriorated in his absence?

He sat up gingerly, wary of the toll the hours splayed out on the couch might have taken on his back, already compromised by crashing on the bench at Grand Central the night before. He felt okay. Almost refreshed. Lou wandered into the kitchen and opened the cabinets, searching for some normal coffee, but settled for a cup of Earl Grey. He drank standing up, looking absentmindedly out the kitchen window. The swing-set still dominated the little patch of backyard, a few over-anxious autumnal leaves a vivid red accumulating at the bottom of the slide despite the heat.

The question was just as Tara had posed when she saw him at her front door that morning. *What the fuck, Lou?* He had no good answer. What had drawn him here, of all places?

The only thing he knew for sure at that moment was that he needed to take a shower.

Lou grabbed a towel from the linen closet and went into the bathroom in the master bedroom. While he waited for the water to warm up, he opened the medicine cabinet. As he expected, everything he hadn't taken two years ago had been cleared out.

Although he knew it wasn't logical, it made him sad. He was heartened to see that Tara didn't have any new prescriptions, just her same thyroid medication and some Ambien. And she hadn't given up the Dior perfume he'd bought her each year at Christmas. Knowing she still smelled the same was reassuring. As his eyes drifted over the shelves, he came upon a half-used white styptic pencil stuck in the corner, the one that he used to stop the bleeding when he would occasionally cut himself shaving. Lou picked it up and put it in his pocket. Then he thought better of it and put it back in its place. A small marker of his existence.

As the water started to steam the mirror, it hit Lou that it was intrusive of him to take a shower—to get naked—in what was now Tara's bathroom. He turned off the faucet and walked down the hall, intending to shower in the other bathroom instead. He was brought to a halt when he passed Bryn's bedroom door. In the brief window of time after Bryn woke up and discovered Lou napping on the living room couch but before she pummeled him and ran out the door, she'd posted a warning addressed to him. It was artfully created on her computer and printed in color, a picture of his face photoshopped onto a cartoon image of a man standing alone on a desert island in the middle of the ocean. The caption read "Get lost, LG."

Bryn's sign hit him like a punch to the gut, a pathetic riff on the game he used to play with her to test the strength of his abs. Why had she banished him to the island when all he'd done was respect her choice to stop the visits? He thought he'd allowed her to assert her independence, but maybe he'd given up on her without enough of a fight. And was it that obvious that he was as lonely as Bryn had depicted him? Bryn was still angry about the divorce, and Lou felt like a fool for failing to understand that. He contemplated grabbing his bags and leaving before Bryn got home from school that afternoon, to spare her more pain. But he needed a few days to sort himself out. And maybe he could mend the fences that he had been too caught up in himself to realize he had broken.

Dejected, Lou climbed up slowly to the dormered-out second floor where two small bedrooms flanked a tiny bathroom. In the early optimistic years of their marriage, he and Tara had talked about more children filling that space, a brother and sister for Bryn. Lou undressed and showered quickly. He didn't want to linger on the empty upper floor where the sadness of unfulfilled dreams permeated the space.

Tara was explicit that Lou not stick around for dinner. He saw her point, especially given Bryn's reaction to his being in the house. But there was no reason he couldn't make her and Bryn a meal, a small gesture in return for her not-exactly-warm but at least not-overtly-hostile welcome. Although the pantry wasn't as chock full of healthy options as when he lived with them, he managed to pull together a nice baked pasta siciliano with eggplant, a green salad, and some oatmeal cookies. When everything was ready, he put it in the fridge and left a note on the table: "Bon Appetit. Your dinner is ready!" He found a bottle of red on the counter still in a wine sleeve but without a card and put it on the table. Then he thought better of it and put it back where he'd found it. This wasn't a romantic dinner, after all.

Lou cleaned up and helped himself to an apple and a couple of cheese sticks. Then he glanced at the clock on the microwave.

"Shit!" It was the first sound he'd made in the hours he'd been tooling around the empty house and he jumped when he heard his own voice. He had no idea where the time had gone. It was 2:45 and Bryn would be back before he knew it. He grabbed his laptop, made sure that the spare key was still in the little lock box he had installed near the front door, and closed the door behind him

Once in the driveway, Lou remembered he didn't have a car. He contemplated calling a taxi or an Uber, but figured a walk would help him clear his head. It was still unseasonably warm, although in the burbs it was less oppressive than it had been in the city. He stood in front of the house for a minute and thought about where he should go to start working on his novel. He was overwhelmed by indecision and a longing for Cafe Zaz until he was distracted by the lace curtain moving a little at the house across the street. What must cranky old Mrs. DePisa think seeing him there after all this time? He didn't want to know.

Lou decided on the Arcade, a mid-sized mall about a mile from the house. Although it was the closest shopping destination, they had hardly ever gone there as a family. They preferred the tonier complex about three miles further away where Tara's branch of the Banana Republic was located. There was something just this side of seedy about the Arcade. The clientele that trolled both the nice mall and not-so-nice mall was nearly identical—rowdy teens, bedraggled parents with small children, elderly cardiac rehabbers—the real difference was in the food court. The bottom floor of the Arcade was devoted to food stalls dishing out bargain-basement quality chow from what seemed like every nation on earth. There was no rhyme or reason to the way the offerings were organized and no acknowledgment that not all types of cuisine played nicely together in the sandbox. It was culinary mayhem. At the nice mall, the food area was comprised of individual restaurants with seating and waitstaff; there was still a range of ethnic options, but the smells were segregated. Oh well. Today, the pungent food court would have to do.

Lou set off on foot, walking at a pace that would get him to his destination in a reasonable time but not make him sweat. He'd spent many an early morning or late afternoon jogging on virtually all of the streets of their immediate neighborhood during the years he was married to Tara. The most direct route was past where the homes became smaller and stood closer together, the yards still neat but cramped. This wasn't poverty. Lou knew the demographics. There were young people starting out and older people who worked hard but never quite made it. Italian, Irish, Greek, they were church-going and proud. They were confident their children would have it better. It was very 1950s in a way. Not exactly Levittown, but not far from it either.

Lost in thought, Lou was surprised when he reached "Petunia Way." Tara had grown up on the block, the modest home ever more snug as her three older brothers grew taller, bigger, and more hairy. Her parents had sold some years back and settled in Vegas where the weather suited them. Tara and her siblings had done as their parents had hoped, each moving out and purchasing a house one step up from their childhood home. One brother in Albany, one on Long Island, another in Jersey. Tara had moved literally half a mile away, buying with her parents' help but "up" nonetheless.

Lou turned onto the street, curious to see if anything had changed. He remembered the first time Tara had brought him home to her parents. Thanksgiving ten years earlier. He'd been so much younger then, just 33, in love with Tara and mad about little Brynny. Tara had insisted that they arrive exactly on time, but when they got there, Lou hung back. Bryn ran to the front door and rang the bell, while Lou was seized with a moment of panic.

"Think this is going to be a reprise of that scene in *Annie Hall?*" When Tara stared back at him blankly, he realized it was definitely a possibility. She knew who Woody Allen was, but the movie reference had gone right over her head. Jews were not within the Donohue family range of knowledge. Lou wasn't convinced that Tara even realized he was a member of the tribe the first several weeks they'd dated, even though he routinely peppered his conversation with Yiddish and exuded all manner of New York Semitic. It had been different with Jackie. She wasn't Jewish either—what must his parents be thinking, watching from above? —but she was New York, through and through. Jackie was Jewish by osmosis.

Lou turned away from the former Donohue homestead. Water under the bridge.

The nose knows. At the food court, Lou let his sniffer lead him to the least offensive olfactory alternative, planting himself at a small table for patrons of "The Bagel Depot." The soothing smell of warm dough and salty smoked fish wafted over him, comforting him like his father's well-worn prayer shawl. Maybe he was meant to fulfill his writing dreams among his own people. He opened his laptop to the document he had started at the Zaz and pondered how totally nuts it was that only a day had passed.

Unfortunately, in the hours since he had given up his Manhattan residency and crashed at the home of his ex, Chapter 1 of his detective story had failed to write itself. Lou stared at the screen. How was it possible that his columns, funny, incisive, sometimes with even a modicum of profundity, came to him so easily, and he couldn't even write the first line of his novel?

"When Detective Harry Moskowitz woke that day, his instinct told him something was amiss," Lou typed. Awful. He deleted and tried again. "Detective Harry Moskowitz awoke, alert and aroused, all of his senses humming." Better, but is that the first thing the reader needs to know about the hero of the novel? That he wakes up with a hard-on? Mundane at best, juvenile at worst.

It seemed so unfair to be judged by a first line anyway. He wondered whether readers were so shallow as to reject a book after one line. Certainly, the advice not to judge a book by its cover must extend to the first line. It was too much damn pressure to come up with something earth-shattering to start the whole thing off. Lou believed deeply in beginnings; Tara had said so this morning. But weren't how things ended more important?

Lou's thoughts were interrupted by grunts of pleasure emanating from somewhere close behind him. The noise was not sexual or obscene, nothing that might have inspired Lou to write a first line with some pizazz. No, these were guttural but less wild, more focused. Whatever the sound-maker was so intensely enjoying, Lou wanted a part of it.

He turned his body slowly in his chair and saw an overgrown teenager, his long legs protruding from cobalt blue satin basketball shorts, crossed at the ankle. He was probably a local college kid, Iona or College of New Rochelle, maybe paying his own way. His shaggy hair hung over his eyes, he needed a shave, and he looked like he might've taken Lou up on an offer to shower in the claustrophobic upstairs bathroom at Tara's house.

In his hands he held a beat-up paperback. He was totally engrossed, his eyes darting away from the page only momentarily each time he took a gargantuan bite of a toasted everything with scallion cream cheese. The grunts came at approximately thirty seconds intervals, in response to what—a funny line? a pithy description? He was a keen reader, although his eyes looked slightly glazed over and a little bloodshot. Now that the police didn't arrest for low-level weed, it seemed to Lou that everyone he met between 15 and 39 was walking through life stoned. Despite the kid's compromised state, Lou realized that what he wanted most in the world was to have someone read a novel that he would write with that level of joy.

"What're you reading?" Although they were sitting a few feet apart, Lou couldn't make out the title because the boy was holding the book at an angle to avoid globs of cream cheese landing on it.

At first, he didn't seem to hear Lou and he didn't look up. Initially that concentration had moved Lou. Now it struck him as rude. Besides, he needed to know what book it was, and, more critically, what the first line was that had sucked this young man in so deeply.

"Excuse me, may I know what you're reading?" Lou's language was polite, but he was almost at the point of yanking the book from the guy's hands when he finally looked up, startled.

"Sorry, bro, I was reading this book. *Slaughterhouse-Five.* Vonnegut's my man. You know it?"

Lou felt about a million years old. He'd once been this kid's age. A 20-year-old college student in 1996, reading Vonnegut by flashlight under the covers in his dorm room. He too had thought Vonnegut was his "man," *Slaughterhouse-Five* already almost 30 years out at that point.

"Yeah, I know it, but it's been a while," Lou said. "Can you read me the first line?"

"Sure," the kid said obligingly. He flipped back to the beginning of the book.

"'All this happened, more or less,'" he read solemnly. "Fucking epic." He sighed. Then he turned back to his book and continued to read and grunt.

Lou closed his laptop. There was no competing with Kurt today. He didn't have it in him.

October

Jackie

Mike leaned into Jackie's robing room, his broad shoulders filling the entryway.

"Almost showtime, Judge." Time had passed slowly for Jackie. September had finally turned into October. The Indian summer had subsided, but it was still warm in the courthouse. The standing fan in the corner blew across Jackie's desk, moving some papers around and messing with her neat hair.

"Thanks. Just a little more coffee before I face the music," Jackie said. She took another swig, and, assuming Mike had retreated to his post in the courtroom, closed her eyes to amplify the warmth and taste. When she looked up, he was still there. Grinning at her.

"What?"

"I'm glad you're using the present I got you. It was gathering dust there on your desk."

It was true. For her 40th birthday a few months back, Mike had given her an oversized mug with the words, "Here Come De Judge" emblazoned in red. She hadn't used it once. Not because she didn't appreciate the gesture and not because Angela had teased her that Mike had a crush on her. She always drank her coffee out of the cardboard hot cups from the carts outside.

"I bought a Keurig." Jackie gestured to the credenza, where her new coffee toy was proudly displayed. Although she'd made few changes at home after Lou's departure—he'd left barely a trace of himself—she bought herself a Keurig for her apartment too. She hoped it would help erase the memory of the day Lou didn't brew the carafe of morning coffee and was never seen or heard from again.

Jackie reluctantly put down the mug. She ran her courtroom punctually and it was 9:00. She'd been trying to establish herself as a no-nonsense judge, professional, serious, fair. She knew that as a result, many of the attorneys who practiced before her perceived her as unfeeling and a bit of a hard-ass. Trying to make up for lack of experience by being tough. Angela had suggested as much. Jackie wondered whether she should or could show more sensitivity like some of the other judges. She wasn't sure she could pull off warm and fuzzy, but Jackie was pretty sure that a change in judicial temperament went hand-in-hand with the personal transformation she needed to make.

Ironically, it had been Lou who'd encouraged Jackie to empathize more with the people she judged. "You need to want to help, to make things better. Not just to fix things to be the way you think is right." When Jackie was first getting her head around the job, it had helped to discuss the challenges of her work with Lou. He was a good listener and he had a feel for the families. He expressed compassion more easily than she did.

"In family court, the jargon is all different, softer. The defendant is the respondent, a trial is called a fact-finding, sentencing is disposition. And when you send the kid off to a facility, it's a placement," Jackie explained one early Sunday morning as they lay in bed reading the *New York Times*. Lou put down the Magazine section and looked at her.

"Who do they think they're fooling?" he asked. Jackie had no answer.

Today was the final day of the dispositional hearing for Moshe F. and Jackie was dreading it. The fact-finding had taken place several weeks earlier, "BLL," before Lou left. She'd determined that the 14-year-old boy had committed arson in the second degree when he set a fire one morning in the library at his Yeshiva middle school. He'd started the blaze intentionally in a large metal trash can, burned some religious books and attracted a lot of attention from the press. The damage would have been minimal, but the sprinkler system went off and doused the place, destroying hundreds of volumes. But what made the charge serious was that the building was full of teachers and students at the time. Thankfully, no one was hurt.

"A kid who starts a small fire now starts a bigger one later," Mindy had commented. Jackie had answered with a non-committal "maybe." She knew, as usual, there was probably something to Mindy's observation.

Today Jackie would decide how Moshe should be punished. Fire setting was classic delinquency that could, as Mindy intuited, lead to a future of criminality. It didn't presage sociopathic behavior at the level of torturing small animals for kicks, but it wasn't far off. She'd heard two full days of testimony from psychiatric experts from both the prosecution and the defense. Their views were so diametrically opposed that they nearly cancelled each other out in Jackie's mind.

Jackie had discussed the broad outlines of the case with Lou one night at dinner. Now that he was beyond her reach, his words, and his frustration with her, came back to her as she geared up to decide the boy's fate.

Lou had served each of them a plate of grilled chicken with a citrus glaze, a side of quinoa and roasted vegetables, and a chilled glass of chablis. Jackie took off her heels and carefully put them away on the shoe rack in the bedroom before she came to the table and sat down opposite him.

"L'chaim!" Lou said, raising his glass in the air and tilting it toward Jackie. He waited for her to do the same, the satisfying clink of glass on glass signifying the start of the meal on a festive note.

Jackie didn't raise her glass but instead gazed distractedly over Lou's shoulder and out the window. When she turned back, she saw a look of concern cross his face. It was sometimes like this. Lou would put his all into preparing a gourmet dinner, but there were evenings when Jackie would have preferred a quick bowl of Wheat

Chex before curling up on the couch with a book. Tonight though it wasn't the menu that caused her hesitation. She was preoccupied with Moshe's case.

Lou tasted the food and, apparently finding it not only unobjectionable but, as he declared, "delicious!," turned to ferreting out what was bothering Jackie. He had a reporter's instinct and zeroed right in.

"Fire-setter getting you down?"

"There's no question he's guilty. Now I have to figure out what to do with him," Jackie said. "I mean, this boy seems to have it all, at least in comparison to the children I usually see. Parents in an intact marriage, a dad with a job, a good school, a religious upbringing, structure. But he could've torched that school with all those kids and teachers inside. And he could do it again."

Lou had been eating steadily and quietly while Jackie talked. Now he put down his utensils and picked up his wine, taking a swallow before he addressed her.

"I don't know, Jackie. Couldn't you cut the kid a break?"

"Why would I do that? Because he's Jewish?" She regretted the words as soon as they had left her mouth. Somehow, it felt like the question had been in the air between them.

"No, not because he's Jewish. Because he's a kid, and kids do stupid things."

"They're all kids, Lou. I'm a Family Court judge!" She got up from the table and walked to the kitchen where she filled a glass with water from the tap and took small sips, as if trying to cure hiccups she didn't have.

"I know that. I mean, you should've seen some of the stupid things that I did at his age."

"You didn't set fires, did you?" Jackie's voice cracked and she realized how much this case had gotten under her skin. She was fighting with Lou about something he had absolutely nothing to do with.

"I used to set fire to my farts at camp," Lou said.

"That's not funny."

"Actually, it was pretty funny. Anyway, all I meant was that sometimes I think you need to apply the law, sure, but also let yourself feel more. You're a good person and a good judge, Jackie, but you don't let yourself be human. Never mind about trying to get inside the kid's head. Try for a minute to put yourself in the shoes of these parents. Think how desperate they'll be when you send their child away. How much they'll feel like they failed him." Lou took several more bites of his chicken. Jackie couldn't possibly think about eating.

"It's funny how you think you can empathize with the parents any better than I can," she said. But in her heart, she thought that Lou would make a good father. Kind and responsible, not a pushover but not too stern either. What kind of mother would Jackie be? The choices she'd made meant she'd likely never find out. Maybe that was for the best.

"Besides, there's no question this kid has to spend some time in a juvenile facility. The statute leaves me no choice. The issue is only how long. And I have very little leeway."

Jackie sat down again at the table and drank her wine, the food rendered totally inedible by the conversation. Lou held her gaze and opened his mouth as though he had something more to say. Instead he ate another forkful of quinoa.

"In the matter of Moshe F.," Mike announced at a volume only slightly above conversational. There was no need to call out. It was the first case on the calendar and the attorneys had arrived on time, ready for the proceedings. The law guardian appointed to represent Moshe sat at one table with the boy's father, waiting for Moshe to be brought in. The attorney from the Corporation Counsel's office, representing the city, sat at the other table. At the sound of Mike's voice, they all rose. Jackie disliked the moment when everyone in the courtroom stood and she was seated. It made her feel momentarily powerless.

"Please be seated," Jackie said.

The side door to the courtroom opened and a court officer ushered Moshe in. The boy had been held in a secure detention facility during the pendency of the hearings and he looked even paler than when he'd first been brought to court for the fact-finding. Jackie watched as Moshe's father leaned toward Mike and spoke close to his ear. Mike nodded, and Moshe's father took his son in his arms, holding him close. The boy wiped a few tears away from his eyes with the back of his hand but stood tall. His father exchanged another word with Mike and showed him something in his hand. Mike examined it for a moment and handed it back to the father, who then placed a black velvet yarmulke gently on Moshe's head. The boy lowered his chin to his chest and looked down at his feet for a moment. Jackie wondered what he was thinking.

"Your honor, I want to apologize that Moshe's mother couldn't be here today." The law guardian addressed the court but looked at Moshe. "Unfortunately, Moshe's twin sisters both have the flu, and his mother couldn't leave them. But Moshe has her full support."

"I'm sure he does," Jackie said. The boy's mother had attended every other court appearance. Jackie thought her absence today was likely due, sick siblings notwithstanding, to her inability to watch as judgment was meted out against her eldest child. Lou's words came back to her as though he were standing next to her, whispering in her ear. Did Moshe's parents feel they had failed him? Had they?

Would Jackie fail him now?

"As you know, the court has taken quite a bit of testimony over the last few weeks in an effort to determine what placement would be in your best interests while simultaneously protecting the community," Jackie said. A tiny whimper escaped Moshe's lips and Jackie realized how close he was to bursting into tears. It was cruel to make speeches. She'd address him directly. She could at least do that.

"Moshe, when I listened to the testimony at trial, I didn't get the feeling that you were trying to hurt anyone when you set the fire. Am I right?"

Moshe looked startled by the question and turned to his lawyer to see if he could answer. She nodded.

"I never meant to hurt anyone. I didn't hurt anyone."

"And it also seemed to me like you didn't intend the fire to spread because you put those books into a metal trash can and lit the fire there. You hadn't figured on the sprinklers. Is that correct?"

"Yes," he said, making eye contact for the first time. Now it was Jackie's turn to be startled, his gaze was so pure and so direct. She wanted to ask him what had gone through his mind at that moment in the library. Was it something in those books or what they represented that fueled his need to destroy them? Didn't he realize that he'd be severely punished? But it was irrelevant; it hadn't been an accident. He would pay for his deed no matter what he'd been thinking.

There was no point in dragging this out. Jackie only had two options, three years in a secure setting, or 18 months in a less secure setting. It was, in the end, a question of whether a show of mercy on Jackie's part was appropriate under the law. She would do what she could and hope she didn't regret it later.

"It is the determination of this Court that you be placed for 18 months in a medium security juvenile facility. I will direct that the Commissioner make every effort to place you as close to your family as possible to facilitate visitation."

Jackie turned to Angela, who was seated to her right, to avoid watching Moshe and his father embrace again before he was handcuffed and taken away. She wasn't expecting the scowl on Angela's face.

"I hope your leniency wasn't misplaced," Angela said through thin lips. "I understand why you'd feel pity for the boy, but that fire could have resulted in tragedy. This child has psychological problems, and you sent him a message that what he did wasn't all that serious." As almost an afterthought, Angela looked toward the back of the courtroom.

"Ms. Lopez from the Judicial Review Panel came in while you were handing down the judgement. She's sitting in the back."

Jackie glanced briefly at the woman and understood how Moshe F. must have felt, as her own actions were judged by someone who simply could not stand in her shoes.

And then Ms. Lopez shook her head, ever so slightly, in disapproval.

Jackie realized, too late, that she should have consulted Angela before handing down her decision, even if only to placate her law secretary's need to feel involved. She couldn't afford to offend Angela and it appeared that Ms. Lopez also felt Jackie's decision was too soft. She should feel chagrined, worried.

Instead, Jackie felt she'd taken a step forward

Lou

They'd settled into a routine. If Lou had been forced to explain it, he wouldn't have been able to, it was so beyond comprehension. But he hardly spoke to anyone so explaining wasn't really an issue.

A few days on the couch had turned into an interim residency, albeit one with strict parameters. On Sundays, Lou went food shopping at the Super Stop & Shop. He loaded up with groceries for the week for the three of them, on his dime. After putting everything away, he'd spend hours walking around the neighborhood, briskly but aimlessly, to stay out of Tara and Bryn's way. Lou wondered what would happen when the weather turned from crisp fall to freezing winter, but promised himself that he wouldn't be there for the change of season to find out.

On weekdays, he trained himself to sleep late, tucked away in one of the tiny upstairs bedrooms that Tara reluctantly said he could use because she didn't like having him sacked out on the couch in the living room. His back hurt from nights tossing and turning on the old futon they'd originally had in their first apartment in Brooklyn. Back then, sleeping on the equivalent of a wooden plank seemed youthful and erotic. Not so much anymore.

After Tara and Bryn left for the day, Lou would come downstairs, make coffee, and reassess his options. Finding no good ones, he'd spend several hours working on the accounts of his paying clients before he made dinner for his ex-wife and her daughter. A meal that he was banned from sharing. Then for the rest of the morning he would look around the house and see what needed repairing, organizing, cleaning; if he needed a part or a tool, he'd walk to the hardware store and pick it up. One day he fixed the drip in Tara's bathroom sink; another, he cleaned the grill. That morning, he'd mowed the lawn. He was like an on-site handyman, which made him feel like less of a burden. Tara didn't acknowledge any of his efforts, but she didn't tell him to stop either.

At 2:30, before Bryn returned from school, Lou skedaddled, walking to the mall and setting up shop in the bagel store. Sometimes he wrote his column, sometimes he made lists of things he needed to do to get his life on track. Look for an apartment, get a few more accounting clients, enroll in a writing class, hang out in a classy bar instead of the rundown shopping center, flirt with a woman to remember you're alive.

He'd yet to write an opening salvo for his book, or any words that might follow, although he'd set plenty of goals. One day he vowed to create a cast of characters. Another time he promised himself he would plot out the storyline. On a third occasion he swore he wouldn't leave his post until he wrote 2000 words. But he was uninspired and good intentions were no cure for lack of imagination. He'd return to the house after eight at night, sometimes dejected and sometimes just baffled at the course his life had taken and his inability to set it right. He'd exchange a few pleasantries with Tara, and then retire to his attic refuge. The next day it would start all over again.

Lou amused himself by switching up the kind of bagel he ordered to accompany his labors. He'd started with the standards (sesame, poppy, onion, plain) and moved on to the more particular (whole wheat, cinnamon raisin, egg, everything). Now he was up to the flavors that no self-respecting Jew would ever order: Oreo, blueberry, shitake mushroom. He was about to bite into a toasted zucchini when he saw her.

Bryn had inherited her red hair from her father, "Froggy," Tara's first serious boyfriend and an aspiring musician. He'd branded his daughter with the unmistakable genetic trait before he walked away from both mother and child. That had been Lou's assumption, anyway. But early in their courtship, when Bryn was a rambunctious four-year-old tearing up the playground and running her single mother ragged, Tara had confided to Lou that she'd never told Froggy she was pregnant. She broke off the relationship before she began to show with the excuse she'd met another guy with better prospects.

"What did I need him hanging around for?" Tara had asked. "Why ruin his big plans?" Lou had been so shocked at Tara's perspective that he hadn't responded. As he and Tara and Bryn became their own family, he was grateful that the man who'd contributed so fleetingly was not part of Bryn's life. Now, Lou couldn't help looking at the situation through Judge Jackie's eyes. Absentee fathers were public enemy number one in her book, the root cause of all family misery. Although off-the-bench Jackie would never admit it, Lou figured this inability to trust in others was part of what kept Jackie from marrying and having children herself.

While he and Tara were married, Lou had proved to be a good father to Bryn. He'd wanted to stay a good father post-split, involved in whatever aspects of Bryn's life she'd been willing to share. But it hadn't panned out that way. And because he wasn't sure that Jackie would understand—might peg him as irresponsible like so many of the men she saw in her courtroom—Lou had never told Jackie about Bryn. It had been better to leave Jackie in the dark and leave Bryn tucked away in a place of heartache only Lou could access.

Lou studied Bryn from the safety of the bagel store as she sat with a bunch of kids in the Starbucks across the way. He counted three boys and two girls, plus Bryn. He didn't recognize any of them as Bryn's childhood friends. He wasn't sure he would at this point, the teens all post-pubescent and altered. Hell, even Bryn was almost unrecognizable. When she was a little girl the bright red hair had merely been a feature that made people smile and want to pat Bryn on the head. Now, in the slightly sleazy mall, her hair was provocative, brazen but also needy. A flare on a sinking boat that screamed "stay away!" and "save me!" simultaneously.

Lou remembered how Tara used to dress Bryn, so cute and innocent. Pastels and floral prints, even the occasional ruffle. Now Bryn's wardrobe was all audacious jewel tones, deep reds and emerald greens and bold purples, worn just a little too tight or a tiny bit low-cut, whatever Tara would let her get away with to fit in. Bryn made Lou feel old and sad and tired.

Lou watched as a barista, a tall teen with a mop top of blond hair and a green apron, approached Bryn's table. He shrugged and pointed to the kids, then gestured around at other customers with coffee cups in their hands. Neither Bryn nor any of her friends had a drink or a snack from Starbucks. The boy was clearly trying to move them along. Lou knew the drill. It was why he was diligent to nibble on a bagel or sip a cappuccino at his table. It was embarrassing to be asked to vacate.

Lou could hear Bryn's voice above the others. He couldn't make out her words, but the tone was flirtatious, pleading. Then she pulled back her shoulders and stuck out what passed for her budding breasts, snug in her electric blue v-neck shirt, in the boy's direction. Apparently unimpressed, the Frappuccino-maker stood with his arms crossed over his chest and feet planted firmly, waiting for the group to get up. They started to gather their backpacks and pick up their cell phones. The boy took a walkie-talkie from his belt and communicated something to someone. The battle had been won.

Bryn and the other girls walked out first, settling themselves onto those mechanical riding toys—a pink pig, a black and white cow, and a yellow duck whose paint had seen better days—the kind that cost a quarter to ride for thirty seconds of pleasure and half the time eat your money without moving at all. The boys stood around looking as awkward as only 14-year-old boys can. Legs and arms too long for torsos, a hint of hair on the upper lip that looks more like dirt than mustache. Lou looked at his watch: 5 p.m. Had the kids come to the mall straight from school? Tara expected Bryn to come home when class let out, eat a snack, start her homework. But he wouldn't get in the middle of this. It wasn't his place.

And then, without any warning, it became his place. Lou watched as Bryn and one of the boys, the tallest one in the Beastie Boys t-shirt, peeled off and headed toward the hallway where the restrooms were located. At first Lou didn't think anything of it. Maybe they both had to use the toilet at the same time. Then he saw Bryn leaning against the wall with Beastie standing too close, almost pressed against her, the palms of his hands spread on the wall on either side of her head. Bryn jerked her head to the right, perhaps avoiding an unwanted kiss. She pushed her closed fists into the boy's chest, barely moving him back an inch. Lou could see the tension in Bryn's arms. She wasn't playing.

In five or six strides Lou was on top of him, pulling him away from Bryn by the back of his shirt.

"Who the fuck are you?" The boy sneered, shaking Lou's hand off his neck but stepping away from Bryn.

"I'm her father."

"You're not my father," Bryn yelled. "Get away from us."

"Do you know this guy?" Beastie asked, all of sudden Bryn's gallant protector. Lou had to restrain himself from shoving the kid further away, his presence so disgusted him. But he glanced at Bryn, who looked completely mortified, and regained his composure.

"She knows me. Not that you deserve the information, but I used to be married to her mother and I'm taking her home now. I don't want to see you around her again." Lou threw out his chest in a more successful version of what Bryn had tried with the barista. He stepped a few inches closer to the boy whose own shoulders were so narrow that his chest was practically concave. At this close range, Lou could see that the kid had the sort of suppurating acne that would not clear up until well into college, if that's where he was headed. Lou felt

94

sorry for him and then remembered that he'd almost manhandled Bryn.

"Let's go," Lou said to Bryn, who was staring at him with pure malice in her eyes. He had no authority over her. He was banking on his intuition that she wouldn't want to make more of a scene in front of her "friends." Sure enough, she headed toward the exit by his side, sullen and silent.

"Do those kids go to school with you?" They were outside the mall, back on his well-worn route to the house. Lou tried for a casual tone, but Bryn wasn't having any.

"Look, Bryn, I'm not going to apologize for intervening. I couldn't let that boy get in your face like that." They walked another block in silence. "Do you hang out at the mall a lot?"

"What do you care?" Bryn finally answered.

"Just making conversation."

"I don't want to make conversation with you. What don't you get about that?"

And then she took off running. For a second Lou contemplated chasing her, but there was no point. She was headed home and Tara would have to deal with her. He wasn't the villain here.

When Lou reached the house, Tara and Bryn had sat down to the dinner he'd made earlier in the day. Bryn's steady stare communicated that she hadn't told Tara what had happened between them and Lou figured that was okay. If he'd succeeded in humiliating her a little in front of the other kids and maybe even scaring her companion, then maybe Tara didn't need to know.

"Are you hungry?" Tara asked. Before he could answer, she'd gotten another plate down from the cabinet and was pulling silverware from the drawer. He wasn't sure why she'd violated her own rule and extended him an invitation, but his cooking smelled good and he'd hardly eaten all day. It was one of his signature menus, teriyaki salmon, Israeli couscous with sautéed onion, and a mixed green salad with avocado, hearts of palms and craisins. His mouth watered.

"Don't mind if I do." He sat down directly across the table from Bryn. He'd taken one bite when she pushed back her chair, cleared her plate to the sink, and raced out of the room.

"Did I excuse you from the table young lady?" The color rose in Tara's cheeks and her tone spoke more of embarrassment than annoyance, as though Bryn's poor table manners were a direct reflection of her mothering.

"I didn't ask," came Bryn's reply before she slammed her bedroom door.

Lou sat back in his chair and closed his eyes, suddenly overwhelmed and exhausted.

"She hates me," he said.

When he opened his eyes, Tara was looking at him with something akin to worry, although it might have been pity.

"Bryn doesn't hate you. She's confused. She doesn't understand why you're here. To be honest, I don't understand why you're here either. Or why I let you stay."

Lou struggled for a response. Their marriage had not been easy, but they'd been truthful with each other. Sometimes the honesty had been so raw they'd barely held themselves together as a couple. Now, Tara was asking him, three weeks after he'd crashed on her couch for a couple of nights, why had he moved in? Why was he taking care of the house, cooking dinner every night? Could he tell her that he'd initially turned to her as a last resort, knowing only that she wouldn't put him out on the street? Should he confess that the smells and tastes and feel of home were seeping into his skin and binding him back to this place, this family, to her? It was all too much to contemplate, too much to handle. He wouldn't go there.

"That makes three of us," Lou said. Tara managed a half smile.

When Lou finished what was on his plate, he didn't take a second helping, his appetite gone. He washed the dishes and silverware, placed the plates carefully back in the cabinet and the cutlery in the drawer. He wiped his hands on the green and white striped dish towel hung next to the sink. Jackie had insisted on paper towels only in the kitchen, for sanitary reasons, and he realized now how much he had missed the feel of this cloth in his hands.

"Good night, Tara," Lou said, softly. She looked away, but he saw the tears.

Upstairs on the futon, he pulled out his laptop and began to write his column.

You Can Have A Roof Over Your Head and Still Be Homeless

As you all know, about a month ago I made some big changes in my life. Although the woman I was with, a woman I loved, did nothing identifiable to hold me back from my dreams, I felt in my heart that I couldn't be with her and become the man and the writer that I was meant to be. I'm sure some of you found my decision to leave her rash, incomprehensible, perhaps even foolish or cruel. I won't try to argue against that. I've had those thoughts myself. I will tell you that it's what I needed to do.

If I'm being honest with myself and with you, which I always try to be, the state of affairs I'm in is so surreal that I'm nearly paralyzed, unable to make progress on my life or my work. I'm not looking for sympathy—I made my own bed, so to speak. By being here, although I am tolerated and try to contribute, I'm causing people that I care about pain and confusion. Though I have a place to hang my hat, I'm more alone than I've ever been. I'm "homeless" in a deeply emotional sense of the word, a person with nowhere he can go where he feels truly loved and accepted and needed. It's a state of being I wouldn't wish on anyone. And I have only myself to blame.

Jackie

"If you help me, it'll take the two of us an hour instead of twice that if I do it by myself."

"I don't understand, Mindy. Who sends paper invitations anymore? Hasn't the PTA discovered email?"

"That's what I said! But I'm not in charge. I'm a worker bee."

Jackie knew it was a ploy. Mindy had been telling her for weeks to stop moping around her apartment and start living her life again. Although not exactly an invitation to the Oscars, stuffing envelopes for the autumn fair at Nicole's middle school was an excuse to get Jackie out of the house. As much as she hated to admit it, she was grateful that Mindy had persuaded her to come over. Even a mindless task was better than another night mired in her solitary thoughts.

"Did you call him back?" They were about half-way through the pile of flyers.

"Who?" Jackie was so engrossed in folding the sheets of orange paper into exact thirds that she'd almost forgotten her sister was in the room.

"What do you mean, who? Adam." Jackie was roused from her reverie by Mindy's impatient tone.

"No, I haven't called him." Adam lived in the apartment at the far end of Mindy's hallway. A divorced hedge fund exec with a kid in Nicole's class, Jackie had met him a few times in the elevator. He was pleasant enough and, at 6 foot 6, hard to miss. Mindy had alerted Adam to Jackie's newly single status and he'd gamely called her. When it wasn't Lou's ringtone, she'd let it go to voicemail.

"Can you imagine us together? He's a giant! I come up to his belt buckle."

Mindy smirked. "Lucky Adam, I'd say."

"Thanks, little sister. Just what I need—juvenile sex jokes."

"Actually, the sex may be exactly what you need. Anyway, he makes tons of money. Let him take you out on the town. Dress up, get your hair blown out. Enjoy yourself a little." Mindy stuffed a few flyers into envelopes. She poured Jackie more wine although her first glass was untouched.

"You know money doesn't impress me. Lou and I always had a good time and he spent almost no money on me at all."

"That's because he didn't have any." They folded and stuffed in silence.

"I mean, don't you think that was part of it?" Mindy stopped stuffing and put a hand on Jackie's, mid-fold.

"Don't I think *what* was part of *what?*" She shook her sister's hand off and finished the crease.

"Part of why Lou left you, silly. The financial disparity. The power issue. Men don't like to be with women who are smarter than they are, or out-earn them, or who have more prestigious jobs. It makes them feel inadequate and weak."

"I don't think so," she said through clenched teeth. Jackie knew where Mindy's conjecture was coming from. Her sister had given up her own promising job in fashion to raise the girls and support Sam in his career. Mindy's understanding of the dynamics between the sexes was traditional and it worked for her. But did Mindy have the right to comment on the choices that an accomplished professional woman like Jackie made, even if her love life had crashed and burned and she was now stuffing envelopes?

Oblivious to Jackie's discomfort, Mindy plowed on. "Or maybe he wanted something more conventional; marriage and children?" Mindy had stopped stuffing envelopes and was now looking up at the ceiling, as though inspiration might appear from above for other theories she could posit regarding Lou's flight. It was more than Jackie could take.

Jackie pushed her chair back from the table and stood up. "I'm done here. I'm going home."

Mindy's next question stopped her in her tracks.

"Do you remember Coach A?"

Jackie sat down again.

"Of course."

Coach A was the gym teacher at their middle school when Jackie was in eighth grade and Mindy was in sixth. He was short and stocky, with one bushy black eyebrow that grew across his forehead and a huge bellowing laugh. When he had a heart attack and died on the school basketball court at age 42, everyone was devastated.

"Do you remember what the principal said at the assembly we had the next day?"

"No."

"I know Lou isn't dead. But she said that if we wanted to remember Coach and keep him in our hearts, then we needed to remember everything about him. Not only the good things, like how fun he was or how he encouraged us to be the best we could be, but the things we didn't like. I used to sit on the floor in my room after school and force myself to think about how Coach sometimes lost his temper and said something mean, like that time I missed all my layups in the semifinals and he called me hopeless. Or how once he told me that I should be nicer to that girl, Sara Fleishman, when he didn't know anything about the situation and it was none of his business."

"Where are you going with this, Min?" Jackie tried to steady her voice, but she could feel the tremble.

"I'm saying that you're creating this totally perfect Lou in your head and blocking out how he hurt you. I know you love him and I'm sure he has a lot of good qualities, but Lou's no saint. He's not that perfect guy in the column. You haven't even allowed yourself to be furious that he dumped you. It isn't normal. It's okay to grieve for a while, but grieve the whole person, not some fairytale version of him that never existed. Then you'll be able to move on."

Jackie awoke the next morning groggy and grumpy. Despite what Mindy thought, Jackie was enraged at how Lou had abandoned her, destroyed what they'd been building, without having the basic decency to explain why. Her self-respect was intact; she hated Lou for treating her like another passing topic for his column—'today I left my girlfriend.'

Jackie also remembered how Lou made her laugh. How they'd held hands like teenagers while they shared an ice cream sundae. How they'd binge-watched five seasons of *Breaking Bad* over Memorial Day weekend in her bed and how Lou had held his hand over her eyes at the scary parts. How she felt when he made love to her, exhilarated and protected. Jackie hadn't forgiven Lou for what he'd done and couldn't imagine that she ever would. But he'd changed her. Revealed the possibilities.

"I decided you were right," Jackie said. It was early to call, but she could hear the sounds of Mindy's already bustling household in the background. *Good Morning America* was blaring on the television and Nicole and Caroline were fighting over the last frozen waffle.

"Sorry, I couldn't hear you—nuts here. What did you say?"

"I said I decided you were right."

"Of course you did. About what?" Mindy said. "Dara, go wash your hands!"

"I'm over Lou. It's been a month since he left. I'm putting the relationship behind me. I need to concentrate on doing my job and getting this ten-year appointment. Love is overrated."

"Not sure that was my advice but getting over Lou would be a good start." Jackie could hear Mindy turn her back on the cacophony of her kitchen. "Call Adam. A cheap fling with an exceptionally tall man would help," Mindy whispered into the phone.

Jackie laughed. "What would you know about that, Miss 'married her average-height high school sweetheart and never kissed another boy'"?

"Just a guess. Have to go. There's going to be a war over breakfast food here in two minutes."

Jackie pushed herself to get ready for work. Angela had reminded her before she wrapped up the day before that the Clark case was on the calendar. The attorney for the city had checked in periodically since the last adjourned date, reporting that Darlene Clark and her girls were still MIA. Jackie had the nagging feeling that she'd mishandled the case, although she couldn't pinpoint where she'd gone wrong. If, in retrospect, holding Ms. Clark in contempt had been too much tough love, it didn't excuse her behavior in bolting with the girls.

Jackie emerged from the elevator and Dennis was by her side with a cheerful "Good morning, Judge!" Jackie had asked the doorman repeatedly not to address her as "judge" in the lobby, but he seemed incapable of restraining himself. This year she might have to link his Christmas bonus to a promise that he'd try harder; she never knew who might be lurking. As if reading her mind, Dennis clapped his hand over his mouth and then said in a hushed tone through his fingers, "Your friend is here. She's in front, just inside the door."

"What friend?" Jackie hardly socialized these days and definitely was not expecting anyone at this hour of the morning.

"I didn't ask her name since she didn't want to go up to your apartment, Judge. She said she'd wait down here for you."

"Okay, Dennis. Keep an eye out."

Jackie walked toward the door and saw a woman lying on the wooden bench curled in on herself, her head resting on her hands and her eyes half closed. She was totally still. Only the smallest sound seemed to float around her, a self-soothing coo. Jackie hadn't recognized Darlene Clark in her courtroom that day after the early morning subway encounter. Here, even more out of context, she knew exactly who she was. Jackie's mind raced to work out how Ms. Clark could have discovered where she lived. But as Mindy had reminded her, her address was all over the internet from the days when she was a private citizen.

Jackie could still feel Ms. Clark's fury as she was led out of court by the officers, a mother's blind rage and fear aimed directly at her. For all she knew, the woman had a gun or a knife, ready to exact revenge. But she looked so helpless, defeated and small. Pity welled up in Jackie, a weirdly maternal feeling toward this woman whose children she, Jackie, had taken from her care. Jackie felt this was a test of her resolve to be a different person, a person who broke through her usual boundaries of what was right and wrong. Could she summon the empathy to relate to this woman as someone who needed her help?

There was a warrant out on Darlene Clark, a warrant Jackie had signed, and the little girls were missing. Jackie knew she'd need to call the police, sooner rather than later. But after so many weeks, a few minutes were not likely to make a difference. She sat down quietly on the end of the bench so as not to startle Ms. Clark and spoke softly to her.

"Ms. Clark. You need to get up."

At the sound of Jackie's voice, Ms. Clark bolted upright. Jackie jumped up from the bench and backed away several feet from her. Dennis, normally kind of pokey, moved faster than Jackie would have thought him capable and was next to her in a flash.

Ms. Clark raised her hands in an "I'm not armed stance," and blurted out, "I came here to talk to you. I need your help." Jackie wondered what it was like to know that you might be perceived as dangerous. Jackie realized that Ms. Clark seemed more vulnerable than anything else and she was moved rather than afraid.

"Let's go outside, Ms. Clark," she said.

"Are you sure?" Dennis said. He needed this job and Jackie could tell he was worried that screwing up this encounter could cost him.

"Yes, it's fine. I know her." Jackie guided Ms. Clark out of the building and to the stoop of the brownstone across the street. Dennis followed them out the door and stood proprietarily in front of the building like a good guard dog. Although the doorman outfit did not inspire the confidence of Mike's court officer uniform, it was something, and Jackie made a mental note to increase Dennis's Christmas bonus. Jackie and Ms. Clark sat down on the steps.

"This is a serious thing you've done by coming here. Listen to me carefully. I can't be the judge on your case anymore. Do you understand that?"

"I don't care about the damn case. I need your help. Isn't that why you have this job?" Ms. Clark's words were challenging but her gaze was fixed on the ground. Where was the feisty woman who had cursed at Jackie in court weeks ago? Jackie had a fleeting thought of what Estella Lopez would make of this flagrantly inappropriate interaction, but she pushed it to the back of her mind. She wanted to help.

Ms. Clark looked slightly disheveled. Her hair was uncombed and hanging loose, her shirt misbuttoned so that it hung unevenly at the bottom outside her jeans. Jackie asked on a hunch, "Ms. Clark, when was the last time you had something to eat?"

"I'm not sure. I haven't been too hungry lately."

"Well, I can't think without more coffee. Let's get a quick bite and then we'll figure out what to do." Jackie extended her hand, helping Ms. Clark up from the stoop. Not the touchy-feely type, she let go as soon as Ms. Clark was on her feet. Still, there had been that momentary intimacy.

They inched down Broadway, Jackie matching herself to Ms. Clark's pace. What must they look like together? The judge, petite but head held high, shoulders thrown back in her tailored beige suit and leather briefcase in hand. And Ms. Clark, the victim? the accused? head bowed, shuffling, gazing at her feet. But this was New York City. No one gave them a second glance.

When they approached Cafe Zaz, Jackie gently turned Ms. Clark toward the door, opened it for her and steered her to a table. She'd been to Lou's "office" a couple of times with him, even met Mia once. This early in the morning, there was a line for take-out, but the tables were mostly empty. Jackie was relieved that Mia wasn't working. She couldn't imagine making chit-chat about Lou's welfare. Out of all the places she could have bought Ms. Clark for breakfast, she didn't know why she'd chosen this one. Maybe going cold turkey on Lou was harder than she thought.

When the waitress brought the menus, Ms. Clark didn't open hers. Jackie ordered coffee for herself, and then ordered for Ms. Clark.

"She'll have oatmeal, a side of cinnamon toast, and a hot cocoa." She had no idea if comfort food was universal, but it seemed worth a try. The niceties of ordering finished, Jackie took a legal pad out of her briefcase and placed it on the table. She didn't want to appear too official, but she needed information. She'd now waited longer than she should have.

"I'm going to try to help you, Ms. Clark. But there's something I need to know right away before we talk about anything else. Where are your daughters?" Jackie's tone was kind, but firm.

"They're with me." Jackie looked around the cafe, half expecting the children to pop out from behind the counter or come running out of the kitchen.

"Where are they now? Where are they living?"

"We're all at my cousin's in Brooklyn."

"They're supposed to be with your sister. That's where Child Protective Services placed them. You're not allowed to take care of them right now." Jackie knew she sounded pedantic. These were serious court orders that Ms. Clark had flaunted.

"I need the girls with me. I'm their mother. And my sister don't know shit about taking care of children." Jackie smiled, despite herself, picturing Mindy saying the same thing about her.

Ms. Clark began to cry. The tears seemed to come out of nowhere. They rolled down her face, big globs taking with them black eyeliner and mascara and dripping onto her hands that lay folded in her lap. She made no sound. Jackie opened her bag and pulled out the pack of tissues her mother insisted a lady always carried. Could she have envisioned this? Ms. Clark took the pack and held it, as though the act of pulling out a tissue was too much effort. It dawned on Jackie that perhaps Ms. Clark was not overwhelmed but might be clinically depressed. She had to do something before the situation deteriorated further.

"Ms. Clark, I need you to write down your cousin's name and the address where you and the girls are living."

Ms. Clark looked up for the first time. She fixed Jackie with a gaze that tried for defiance but telegraphed desperation.

"OK." It was just one word, perhaps all she could manage. But it was buy-in and Jackie knew the rest would be easier. After Ms. Clark had neatly printed the information on the legal pad, the food arrived. Although still listless, she ate most of the oatmeal and drank some of the cocoa. She didn't touch the cinnamon toast. After a decent interval, Jackie took a piece from the plate, savoring the warm, sweet crunch.

"When you said you wanted my help, what did you have in mind?" Jackie, who was so proficient at interrogating witnesses in depositions, in courtrooms, and now from the bench, was uncomfortable speaking with this woman across the table. With the formal barriers removed, the interaction was so personal.

"Sometimes I need to stay in bed. I can't face the day. When I'm like that, I don't take such good care of the girls. I forget they need breakfast or to get to school. With my cousin there, the girls are safe, and they still have me around. I want you to fix it so I can stay with the girls at my cousin's."

Jackie thought about what Ms. Clark had said. It wasn't unreasonable. As long as she was also getting mental health care.

"Let's walk." Jackie couldn't promise anything, but she'd find a back channel to suggest that the girls be officially placed with Ms. Clark's cousin. As for her being allowed to live there too, first she needed to clear the warrant so the woman wouldn't be arrested. Then Ms. Clark needed a psychiatric evaluation. Jackie had to get her to the 20th precinct before she turned tail. It was the only way. If Ms. Clark took off once she realized where Jackie had brought her, at least Jackie knew the location of the children. The police would take it from there.

"Ms. Clark, how long have you been feeling so out of sorts?" Jackie asked, hoping the answer would not be "from the moment you took my kids and held me in contempt." She took her elbow and guided her around a puddle of coffee on the sidewalk.

"On and off since I was a teenager," Ms. Clark answered. "It comes and goes. It's bad now."

They walked on in silence for a few minutes.

"You got a family? Kids?" Ms. Clark asked.

"I can't answer that question," Jackie said. "Why?"

"Love is the most painful thing in the world and the only thing that matters. That's what I think, anyway. It feels like you might understand that."

Jackie looked away and focused her attention on the middle of the block where a driver was trying to maneuver into a parking space that was an inch larger than the car. The utter weirdness of Ms. Clark's commenting on Jackie's views on love was palpable. Try as she might to evade him, she could feel Lou by her side.

Ms. Clark didn't ask where they were going and Jackie took that as a sign that she trusted her to do what was right. She accompanied Jackie into the precinct without resistance.

"Are you ready? We need to let the police know where the girls are. And we're going to get you some help so you can feel better."

Ms. Clark nodded, standing submissively while Jackie explained the situation to the desk sergeant.

"Officer, this is Darlene Clark and I'm returning her on a family court warrant. Her children are with a relative—" she handed him the legal pad after quickly taking a photo with her cell—"but AWOL from their foster care placement. And she needs a psych evaluation."

The cop, young and cocky, looked Jackie up and down. "Who the hell are you?"

"I'm a concerned private citizen. Please take care of Ms. Clark."

With that, Jackie put a hand reassuringly on Ms. Clark's shoulder. "It'll be okay," she said, as much for her own sake as for Ms. Clark's.

That night, the events churned inside her. With no one at home in whom to confide, Jackie called Mindy. She listened patiently to the whole story.

"Maybe sometimes being a great judge means stepping out of the robe and being a human being," Mindy said.

Later, Jackie lay in bed and thought about what Mindy had said. Maybe her job entailed more than sitting on high and telling people how to live their lives. She'd helped Darlene Clark more in an hour on the Upper West Side than she could have in months of handling her case in the courtroom. There was a lesson in there somewhere.

And was pain what Jackie could expect out of love as Darlene Clark said? She'd had enough of heartache. Jackie wanted something more.

Lou

Lou hardly ever had insomnia. Even when he had a lot on his mind, he could turn off his thoughts when his head hit the pillow, his body prone and relaxed. But when he did have trouble sleeping his eyes would simply refuse to close and he'd stare at the ceiling for hours. It was unbearable. On the night of his encounter with Bryn in the mall, he knew he was in for it.

After a valiant, albeit unsuccessful, attempt to drop off, Lou went downstairs. It was past midnight. The ground floor was dark except for a strip of light emanating from underneath Bryn's door. He could hear music playing and pictured her lying on the floor, texting her friends. Was she telling those kids he saw her with that he was a jerk? Was it true?

Tara's door was slightly ajar. When they'd first gotten together and Bryn was little, Tara had insisted that they sleep with the door cracked in case her daughter needed her in the middle of the night. It had annoyed Lou. He preferred at least the illusion of privacy when they were in bed. And it was as if they had taken a vow of silence during sex, which Lou found inhibiting but Tara didn't seem to mind.

"Can't we close the door and teach her to knock? We don't even have to lock it," he once suggested.

"I don't want her to feel shut out. You're the guest here, not Bryn."

It had continued like that even after they were married, when Lou wasn't a guest anymore and long past the age when Bryn might conceivably need her mother for a glass of water or an extra kiss goodnight. These days, the teen rarely sought comfort or help from

Tara. Her online companions, friends or strangers, were much more clued into her needs. Still, her mother's door remained open.

Lou peeked in to make sure Tara was asleep and then tiptoed into her bedroom en route to her bathroom. Tara slept on the brink of wakefulness—a car starting two blocks away roused her in an instant. Although he'd barely made a sound, she sat upright. Her eyes wide, she pulled the blanket up to her chin.

"Lou! What are you doing in here?"

"Jeez, Tara. I'm sorry. I didn't mean to scare you. I can't sleep. I'm just getting one of your Ambiens." He walked into the bathroom and opened the medicine cabinet.

"How'd you know I even have any?"

"I took an inventory when I arrived." Lou liked to tell the truth when he could. He wondered if he should have been more honest with Jackie. He decided not to go down that road, should sleep further elude him.

"Oh. Okay. But Ambien gives you crazy dreams, remember? Are you sure you want to take it?" Tara got out of bed and walked to where Lou was standing in the bathroom in his boxers. Her nightshirt had fallen off her left shoulder and she pulled it back in place. Lou's eyes lingered momentarily on the spot where the skin peeked out. It was the closest they'd been to intimacy in a long time and Lou felt a little tingle in his shorts.

"Thanks for the warning. I'll just take one." Lou popped the small pill in his mouth and cupped his hand under the faucet to avoid using the cup Tara kept by the sink. That might have been more intimacy than she could take.

"Go back to sleep," he said. "Do you need one of these?" He held the bottle of pills out toward her.

"No. For some weird reason, I sleep better with you in the house. Who would have thought?" Tara turned her back and fell back into her bed. She pulled the covers over her head.

Lou shrugged, but didn't attempt a reply. Sometimes saying nothing was the better course.

He returned to his attic cell and lay stiffly on the futon, waiting for the Ambien to kick in and sleep to release him . . .

He knocked loudly on the apartment door but no one answered. Lou had begged his father, who'd been fitted for hearing aids in both ears but never wore them, to install one of those amplified doorbells.

"What're you, nuts? That's all I need. The doorbell would ring and give me a heart attack."

Lou hadn't been amused by his father's stubbornness at the time, but he smiled at the recollection. If only his Pops had died of a doorbell-induced heart attack, quick and merciful, instead of slowly wasting away from stomach cancer. He'd been dead for eight years, the apartment sold to a young Chinese couple named Wang. Yet the mezuzah was still nailed to the doorpost. Lou reached up to touch it, bringing his fingers to his lips for a kiss. Old habits die hard, he thought. Lou felt something materialize in his pants pocket and pulled out a single brass key. He fit it into the lock and opened the door.

He stepped into the living room. The enormous hospital bed he'd rented for the last few weeks of his father's life stood in the center of the room. His father's body tucked under the covers.

"Helga!" Lou approached the hospice worker who sat on the plastic covered couch doing *The New York Times* crossword puzzle in red pen.

"Well, look who the cat dragged in," she said. "Come here, Lou, and let me look at you."

When he got within range, Helga reached up and slapped Lou hard in the face.

"Hey! What was that for?" Lou brought his own hand up to his cheek and rubbed. When he looked back at Helga, she had vanished.

"What the hell—"

"Don't curse, Louie. Bad language makes a bad impression." His father sat up in the hospital bed and fluffed his pillows and then lay back on them. After a moment, while Lou stared in silent shock, his father got up and went into the kitchen. He fixed himself two eggs, pulling them from the boiling water when a small bell dinged.

"It's critical to precisely time the soft-boiled eggs. Otherwise, the yolk gets hard, and then what?" He looked at Lou expectantly, as though his son might have a counter-argument on the doneness of the eggs. But Lou had bigger things on his mind.

"Dad, I don't understand. You're supposed to be dead." Sweat poured down Lou's back as a wave of dizziness came over him. He sat down on the couch where Helga had been a moment before and pulled a pink and purple afghan over his legs. Where did this come from? Did Ma make it?

"Of course I'm dead, Louie. Why else would you have gone to shul three times a day and recited the mourner's Kaddish for me?"

Lou's stomach churned. "Dad, I tried, I really did. For the first two weeks I went every day, at least once. I stood next to that guy Zwirling, you know, the chiropractor, who was also praying for his father. I thought he'd be a good influence. But Zwirling's his own boss and could arrange his schedule around the services. I had to take off time from that job I had and I couldn't afford to—"

"It's okay, Louie. Water under the bridge. You're here now and we have work to do." With that, his father walked briskly out of the kitchen. He was fully dressed in the outfit he wore for forty-odd years as an adjunct professor of accounting at Yeshiva University in the night school, a second job he worked to earn some extra money for the family. Khaki pants, a white shirt in need of ironing, brown and beige plaid sports jacket, signature bow tie. He looked spry and happy. Lou felt a surge of joy because clearly Mordy Greenberg wasn't dead.

As if reading his mind, his father sat on the edge of the bed and patted Lou's knee. "I'm still dead, Louie. But we have things to talk about, decisions to make." Mordy stood and headed to the bedroom. Lou got up to follow, afraid his father would disappear like Helga had. "Sit down, Louie. I'm getting the chalkboard."

Lou's wonder turned to irritation. The chalkboard! It was one of the few things that Lou didn't miss about his father. Ever the accountant, Mordy had insisted that all major decisions had to be made with use of a visual aid—more specifically, the chalkboard. Mordy would write each option out with white chalk in big block letters. Then he'd record points in favor of one or the other alternative. There was little room for nuance or even much argument because Mordy decided how many points to award. Despite appearances of objectivity, the fix was in from the start.

"You know, Dad, not everything in life can be decided on a balance sheet."

"Of course it can. Pros and cons, pluses and minuses, debits and credits. And if you'd studied accounting like I told you, you would have taken over my business and have a decent job now. Instead of writing for some fluffy women's magazine." His voice got fainter as he retreated further into the apartment and Lou was scared again.

"I did study accounting, remember? I just wanted to go out on my own. Don't leave, Pops," he yelled.

"Leave? We haven't done the assignment yet. Sit down." Mordy wheeled a gigantic chalkboard out of the bedroom into the living room. On the left side he wrote, "Tara," and on the right, "Jackie." There was a line down the middle dividing them.

"Dad, I hate to tell you this, but you've got it all wrong this time. This is pointless. Tara and I split up over a year and a half ago; the divorce was final last March. You're confused because you're dead. I mean, I guess you didn't know how that all turned out. And you never met Jackie. We were only together for six months. That's over too. I'm not choosing between Tara and Jackie."

"Yes, you are, Sonny. You just don't know it yet. But I'm going to help you make the right decision, don't you worry. Like I helped you pick which college to go to, remember?"

Oh, Lou remembered. His parents inexplicably had allowed him to apply to Georgetown University in addition to Yeshiva University where his father taught and where Lou would be eligible for a full ride. On the chalkboard, Mordy had awarded Yeshiva University 10 points for affordability, 10 points for its accessibility to the Jewish community, 10 points for its proximity to home, and 10 points for not being Jesuit, like Georgetown. This was Mordy's idea of balancing the books. Lou had spent four nearly insufferable years living at home while dreaming of Washington D.C. and pretty blond girls with names like Claire and Savannah.

"Speaking of *shikses,*"Mordy said, "they're both in the hole. Tara and Jackie start off with minus 5 points."

"That makes no sense, Dad. They're both not Jewish. That makes them even."

"Exactly. They are both unacceptable to your mother and me in this regard." Lou's heart skipped a beat.

"Is Mom here too? Where is she?" Lou looked under the afghan but saw only his own legs.

"Don't be silly, Louie. Mom died years ago. You remember, you helped me bury her out at Beth David in Elmont."

"I know. But I buried you out there too and now—"

"Pipe down. There're more categories. Jackie gets 5 points for superior intelligence and ambition. I mean, imagine me telling the guys in the temple Men's Club that my daughter-in-law is not only a lawyer, but a judge."

"She won't be your daughter-in-law, Dad. She doesn't want to get married. All she cares about is her career. She's probably a little bit glad I'm not there distracting her from her work."

"Don't be stupid, Louie. Haven't you learned anything from writing for that women's magazine? Everyone is looking for love.

114

Jackie is no different. I'm not saying she isn't a successful professional. I'm saying she also wants what her sister Mindy has. A husband with a good job and a family."

"Dad, that's ludicrous. You're living in another era. Besides, Jackie seems clear on this one. And how do you know about Mindy?" Lou couldn't believe he was arguing with his dead father over this, but here he was.

"She may believe that, Louie, but you'll see. After you're gone, she'll want you back."

"Okay, Dad. What about Tara? She works incredibly hard. And she has Bryn. She already gave you a grandchild. She must get points for that." Might as well play along, see where the old man was going.

"Exactly! Tara gets 2 points for sticking it out at the Banana Republic and making an honest day's wages, becoming a manager. And for putting up with that guy Simon who's always trying to pinch her ass behind the sweater display."

"He does that? I'll kill him!" Lou shouted as he rose from the couch and flung the afghan to the floor.

"Well, it really isn't your business, anymore, is it son? She can *shtup* Simon right there in the fitting room for all you can do about it now. But see how upset you are? Doesn't that tell you something?"

Lou rubbed his temples. He felt confused and his dad was running circles around him with his bizarre logic as he always did.

"Okay, Dad, let's move on. What about giving Tara credit for Bryn?"

"Tara gets 3 points for having Bryn and trying hard to be a good mom all on her own. She gave you a ready-made family, although I would have liked the Greenberg genes carried on into the next generation. Bryn is a handful, but she's spunky. I like that in a kid. I liked it in you. Are you still spunky, Louie?" His father came closer and tousled Lou's hair.

Lou began to cry.

"It's okay, Son. Everything's okay." His father sat down on the couch and put a comforting arm around Lou's shoulders.

"Nothing's okay, Pops. Everything's a mess. I'm a failure." Lou sobbed, barely able to catch his breath.

"No, Lou. You're not a failure. You need to make some choices and live your life like a *mensch*. You *look* like you're making decisions by walking out on the people in your life and moving on. You're going nowhere, or in circles at best. It's not all about happiness and self-fulfillment—whatever the hell that is. Go where you're needed. That's the most important, to be needed. To be part of something bigger than yourself."

Lou took a deep breath and looked up at the chalkboard. The score was even. Zero to zero.

"Dad, we can't stop here. There's no winner. You have to help me pick!" Lou, frantic, pulled his father to his feet and dragged him to the chalkboard.

"Careful, Louie! I'm a sick old man. Help me get into the bed. Where's Helga? What have you done with Helga?" His father's voice was getting weaker.

"Dad, don't leave me."

"You have to choose, Louie. I can't make this decision for you." With that, the chalkboard disappeared.

Helga called Lou over to the bed. "Give your father a kiss. It's time for you to go now."

Lou woke on the hard futon, his lips pressed to the wet pillow.

When he came downstairs, Tara was preparing to leave for work. Bryn was already off to school.

"Shit, Lou. You look terrible. Did you sleep at all?"

"I slept. You should get two points for telling me not to take the Ambien," Lou said. He realized what he'd said and he shook his head. "It can't be, Dad."

116

"What did you say?" Tara grabbed her car keys. "Maybe you should go back to bed for a while. You don't seem right."

"Yeah, maybe." He went back upstairs, silently willing Simon to leave Tara alone.

Jackie

Jackie could count on one hand the number of times she'd taken the subway home from work at rush hour, especially on a Friday evening. Even if it meant she sat in her robing room for an extra hour after an already long day it was worth waiting to avoid the crush. Today she had no choice. Jackie had convinced Mindy to hire a babysitter for a couple of hours so they could have an adult conversation over Thai food. It seemed the least she could do to safeguard her sister's sanity. Truthfully, Jackie's motivation was more selfish. It was she who needed a break from the loneliness; Mindy was doing just fine.

When Jackie got down to the platform at the Brooklyn Bridge station, it was worse than usual. People were standing three deep. The ones closest to the edge leaned over precariously, staring down the tunnel or looking impatiently at their watches or phones. The disembodied voice of the MTA employee intoned that the cause of the delay was a sick passenger at Borough Hall. A man pressed too close to Jackie for comfort muttered, "God damn it," under his breath. Jackie tried to nod politely without expressing too much solidarity. Certainly, one should have sympathy for a sick passenger even if it meant that the subway was all screwed up.

She let a few trains go by and Darlene Clark and her girls crossed her mind. The new judge assigned to the case had allowed Clark's children to stay in the cousin's home with an eye toward reunifying the family when Clark's psychiatric condition stabilized. Jackie felt like things had resolved about as well as they could have. Still, only she knew it had been Clark who'd made the difference by proactively seeking Jackie out. Of course, she'd recused herself immediately, admitting only to a brief *ex parte* contact, and said nothing about oatmeal at the Zaz. If the extent of her out of court interaction was discovered, there'd be further repercussions.

But that was a problem for another day. The issue at hand was that she was sweaty and claustrophobic. The longer it took for the next train to come, the more her fellow straphangers grumbled, cursed, and stamped their feet in impatience. The platform had the feeling of a riot in the making.

It was getting late. When the next train arrived, Jackie shoved her way on and took an immediate turn to the right where she saw an empty space. Except it wasn't an empty space after all. One of those bulky infant carrier seats was on the floor of the subway car, a baby wrapped in a light blue blanket and buckled in snugly. The mother sat facing her child. Her feet were planted firmly and protectively on either side of the carrier as she gabbed with her friend who stood next to her and held on to the pole. People continued to pour into the subway car. Unable to see the baby, they surged forward, trying to cram Jackie into what they thought was a pocket of air.

"Cut it out," Jackie said, sharply. "There's a baby here." Someone behind her snorted, and Jackie was aghast at the rudeness of most New Yorkers these days. She glanced at the mother, making sure not to make eye contact. Jackie knew all too well from the people who appeared in her courtroom that few liked to be looked at directly. Everything was perceived as an accusation. That she was just any other tired and bedraggled commuter didn't occur to Jackie. She felt the weight and authority of her position at all times and subconsciously assumed that others around her sensed it too.

The quick peek revealed that the mother was young and grossly overweight—Jackie wondered if it could be from the recent pregnancy, but decided that couldn't account for it entirely. Another look, and Jackie realized that the woman was a girl, not more than 15 or 16. A huge girl in a sloppy sweatshirt with St. Alban's High School in yellow cursive letters stitched across her chest.

Jackie knew she should be immune to the spark of anger that invariably mixed in with the sympathy she felt toward this girl. So many of the mothers accused of neglect or worse in her courtroom were overgrown children themselves. But somehow, it never failed to shock and irritate her. She understood the emotional needs and the hormonal impulses that would lead the teens to have sex. But Jackie couldn't fathom the recklessness of *unprotected* sex. She contemplated what kind of high school experience this girl could have as a mom. Who would take her to the senior prom? Maybe even the boy who helped her get into this predicament would have a better option. A girl who didn't have to race home to take care of an infant.

Jackie stole another glance at the baby. He was wrapped tightly in his blanket, like a little sausage. And he wasn't fussy, not a peep out of him. He gazed steadily at his mother, as though she were the most beautiful girl he'd ever seen. Jackie was so lost in thought that she didn't realize she was staring at the baby. Her eyes locked on his, unblinking. Unblinking. And then it dawned on her. Not only was the baby not blinking, he wasn't breathing or moving either. Because the baby was a plastic doll. A damn realistic one, but a doll nonetheless.

Fury welled up in Jackie and practically choked her. She felt duped, having steadied herself so carefully in the crowded car so as not to disturb a fucking plastic doll. Then she understood. Jackie knew all about these programs they had in the high schools. The kids were given a baby doll or even an egg. Something fragile to protect so they would get an idea of how hard it was to take care of children, to discourage them from risky behavior. Jackie was all in favor of these programs, wished desperately that the message would get through.

But this was too much.

Jackie knew she should swallow it, but the bile kept rising in her throat. She held it together until the girl started talking to her friend about the baby as though he were real. Telling her that she hoped he would sleep well tonight after this long subway trip. Jackie looked the girl full in the face and spat out, "That's not a baby. That's a doll." The girl registered Jackie for the first time, although she'd been standing in front of her for a good ten minutes.

The teen got up quickly for someone her size and reached down for the carrier. "You want to sit, old woman?" she said, sneering. "I'm getting off." The girl pushed past Jackie and made for the door. Jackie didn't want to accept the offer, but the blood had rushed out of her head and pooled in her feet and she collapsed into the seat the girl vacated. She watched as the girl and her friend exited at Grand Central. Despite herself, Jackie wondered where the girl was headed and if the baby would be safe.

When she next noticed, the train had slowed to a halt. Jackie realized she'd gone way past her stop and was now somewhere past Yankee Stadium in the Bronx. She pictured Mindy sitting in the Siam Gardens restaurant on 74th Street, dressed for a rare dinner out, checking her cell phone every few minutes for a text from Jackie. She got out at the next station, crossed the platform, and boarded the nearly empty car for the ride back downtown.

When Jackie caught sight of her reflection in the window opposite, she realized from her smeared eye make-up that she'd been crying. Maybe that girl was on to something. Maybe Jackie was just an angry old woman with aging eggs and a blaring biological clock who would never know the joys of love and motherhood herself and took it out on those around her. Maybe this was what Lou had understood, why he'd moved on.

When her cell phone rang the next morning, Jackie was already showered and dressed, sitting at her kitchen table doing the crossword puzzle in ink. She'd apologized profusely for being so late that Mindy had to go home to relieve the babysitter, their evening ruined. Her sister had said it was no problem. So why on earth was Mindy calling at 7 a.m. on a Saturday? Jackie muted the ringer and put the phone on the counter. Whatever Mindy wanted, it would have to wait until a more civilized hour.

Twelve letter word for without reason, defying logic: 'Unfathomable.' Jackie filled in the spaces in all caps. After six weeks—that was still what Lou's leaving her was. Unfathomable. She stood up and wandered the length of her living room. Her hand brushed lovingly along the bookcases that lined one wall. They'd been her only real extravagance when she furnished the apartment—floor to ceiling bookcases custom built in beautiful, rich mahogany, that she kept polished to a high gloss.

As she looked over her collection it hit her. Although Lou had been too cowardly to tell her either in person or in his note why he was leaving, he'd made quite a bold and specific claim in his column. He'd told thousands of women who hung on his every word that he needed to leave Jackie to uncover his inner novelist.

But did he even read novels? The books were all hers. Lou had brought none with him when he moved in and took none when he moved out. Jackie could picture the occasional book resting on Lou's bedside table, pulled from these shelves. She scanned her library for clues to Lou's yearnings. She ran her hand over the spines as though she might feel remnants of his energy, but she felt nothing. After ten minutes of searching, she noticed that her copy of *Bonfire of the Vanities* had spots of spaghetti sauce on the cover that suggested that perhaps Lou had been reading it while making or eating dinner. It wasn't much to go on, but it would have to do.

Jackie sat down on the couch and flipped through Wolfe's book that she'd read so long ago. She wondered if this was what Lou envisioned for himself. Would he succeed? Write a bestseller that would eventually be turned into a movie, maybe send her a signed copy in the mail? She tried to picture the cover of Lou's novel, but all she could come up with was a solid red rectangle, like a Mark Rothko painting but without any depth or nuance. In her mind's eye she opened Lou's book to the dedication: "For Jackie—I never could have done this without you." Perhaps, more likely, "For Jackie—I never could have done this with you." Would she put Lou's book on her beautiful bookshelf, alphabetically sharing space with Goethe and Gogol? Or give it away to the doorman on the way out to work one morning?

Jackie jumped when she heard the intercom buzzer. She checked her watch; it was just shy of 7:30. She pressed the button on the wall. "Yes?"

"Judge, your sister is here." Jackie heard in Carlos's tone a recognition that this would not be welcome news at this hour. For a second, she contemplated turning her sister away and then she came to her senses.

"Please send her up."

Jackie opened the door to her apartment and then went into the kitchen to make her sister a cup of coffee. She had a pang of longing for her old Mr. Coffee machine, the pot of 12 cups that she and Lou would work their way through on a weekend morning. But she shook it off. All that was gone. Mindy would get one individually brewed pod. Jackie would get to the bottom of what had been so urgent that her sister had blown past getting sent to voicemail.

"Jacks?" Mindy called from the foyer.

"In here. I'm making you coffee."

"Thanks, but I don't have time," Mindy said.

Jackie walked into the living room, steam rising from the mug in her hand. "What do you mean, you don't have—" she said, looking around for Mindy. She was standing in the doorway, apparently about to make a run for it. Jackie's three nieces sat on the couch. Nicole was dressed in jeans and a Marge Simpson sweatshirt; the two younger girls were still in their pajamas. They had all clearly been yanked out of their beds and dragged to Aunt Jackie's. Now the question was why. Jackie took a gulp of Mindy's coffee, nearly scalding the roof of her mouth.

"I need you to watch the girls," Mindy said. "Sam's father tripped getting out of the shower and broke his hip. He's having emergency surgery this afternoon."

"But Sam's parents are in Boston." Jackie had never watched the girls for more than a few hours in their apartment. She wasn't sure she'd know what to do with them in her place.

"Yes, I know where my in-laws live. I'm going with Sam. Even if he stays longer, I promise I'll be back tomorrow. I'm sure it'll all be fine, but Sam can't meet with the doctors and be with his dad and also help his mom. He's only one person."

She recognized that everything her sister had said was totally logical. Being a spouse entailed these sorts of obligations, done willingly and lovingly. The jump she had trouble making was how that translated to babysitting her three nieces, ages 11, 8 and 4, in her apartment for the weekend. It wasn't a role she'd played before. It seemed—what was that word again? Unfathomable.

Jackie watched as Mindy swept each girl into a hug and reassured them that Grandpa would be fine. "I'll be back for you on Sunday. Behave for Aunt Jackie."

"You'll be fine too," Mindy said as she hugged Jackie, apparently unfazed by her silence. "Nicole knows what they each like to eat, what they're allowed to look at on the internet, and what time they go to bed. Actually, I think Caroline and Dara would go back to sleep now for a while, if that's okay? Come on girls. Go lie down in Aunt Jackie's bed." With that, Mindy shooed them toward Jackie's bedroom, and, after settling them in, softly closed the door.

"Okay, I'm off. If it gets late tomorrow and I'm not back, let the girls go to sleep and I'll wake them when I get here. I know you have to be at work Monday morning." As if she were afraid that any hesitation might unravel her plan, Mindy was out the door in two quick strides.

Jackie sank down onto her big comfy reading chair and put the mug carefully down on a coaster. She rubbed her eyes and then opened them slowly, wondering if the interlude might be a dream. But there was Nicole, her sharp pre-teen voice piercing through Jackie's disbelief.

"Well, I guess you weren't expecting us," Nicole said, stretching out her long, stringy legs on the couch into the space her younger sisters had vacated.

"Get your sneakers off the couch, Nicole." Jackie slipped into judge mode and she felt bad. But shoes on her furniture, even her Ikea sofa, was too much.

"If you'd answered the phone when Mom called this morning, you would've had fair warning."

Jackie knew Nicole was baiting her. Like a kid tormenting a clueless substitute teacher, Nicole was waiting for that inevitable slip-up of a person unused to having children around. She'd give Nicole no satisfaction. Jackie was determined to keep her cool.

An hour later and the girls were all awake and clamoring for breakfast. Jackie didn't even go through the motions of checking her kitchen cabinets to see if there was something she could rustle up. Her tastes ran to plain omelets made with egg whites out of a green and white carton, or cereal without added sugar.

"Get dressed, girls. We're going out for breakfast." Caroline and Dara clapped. Maybe this wasn't so hard after all. Jackie was a fun aunt, at least for a circumscribed period of time. She bent down to help Dara do up the Velcro on her sneakers. What a brilliant invention. Who needed to learn to tie shoes in this day and age anyway? Jackie wondered if fewer boys would end up in her courtroom on assault charges because some kid had dissed their sneakers if everyone were wearing Velcro shoes. It seemed like it would level the playing field.

Either out of lack of imagination or some inchoate need to be near the spirit of Lou, Jackie marched the girls into Cafe Zaz. It was crowded, but luckily in a few minutes they were seated in a booth perusing menus. All except for Dara, who, at age four, couldn't read.

Instead, she pointed forcefully at a stack of silver dollar pancakes in front of a small boy at the next table.

Nicole looked around the cafe disdainfully, suggesting through her slouch that the place was not as posh or the clientele as chic as she'd hoped it would be.

"Is this where you used to come with Loooooou?" Nicole dragged out his name with pursed lips and a coy smile.

Jackie raised her eyebrows, but kept her voice modulated. "No, this is where he used to come by himself to do his work."

"This was Uncle Lou's office?" Caroline asked. Who had told the girls to call him "Uncle Lou?" Mindy, or Lou himself? Jackie tried to remember. She knew she hadn't been the one. It upset her that Lou would've encouraged the girls to consider him part of the family and then so abruptly walked away not only from her, but from them too. The more she tried to understand his behavior, the less things made sense.

Something about the idea of Lou at work in the cafe gave Caroline the giggles. They quickly spread to Dara.

"It's not funny, Caroline. Lou ditched Aunt Jackie and she's devastated. You don't know anything about love."

Jackie stared at Nicole, stunned, even as she realized that she must be repeating something she'd heard Mindy say.

"And do you girls know about love? Tell me what you know," Jackie said.

The girls all looked at her shyly, even Nicole, perhaps wondering if they were in trouble. But as Jackie sat back in her chair, her hands folded patiently on the table, they seemed to perceive that she was listening. She wanted to know what they thought on this weighty subject.

Dara, who had continued to look longingly at the pancakes, said, "I think love is when you want something so bad. Like I love those pancakes."

Caroline poked her little sister in the ribs. "That's silly. That's not love. That's just your tummy talking. I think love is when you can't imagine one person without the other person. Like how I can't imagine mommy without daddy. Isn't that right, Aunt Jackie?"

Jackie smiled, waiting for Nicole to speak. At 11, her niece had perfected a world-weary posture that could put the most cynical adult to shame. Jackie hoped for something different, something more.

"I think love is when you'd give up everything that means something to you to have a second chance."

Jackie put her finger to her lips to peremptorily shush Mindy when she returned the next night.

"They passed out," Jackie said, gesturing to the girls sprawled out on the couches in the living room.

"It's not even eight; what did you do, drug them?" Mindy asked.

"Sort of. Sugar coma."

Jackie's kitchen looked like a war zone. Dirty bowls and spoons were piled in the sink. On the counter were four different uncovered, half-empty pints of ice cream sitting amidst scattered colored sprinkles and streaks of chocolate syrup. A big glob of whipped cream had landed on the handle of the freezer and unceremoniously slid to the floor.

"Oh my God, Jackie—I'm so sorry! The girls ran circles around you and they left your kitchen such a mess. You sit—I'll clean everything up. I'm so embarrassed."

"Don't be. It was fantastic. I loved every minute."

"Are you feeling okay?" Mindy stepped close to Jackie and put her hand on her forehead. "Are you sick?"

"I've never been better. I let go."

127

Lou

Lou couldn't believe the number on the scale. He'd bought it at Target the day before, one of those digital ones, accurate to a tenth of a pound. 176.4!

In the seven weeks since he'd landed on Tara's doorstep, he'd put on ten pounds plus. What did he expect to happen when he sat in the mall eating bagels and nursing cappuccinos all day? All the while unsuccessfully trying to write. His waistband was tight. Worse, he looked old.

Lou needed to exercise. Somehow, though, the idea of doing another activity alone was overwhelming. What Lou needed was a friend.

He pictured the early days of his and Tara's marriage. They'd hire a teenage babysitter, some girl in fashionably ripped up jeans and pink high-top sneakers. She'd be glued to her laptop for three hours while Bryn slept and Lou and Tara went out with some other similarly-situated couple. First a movie, and if time allowed, a beer afterwards at the faux-Irish pub on Main Street. Where were those guys now? Would anyone come play with him?

Plenty of couples who split up divided the mutual friends between the husband and wife, more or less equitably and usually along gender lines. But Lou and Tara's situation had been different. Being a stay-at-home dad, Lou had interacted mostly with the stay-at-home moms. They'd liked him and been cordial in arranging playdates and carpools, but Lou didn't hang out with the women—grab a coffee, get a manicure. And the fathers of Bryn's friends were even less inclusive. These were guys who commuted to New York City every day in suits and ties, clawing their way up the corporate ladder. They didn't respect Lou's piecemeal accounting jobs and they didn't like him hanging around their wives.

So, Lou had let Tara have the friends, both the men and the women. What did he need with these people in New Rochelle when he was moving to the big city to start over again? And now, here he was, not a soul to speak to or take a run with on a cool fall morning.

Except, maybe, for a guy named Harrison. Harrison was the most un-Jewish Jewish dude Lou had ever met. He was incredibly fit. Not the kind of person who ran marathons. The kind that snowboarded in the Rockies and scaled mountains in the Himalayas, went scuba diving in the Mediterranean and rock-climbed in New Mexico. X-treme sports, Harrison used to call it. Despite his travel, Lou had found Harrison x-tremely unworldly, but a decent enough guy at heart. His wife, Anastasia, was wacky in a different way. She was a woman who was so convinced of her inner beauty that she didn't pay a moment's attention to her appearance. She didn't shave her legs or armpits, wear make-up or deodorant, or even wash her clothes regularly. Lou was sure that Tara hadn't held on to either Harrison or Anastasia after their divorce.

Lou picked up his phone, hoping that Harrison still lived in town. After three or four rings, he was about to disconnect when Harrison answered.

"Harrison, hi. It's Lou. Lou Greenberg."

His declaration was met with silence.

"Remember me? I was married to Tara, lived a couple of blocks from you..." Lou thought about hanging up. He could pretend the whole thing hadn't happened.

"Of course, I remember you, you loser. We were friends and then you totally fell off the face of the earth almost two years ago. You dropped me like a hot potato when you went to New York and started writing that bullshit column of yours. You know, Anastasia read some of your crap about not waiting all your life to be happy

129

and getting out from under whatever is weighing you down. You gave her the idea of leaving me. She moved out a few months ago."

Now it was Lou's turn to be silent. What could he say, I'm sorry your wife took me seriously? I never meant for anyone to follow that lame advice I dole out? He knew there were women who actually made decisions in their lives based on things he tossed off as he sat at the mall trying not to get cream cheese on his keyboard. He'd been so out of touch he hadn't heard that Harrison and Anastasia had split.

"Well, anyway, what's done is done, I guess," Harrison said. "What can I do for you?"

Lou had acted so impulsively in calling that he hadn't even thought through his ask. But he figured Harrison was probably a seat of the pants guy himself, so he forged on.

"Well, you won't believe this, but I'm actually in New Rochelle. Not living here or anything, just crashing for a while as I sort out my next move. Are you still on Spruce?"

"Hold on, Bud. Stop right there. Are you back together with Tara?"

Lou didn't peg Harrison for the gossipy sort. He guessed his reappearance was a shocker that required some explaining.

"Nah, nothing like that. Honestly, she barely talks to me. I'm sleeping in the attic, and I try to stay out of Tara's way as much as I can. That's why I called you. I need to do something active today. Not your kind of active, exactly, but something. Thought I'd ask if you'd keep me company."

Lou felt like a shy seventh grader asking a pretty girl to the school dance. He wondered how and when his machismo had abandoned him, leaving him to beg for the attention of a guy like Harrison. Yet here he was.

"Huh. Well, sure. Still know how to ride a bike?"

Lou happily discovered that Tara had not trashed his hybrid mountain/touring bike that he'd bought when they'd first moved to suburbia. He filled the tires with air and half an hour later he did a circle around the block to shore up his balance. Then rode over to pick up Harrison.

Although the meeting was a little awkward at first, both men sized each other up, checking for weight gain (Lou,) hair loss (Harrison,) and other less obvious signs of decay (a little bit on each of them.) The fact that they were on bicycles allowed for only a quick high-five before they hit the road.

They cycled a familiar loop, the twenty-five miles or so a challenge for Lou and a piece of cake for Harrison. They kept pace with one another but didn't talk much. Still, Lou was grateful to have another person around.

When they reached the park near the center of town, they dismounted and leaned their bikes on a small incline. Harrison had his padded bike shorts on, of course, and was feeling no pain. He sat down on the ground and motioned for Lou to join him. Lou hadn't foreseen ever riding a bike again, hadn't the foggiest notion of what had become of the absurd spandex and foam contraption he used to own, and could barely move without crying out in agony.

They sat in amiable silence for a few moments, drank from their water bottles and stretched out their legs. When Harrison spoke, Lou was almost surprised to find he was still there.

"You know, I used to think of calling up Tara after Anastasia and I separated," Harrison said, picking at some weeds and looking away from Lou.

"What for? Like to shoot the breeze?"

"No, you bonehead. To see if she would get together with me. She's a great girl, beautiful, put-together, keeps herself in great shape."

Lou had a vision of Tara going off to work in her Banana Republic outfit, hair carefully done and make-up perfect, standing

131

next to Anastasia, in all her bohemian glory. He could certainly understand Harrison's attraction to Tara, but he hoped to God he hadn't acted on it.

"So, did you call her?" Lou tried to sound as though he didn't care.

"Nah. She's not my type."

Lou felt a buoyancy in his heart, an unexpected rush of affection for his ex-wife and good will toward Harrison for staying away from her. He shifted onto his other elbow to relieve some of the pressure on his left butt cheek. He noticed Bryn sitting in the middle of a group of kids about 100 feet away. The red hair blazed in the autumn sun and distracted him for a moment from the fact that she was smoking something.

Lou's gaze drew Harrison's in the direction of the kids.

"Is Chase in that group?" Lou asked.

"No. I don't think he and Bryn hang out in the same circles much anymore," Harrison said. Lou tried to read meaning into his tone of voice but couldn't. He thought about asking why the kids weren't friends, but it was his least pressing concern. For all he knew, Chase had turned out like Harrison—brawny, good natured, and boring as hell.

"What are they smoking, do you think?" Lou asked, trying for casual. "I don't smell weed or cigarettes."

"Where you been, man? They're vaping, e-cigarettes. It could be THC, but at a minimum it's nicotine all right, and as addictive as hell. I'd beat the shit out of Chase if I caught him doing that."

Lou didn't know what to think. Where had he been? The question was more where he hadn't been. He hadn't been parenting a teenager for the past two years. And he wasn't parenting one now either.

"Is it legal?" Lou felt stupid asking. The conversation had already gone so far with Harrison he no longer cared about making a good impression.

"Not for kids it isn't. But it's lung cancer either way, you know." Lou wondered if he'd ever told Harrison that his father had died of cancer. The words started to form. Then he remembered this was just a bike date gone on too long. "C'mon, let's get out of here." Lou got up carefully from the grass and righted his bicycle.

"Aren't you going to go get Bryn? You're going to leave her there with those delinquents, smoking that crap?" Harrison's face had turned bright red. Lou was afraid Harrison might throttle him.

"Everything's different now. It's not my call." He hoped he sounded nonchalant, but his heart was racing. Lou got on his bike and started to ride. When he looked back, Harrison was still sitting on the grass, his padded ass comfy, a perplexed look on his face.

Lou returned to the house to find Tara sitting on the living room couch in denim cut-offs, a beach blanket spread underneath her, touching up her pedicure with hot pink nail polish. At the sound of the screen door closing, she looked up. Lou made his way toward the stairs to his room.

"Hey, why are you walking like you got off a horse?" Tara asked.

Lou stifled a smile. "I went for a bike ride. Thanks for not getting rid of my bike."

"You're welcome, I guess. I never got around to selling it," she said, shrugging.

"I went with Harrison Weinstock." Lou watched Tara for a flicker of interest, but there was none.

"That's weird."

"Yeah. You want to hear something else weird? Harrison said he almost called you when he and Anastasia split, to see if you'd be into hooking up." Lou knew he was making it sound a lot crasser than Harrison had. Why shouldn't someone like Harrison be interested in dating Tara? She was a great girl, like he'd said. But Lou couldn't help himself.

"Well, I don't think that would've worked out. He's not my type." Tara finished the right foot and turned her attention to the left. Lou moved into the room and sat down gingerly on the soft chair opposite her.

"Hey, Tara, something else weird happened in the park."

"What's that? Shit! I messed up my big toe. Can you hand me that nail polish remover over there?" Tara pointed to a small table next to Lou's chair. He inched his way over, trying not to groan in pain with each chafing of his thighs. He handed Tara the bottle.

"Thanks. You really did a number on yourself, didn't you?"

"Yeah, I did. But listen. I need to tell you something." Lou took a deep breath and waited for Tara to look up from her feet, now waving in the air to dry, perilously close to his face.

"I saw Bryn in the park with a group of kids."

"So? Fresh air, it's good for her."

"Not such fresh air. She was vaping. They all were. It didn't look like the most wholesome crowd, Tara. The kids looked older than Bryn, kind of rough. You need to do something."

Tara put her feet down on the carpet and examined the pedicure one more time. Then she stood and folded the beach towel neatly. She picked up the nail polish and for a second Lou thought she was going to hurl the bottle at his head.

"I should tell you to get the fuck out of here, right now, you fat freeloader. Should have told you weeks ago. If you're going to stay here for even one more night, don't ever tell me how to raise my daughter again."

November

Jackie

Jackie stood in front of the three-way mirror in her bedroom. She turned left and right and examined herself in her heather gray Calvin Klein with the black piping. She wasn't normally the type of woman who stressed over what to wear in the morning. This new indecisiveness was not only irritating, it threatened to make her late for work.

She pulled the dress off and lay it neatly on the bed. She reached for the new navy one she'd bought a couple of weeks earlier, retail therapy at Bloomingdales after she'd sent Moshe off to residential placement. In the dressing room, she'd felt confident and sexy in this one. As she put it on now, she worried that the v-neck showed a bit too much cleavage. Jackie knew it was illogical, that her robe covered everything. She picked up her keys and briefcase, headed for the door, and then stomped back to the bedroom. She unzipped the dress and left it in a pile on the floor.

Jackie grabbed the first thing she put her hands on in the closet. As she struggled with the side zipper, she heard Lou's voice in her head. *It's fine. Now go. You're late.* Most days, she tried valiantly to banish Lou from her heart and her mind. Then there were the days when she'd silence her own thoughts and run through outfit after outfit just to hear him.

Jackie put on a pair of heels and took the elevator down to the lobby.

"Have a great day, Judge." Dennis opened the front door for her.

"Thanks. I'll try." It didn't seem likely.

True to her instinct, it didn't take long for things to go south. As Jackie raced down the stairs to the subway, she twisted her ankle and the heel of her left shoe broke.

Thirty minutes later, Jackie hobbled into the courthouse, feeling calmer as she got closer to her robing room and her spare pair of pumps. Until Estella Lopez stepped into the judges' elevator with her. A fraction of a second longer and Jackie would've told Ms. Lopez that the judges' elevator was for judges, not court evaluators out to find fault with judges. But she held her tongue. They nodded at each other and rode in silence.

The elevator reached the eighth floor. Jackie exited and walked unevenly toward her robing room, her ankle twinging in pain with each step. Out of the corner of her eye she saw Ms. Lopez make her way to the spectator section.

Jackie tottered past Angela in the outer office.

"I know. I'm late." She flung herself into her robing room, closed the door behind her, and sank into her chair. She kicked off both shoes and buried her face in her hands, trying to regroup. Jackie contemplated asking Mike to get her some ice. Instead, she popped three Motrin from her stash in her desk and washed it down with a swig of yesterday's cold coffee. There was no time to sit around feeling sorry for herself; there were people waiting for her help.

She put on her robe and her spare pair of shoes and stepped into her courtroom. If she were the sort of judge to wield a gavel, she would've banged it noisily and repeatedly. Instead, she merely turned to Mike and said, "Good morning. Call the first case, please."

"Everything okay?" Mike stepped up to the bench and leaned in toward Jackie. "You seem a little flustered. Bad commute?"

Although Jackie was touched that Mike was keyed into her emotional state, she didn't want to encourage him to get too personal. His attention made her nervous.

"I'm fine. Let's get rolling."

On a rotating basis, one judge each week was assigned as the duty judge. It was Jackie's turn to hear the emergency petitions filed by people seeking ill-defined but immediate judicial intervention because a situation had blown up at home. There wasn't a lot of time for considered reflection. Mike's job was to squeeze the urgent cases into the gaps of Jackie's already packed docket. Crisis management or disaster avoidance, it was difficult work that required a clear head— something Jackie wasn't sure was in the cards.

"Judge, there's an order of protection that's ready to go. Do you want to do that first?" Mike tilted his head slightly toward Ms. Lopez sitting in the back row. Was he warning her that it wasn't a good idea to hear the domestic violence matter in front of the evaluator? That maybe if they waited a while, the snoop would leave? There was no way for Jackie to ask. She'd have to roll the dice.

"Sure."

Angela pulled up the petition on Jackie's screen. It looked fairly straightforward. Patricia Chang had filed for a restraining order against her husband. Like many of the women who came into court seeking protection against their spouses or partners, Ms. Chang didn't have an attorney. If she couldn't afford one, Jackie would assign one to her later. And because this was the initial appearance, Mr. Chang was not present in court; Jackie would see them both next time and the hard work would begin. Today was a band-aid, meant to get the ball rolling. Ms. Chang stood with her head held high, but her eyes darted around the courtroom and her lower lip quivered.

Jackie read the allegations. The night before, the husband had yelled at Ms. Chang in front of their two young children and then he'd shoved her. She hadn't called the cops or needed any medical attention, but it was the first time things had gotten physical and the incident had scared her. In the panoply of abuse, though definitely unacceptable, this was low level.

The rest appeared to be nothing new. A pattern of verbal abuse and control issues that had gone on for the entirety of the couple's ten-year marriage. Mr. Chang often called his wife stupid and useless. He restricted her social life, texted her when she went out with family or friends to monitor her whereabouts. Like many of the cases Jackie saw, there was a cultural element at play. Mr. Chang believed that a good Chinese wife's duty was to stay home and take care of her husband and children. He didn't allow her to work or volunteer outside the home. He yelled at her when the laundry didn't get done or dinner was not to his liking. In short, he was a jerk.

Jackie took a deep breath and reminded herself that she wasn't in a position to make each family a model of stability and peaceful living. She could only do what she could do—her new mantra—though it was sometimes so frustrating. She chose her words carefully, both for the petitioner's sake and for the ears of Ms. Lopez. "I've read your allegations and I think I get the picture. The question I need your help with is this. You've asked that I issue an order removing your husband from the marital home. That's a very severe remedy."

Ms. Chang nodded.

"You need to answer out loud for the court reporter," Mike said.

"Yes, that's what I want." Ms. Chang said, her voice shaky.

Jackie went into her best patient schoolteacher mode.

"I'd like to explain to you what that means. If I were to grant this order, the police would come to your house tonight and serve these papers on your husband. The cops would watch as he packs one bag of his belongings. Then they'd physically remove him from your apartment, from you and your children. The allegations in your petition, at least as I'm reading them, don't support the drastic remedy of banishing your husband from the home that you share. I understand that your relationship needs work, but throwing him out could be the beginning of the end of the marriage. Is there more you want to tell me? Has there been other physical violence?"

Ms. Chang bowed her head. When she raised her eyes, her quivering lip had spread and her whole body was trembling.

"I'm afraid he's going to kill me."

Jackie tried to ignore her throbbing ankle and focus on Ms. Chang. She was a slight woman, neatly dressed, a year younger than Jackie according to the information in the petition. How had she met Mr. Chang? Had they courted and fallen in love, or had someone matched them up without enough attention to compatibility? Jackie wondered what sort of parents they were. She pictured Ms. Chang preparing a healthy dinner for the kids, helping them with homework and projects. In her mind's eye, she saw Mr. Chang, coming home late from work or elsewhere, and expecting his wife to wait up.

The marriage didn't sound ideal, but it was a recognizable model. And it was a huge leap from one shove to fearing for her life. Did Ms. Chang understand that if Jackie threw her husband out of the house, maybe he wouldn't come back? He might find some other woman, younger or a better cook or more subservient, and he wouldn't need her anymore. This woman didn't get that if she started down this road, she might end up alone.

Jackie turned back to the computer. She didn't make eye contact with Ms. Chang, who she could hear sniffling.

"I've considered your allegations, Ms. Chang. I don't feel that the situation you've described justifies the extreme remedy of vacating Mr. Chang from the marital home. I'll grant you an order saying that your husband must refrain from committing any family offense against you. This includes, harassing, stalking, slapping you, pushing you, calling you denigrating names, yelling at you, controlling your outside contacts. But he can stay in the home for now. You need to have the police serve these papers on your husband for them to take effect. I'll see you both in court on the adjourned date. We'll take it from there."

"That's one week from today, November 2," Angela said. She handed Ms. Chang her order and her service papers.

"What's next, Mike?" Jackie said, as Ms. Chang left the courtroom.

Less than half an hour later, Mike stepped up close to the bench and signaled to Jackie to cover her microphone.

"Judge, we have a recall on Chang."

"Why?" Jackie tried to keep her voice neutral. Mike was her most stalwart ally in the courtroom. She couldn't afford to alienate him.

"Apparently the husband followed her to the courthouse this morning and was waiting in the hall. When she came out, he put his hands around her neck, choked her. Right in front of me and a couple of other court officers. We pulled him off quickly, but she almost passed out and she's got visible red welts on her neck. Security called the cops and Mr. Chang's been arrested, but who knows how long they'll hold him? Angela told Ms. Chang to come in and get your order modified to a vacate. To be on the safe side."

Ms. Lopez sat in the back of the courtroom with her arms folded across her chest, her expression inscrutable.

"Listen, Jackie, you're exaggerating, making yourself too central to this story. It's that perfectionist thing again that I thought you were trying to let go so you can be fallible like the rest of us." Mindy stole a quick glance at her watch

"But I swear, if that woman had been killed outside of my courtroom, or later when she got home, it would've been my fault." Jackie took a deep drink of her wine and put her hand over her eyes, trying to block the painful vision.

They were sitting at the bar of the small Italian restaurant on the ground floor of Mindy's building. Her sister had left Nicole in charge of the younger girls, telling her she'd be back in fifteen minutes.

"That's all the time you have for me? Fifteen minutes? I had a terrible day. I need to talk about it and you're the only one I trust." Jackie wished that weren't true, but it was.

"Then let's talk in the apartment. You can stay as late as you want. I can't leave the girls on their own for too long," Mindy said.

"I don't want to talk in front of them. Don't you get it? When this woman needed my help in a matter of life and death, I totally dropped the ball. Instead of really listening to her, listening to what she *wasn't* saying, I decided I knew what was best for her. She could be dead now because of me."

"So, what do you think happened?" Mindy took the wine glass out of Jackie's badly shaking hand.

"I thought I was saving her from being alone."

Lou

A certain sort of man would have packed his bag and never looked back after Tara's outburst. Lou, in fact, had been exactly that sort of man. But something had changed. There was truth to the epithet she'd hurled at him, fat freeloader. So, he set about trying to do better, to be better.

Despite the fact that the weather had turned sharply cooler, he bought himself an inexpensive pair of those ridiculous padded shorts and rode his bicycle every morning. He left before Tara and Bryn awoke and returned well after they'd gone out of the house for the day. At first he followed the same route he had taken with Harrison. As he grew stronger and less winded, he pushed himself to 30 miles, then 35, then 40. Thanksgiving approached and Lou had firmed up, dropping eight of the ten pounds he'd gained sitting around at the mall, and was almost back to his wedding weight.

As for the freeloader status, well, that was a harder nut to crack. And a more painful accusation. His marriage to Tara had disintegrated in almost direct proportion to his ability to contribute more financially to the relationship. It wasn't that she'd expected him to bring home the same exact paycheck she did. Tara understood that Lou serving as Bryn's primary caretaker was a huge value-add that couldn't be monetized because he wasn't a babysitter or a daycare worker. He loved Bryn. But as she got older and spent more time in school, Tara had demanded Lou step up and find more and better paying accounting jobs to do in his free time. She didn't want to be tied to working the late shift at the mall, supporting all three of them. This time around, as much as he tried to be helpful in the house, here he was putting Tara in the same position again.

But Lou wasn't ready to give up the dream of working on his writing in order to get some more conventional job. He called his editor at the *Balabusta.*

"Harriet, I need a raise."

"So do I, Lou."

Lou had never asked for a raise before. It had been almost two years and his column was more popular than ever. The mystery that surrounded his whereabouts and his love life kept the women reading. Either out of prurient interest, or because they were Jewish mothers who were truly worried about him. Surely, between the *Balabusta* and the syndication, they could cough up some more money. He tried again.

"Listen, Harriet, my ex-wife has filed for spousal support and there's no way of getting out of it." It was a lie, but not far from the truth. Lou asked for an additional $1000 a month, a lump sum to which all the websites on which his column ran would kick-in. Harriet bargained him down to $750. He told her to make the check out directly to Tara Donohue.

The situation was still far from ideal. If Lou had made himself scarce in the days before he put his foot in his mouth about Tara's parenting skills, now he was practically a ghost in their lives. He left early and came home late, stole in the house in the middle of the day to make them dinner and then disappeared. He wondered if he would ever live a normal existence again.

Lou's column became his refuge, the place where he connected with the outside world in a critical way that hadn't mattered so much before when he had a lover, poker buddies, even a cute young waitress in his life. And because he needed to believe in this virtual community, he poured his love into his words. What had once been a chatty, folksy offering was transformed. Lou Greenberg was still lighthearted and clever, but he was also genuine and thoughtful, bordering on wise. The women took notice. He earned his new salary.

A Bike Ride Can Be So Much More Than A Road to Physical Fitness"

When I recently took up cycling, my immediate goal was to lose weight. Like many of you, although I try to stick to a healthy Mediterranean diet, a sedentary lifestyle as well as various stresses in my life had taken their toll on my physique. And, as I get older, my metabolism has changed and losing the weight has become more of a challenge.

But as much as the bike riding started out about the external, it's the internal effect that I want to share with you.

When I leave my immediate neighborhood, away from the cars and the school children and the traffic lights, I reach long stretches of quiet road. I get into a physical groove where I no longer have to concentrate on pedaling or steering. It's as though my body and the bicycle merge. I move through space with a fluidity that I can only liken to swimming in a still lake. I'm calm and I'm whole. My legs begin to ache, starting in my calves and continuing all the way to my thighs. It's a delicious ache. That feeling in your extremities after you have just made love to someone very special to you. And my mind, too, is free. Although I still hear the twittering of the birds and the whoosh of the wind, the song of my soul calls out. I am both greater and lesser than myself.

This is my experience. It doesn't have to be cycling. Forget yourself in something physical. It will bring you the whole world. If only for a little while.

Lou hit send and shut his laptop gently. He stretched out on the hard futon and stared at the ceiling. Despite his upbeat column, a sober assessment of his circumstances left him deflated. In the two and half months since he'd left Jackie, he had no more to his name than when he'd packed up his suitcase in September. He had no brilliant start to a novel nor even a coherent idea for one. He hadn't struck out on his own or given himself the mental or physical space to think. He had no relationship to speak of with his ex-wife or the child who'd been like his own daughter. He had no friends except for Harrison, and he wasn't sure that counted. Who was the real Lou now? He'd left a wonderful woman who loved him and whom he might have loved if he'd given it a chance. He was so out of sorts he wondered if Jackie would recognize him now.

Lou must have dozed, because he was startled when Tara knocked on his door. It was the first time she'd ventured up to his room since allowing him to stow away there. And the first time she'd said more than two words to him since the "FF" fiasco.

"Lou, can you come downstairs?" Tara asked through the closed door.

"What time is it?"

"A little after midnight."

Lou was surprised to find that he was still fully clothed. He listened to Tara go downstairs and went into the bathroom to splash some cold water on his face.

He found Tara sitting at the kitchen table, a mug of coffee in front of her and one waiting for him.

"Why are we drinking coffee at this hour?"

"Bryn isn't home." Tara was gnawing on a Bic pen, a nervous habit of hers that Lou had forgotten but always detested. He used to envision the pen exploding, dark ink ghoulishly spilling from the corners of Tara's mouth.

"So she's sleeping over at a friend's house. What's the big deal?" The caffeine had stimulated Lou's appetite and he absentmindedly wandered over and opened the fridge. The tuna casserole he had made for dinner was on the middle shelf. Untouched and covered in saran wrap.

"She didn't come home for dinner?" Lou asked.

"She didn't come home from school." Tara had moved on from the Bic pen and was now chewing on a strand of her hair while she tapped her foot rapidly on the kitchen floor.

"I don't think you need this right now. May I?" Lou took her cup of coffee and spilled it into the sink.

"I'm sorry I called you that terrible name," Tara said. Her foot was going so rapidly that Lou had the sensation that she might build up enough momentum to fly out of her chair.

"Don't be sorry. You were right. Listen, we can go pick up Bryn if you'd rather she sleep at home. I'll drive. You tell me where to go." He went to the key rack and took down Tara's keys. When he looked back, she was crying.

"I don't know where she is. I've texted her and she doesn't answer. I told you, she's hanging out with different kids now. Kids I don't know."

This wasn't entirely news to Lou. He hadn't recognized any of Bryn's crowd at the mall or in the park; they seemed older and edgier. Lou felt a pang of guilt. For most of Bryn's young life, he'd been a stable presence. The divorce had left Tara doing the job of two parents. It wasn't fair to anyone. It certainly didn't seem to have done Bryn any good.

"Look, I'm sure she's fine. She probably stayed up late at some girl's house watching TV, didn't have a way to get home, and fell asleep. I used to do it all the time as a kid. There's no point in panicking"

But it was too late for that. Tara had broken out into a sweat and was shaking her head and muttering "no, no," as though she'd received terrible news. Lou knew he should intervene, to force her to focus, but he didn't know how.

The telephone rang.

The caller i.d. read "NYPD 6th PCT." Tara stopped tapping her foot but made no move to answer. Lou reached for the phone. He picked up the pen from where Tara had left it on the table, wet with her saliva, and grabbed a pad of paper from the drawer. He took notes as the cop spoke. When it was over, he thanked the officer and hung up.

"Bryn got arrested. Some girl claimed she pulled a box cutter on her. What was Bryn doing in Greenwich Village?"

Tara ignored his question, which Lou thought was fair enough.

"What else did the cop say? Where is she?"

"She's going to spend the night in a juvenile detention center. She'll be in Manhattan Family Court tomorrow morning."

"Can I see her?" Tara was calm. At least she knew Bryn wasn't lost or out on the street. Though it might be the beginning of a terrible nightmare, locating her was such relief it seemed to have pushed the panic away.

"No. The officer said no visitors. You'll see her tomorrow in court. I think you should go to bed for a few hours. She's going to need you to be functioning." Lou reached across the table and tucked the wet strand of hair behind Tara's ear. When she didn't make any move to get up, he gently took her elbow, helped her from the chair, and walked her to the bedroom. She sat down tentatively on the edge of the bed, looking around as though she wasn't quite sure where she was.

"Try to get some rest," Lou said.

"I'll try," she said. "Thanks, Lou."

"No worries. Bryn will be fine," he said, with as much confidence as he could muster.

Upstairs, he lay on the futon, now completely wired, his mind playing old movies of Bryn when she was a little girl. The birthday parties, the scraped knees, the holiday meals with Lou's dad, the tearful homework sessions. Lou felt his heart would burst.

When Tara knocked this time, she didn't wait for his answer. She came into the dark room and lay next to him on the futon. Her newly svelte body fit seamlessly into his, differently than it had before.

"Hold me," she whispered.

147

Jackie

"It's like when you fall off a horse. You've got to just get back on."

Mike stood in the doorway to Jackie's robing room and held out her black robe. She knew he was right. Although the Patricia Chang episode had been a personal failing for Jackie and could have ended in tragedy, it hadn't. Mr. Chang had been arrested and the District Attorney's Office was actively pursuing criminal assault charges against him with Ms. Chang's cooperation. The Family Court order of protection vacating him from the marital home was icing on the cake. He'd be locked up for a good long time and Ms. Chang probably wouldn't ever need to use Jackie's order. Still, Angela had let slip that the court evaluator had not missed a beat in informing the supervising judge that Jackie had screwed up by seriously underestimating the lethality of the situation. Near fatalities in the courthouse were not something to be taken lightly. Jackie's status was in jeopardy.

But it was 9:00. Time to get back on the horse.

"There you go." Mike helped her into her robe and gave her shoulder an encouraging pat. Jackie walked out and took her seat. She scanned the room for Ms. Lopez and was relieved to see she wasn't there. Maybe she'd been assigned to torment someone else today, or maybe she already had so much dirt on Jackie that her job was done. Either way, she had caught a break.

The respite didn't last long.

"You have a newly filed juvenile delinquency case coming in first." Angela nodded her head brusquely toward Jackie's computer where a petition popped up. "In the matter of Bryn D."

Jackie scanned the allegations, trying to ignore Angela hovering over her. A fourteen-year-old girl was accused of brandishing a box

148

cutter and threatening another teenage girl at a bowling alley in Greenwich Village. The supporting affidavit from the cop indicated that there were no injuries and no property was taken. A classic "girl fight," Jackie thought, undoubtedly over a boy. But the combination of the weapon and the threat, if proven, was serious. This girl had some explaining to do.

"Are the parties ready?"

"Mr. Lane, the attorney for the City, is here in the courtroom, Judge." Mike gestured toward a tall man with thick glasses wearing a slightly shiny grey suit. "And the girl's mother is outside in the waiting area. The arrest was after 11 p.m., they had to hold the respondent overnight. The bus isn't here yet from the detention facility. Should be another ten minutes or so and then I'll corral the legal aid attorney."

Mike was his usual calm and capable self, getting everything set, and Jackie felt better. The situation was under control.

"Let's bring the mother in and have her put her appearance on the record. Then we'll be ready to roll when the bus gets here." Jackie took a long drink from her water bottle. The wine she'd had the night before with Mindy had loosened her tongue but hadn't calmed her nerves. She was left with only the dehydration.

Jackie turned to her computer and pulled up the Penal Law. Nine months into the job, she felt more comfortable each day with the rules of the Family Court that she had to apply in the cases before her, but the delinquencies still posed the greatest challenge. She made a point of rereading the criminal law statute to make sure all the specifics were fresh in her mind. She ran through the sections that defined weapon possession, harassment, and menacing, to see how the charges in the petition might fit into the various categories of family offenses. She watched out of the corner of her eye as Mike showed a woman to the defense table. The court reporter put away her protein bar and began to type when Mike spoke.

"Miss, please state your appearance for the record and your relationship to the case."

"Tara Donohue. Bryn is my daughter."

Jackie was so absorbed in the regulations in front of her that at first the name didn't register. But it didn't take long. She looked up slowly, as though any quick motion might frighten the woman away. Still, she wasn't one hundred percent sure—the name was common enough. The photo Jackie had seen on the internet showed a younger, fuller-figured woman with long shiny hair, smiling and confident, "Manager of the Month." This woman seemed older, thin almost to the point of boyish, with a sophisticated haircut. Her face was pained. Her eyes were puffy, her cheeks red and raw, and her make-up hastily applied. The outfit, however, was pure Banana Republic.

Jackie watched Tara for a sign of recognition but saw none. She felt a rush of relief. Certainly, if Lou had been in touch with his ex-wife after their divorce, Tara would know who Jackie was. Lou had told her it was a clean break, that they'd had no contact, and apparently, he'd meant it.

Mike opened the side door to the courtroom and ushered in a girl as angular as her mother but in an adolescent way, with the brightest red hair Jackie had ever seen that hadn't come out of a bottle. Bryn was dressed for a night out on the town: black skin-tight leggings, a black t-shirt with YOLO in hot pink letters stretched across her chest, a denim jacket, and Doc Martens. She looked like a less pampered version of Nicole, and Jackie felt sorry for her and for Tara.

Jackie turned away as Tara took Bryn in her arms, the girl shirking her tough-girl image and openly crying. She called Angela over and asked quietly, "What's YOLO?"

"You Only Live Once," Angela answered, suppressing an eye roll.

"Well, I guess there's some truth to that." Jackie wished she could tell Bryn that living once didn't have to include being locked up in a juvenile facility. She hoped it wouldn't come to that.

As Jackie worked to wrap her mind around Tara Donohue and this mystery child in her courtroom, she thought of her favorite law school professor, Raymond Pearl. A highly respected judge who'd taught her class on the judicial system, his lessons had stayed with Jackie and his words came unbidden now. "A judge must avoid even the appearance of impropriety." What would Judge Pearl say about the scene playing out here?

Jackie studied Tara and Bryn. She had no connection to *them*. She'd never laid eyes on them in her life, didn't know that Bryn existed until five minutes earlier. Jackie thought she could be as impartial toward Bryn as any other judge in the courthouse. And she yearned for the insight this case might give her into Lou's past. But with the scrutiny she was already under, it wasn't worth taking the chance. She turned her chair around half-way so she was facing her law secretary's desk.

"Angela, I believe I may be familiar with the—"

The door to the courtroom opened and Jackie, distracted, didn't finish her sentence. Lou walked in and took a seat in the back row. Jackie turned her chair back around to face the courtroom and hoped she didn't look as shocked as she felt. Longing and anger welled up in her in equal measure. Her heart raced and she tamped down the urge to catapult the bench and throw herself at Lou, unsure if she wanted to embrace him or throttle him. Jackie felt her chest constrict and she coughed to regain her composure.

"Judge, you need some water?" Mike asked.

"No, thanks. I have." Jackie brought her water bottle to her lips and hoped her shaking hands would not betray her. In a flash, Lou's arrival had transformed Jackie's role from an appearance of impropriety to outright misconduct. She had to put an end to this craziness immediately. She told herself she would. When she did nothing, Mike stepped in to fill the silence.

"Sir, state your name for the record please and relationship to the case."

"Lou Greenberg. I'm a friend of the family."

Jackie stared at Lou, forcing him to hold her gaze. He didn't flinch. She thought she saw fear in his eyes.

"Are you the biological father of this child?" Jackie kept her tone even, looking away only when she couldn't stand the strain.

"No."

Jackie felt herself relax slightly, although she was well aware that DNA was only one indicator of fatherhood. Lou and Tara exchanged a look that Jackie couldn't decipher. Was it leftover intimacy from a marriage gone sour or new intimacy from a relationship rekindled? As Jackie studied them, an overwhelmed Legal Aid Society attorney rushed into the courtroom, arms full of files for the many cases she would handle that day.

"Clarissa Reynolds for the Respondent." She scanned the petition Mike handed her and came up with the girl's name. "Bryn D."

"Why don't you take a moment to read the allegations, Ms. Reynolds, and to speak briefly with your client. Then we can figure out what hearings you are requesting. We'll set an adjourned date and discuss the remand status."

"Thank you, Your Honor."

Maybe if Jackie plowed on as if this were any other family and any other case—she couldn't even get through the thought it was so absurd. But there was plenty of time to recuse herself. These were just the preliminaries.

While the legal aid attorney got up to speed, Bryn put her head down on the table and closed her eyes. Teenagers were notorious for being able to sleep anywhere and Bryn looked to be on the verge of dozing off. Jackie wondered whether juvenile lock-up was an exception to that rule. How could a girl like this, from a comfortable suburban home, fall asleep on a cot in a locked room filled with other girls in trouble with the law? Tara smoothed the child's hair and Jackie heard Lou sigh. What was going through his mind? He had to be as stunned as she at the circumstance they found themselves in. Yet his usually expressive face was a controlled blank.

Ms. Reynolds tapped Bryn lightly on the arm to get her attention and they exchanged a few hushed words. Tara leaned in and Jackie gave the three of them a few minutes to speak.

When it was time to move things along, Jackie nodded to Mike. He briefly approached the City's attorney and the defense table in turn, consulted with each, and gave Jackie a thumbs up. She began, grateful to have the legal procedures to fall back on to shield her emotions.

"Okay. Ms. Reynolds, I will give you until the end of business tomorrow to file additional motion papers in case you have other requests. But for now, I presume you want a hearing seeking to suppress the boxcutter, correct?"

The boxcutter would be the central piece of physical evidence in the case to support a conviction on the top charge, weapon possession. The defense was entitled to a hearing to determine if the police search that resulted in the recovery of the weapon was legal and justified under the circumstances.

"Yes, Judge."

"Fine. Mr. Lane, was there a line-up in which the other girl identified this Respondent as the person who threatened her with the boxcutter?"

"No, Judge. The victim spontaneously pointed out the Respondent when the police arrived at the bowling alley. The officers were not involved in arranging any formal identification procedure. There's no need for the court to determine the propriety of the police action in this regard."

"And what about a statement? Did the Respondent make any incriminating statements in response to police questioning that you plan to use against her at the fact-finding?" Jackie liked to get her ducks in a row. So far, apart from the cast of characters, this was panning out to be a straightforward case.

"No, Judge. No statements. The police didn't question the Respondent because she said she didn't want to talk to the cops without her mother present."

Tara put her arm around Bryn's shoulders and gave her a little squeeze. Jackie wondered how the girl had gotten so savvy.

"Has the Respondent been the subject of any juvenile delinquency proceedings before?" she asked Reynolds.

The attorney leaned over and conferred with Tara and Bryn before answering.

"No, Judge."

"All right, then. We'll hold the suppression hearing on the physical evidence and see where we go from there. Mr. Lane, where do you stand on the question of remand?"

This was always the most difficult moment of the initial appearance. Jackie had the option to keep the child in detention during the pendency of the case or send her home and rely on the parents to get her back to court the next time the case was scheduled. It was the first juncture in the case where the judge had to make a judgement call. Ordering the suppression hearing had been standard; every judge in the courthouse would have done the same. Deciding whether to hold Bryn or send her home was subjective—a very personal decision about Tara and her daughter.

"The Corporation Counsel requests that you hold the Respondent until the pretrial hearing, Your Honor. These are serious charges. This child was out at night, in Manhattan, a commuter train ride away from her home in Westchester County. Likely without her mother's knowledge. This raises serious questions about Ms. Donohue's ability to supervise the child. We feel that the safer course is to remand the Respondent."

Of course, he had a point. Nonetheless, Jackie thought Lane, who couldn't have been more than 26 or 27, sounded way too self-righteous for someone who probably had about as much real-life experience with supervising teens as Jackie did.

"Ms. Reynolds, what's your position on remand?"

"Judge, this is Bryn's first encounter with the legal system. She's never been in any trouble before and we don't believe a remand is justified in this case. Ms. Donohue is present in court and she assures me that she will keep a close eye on Bryn and have her here on the next date."

Jackie couldn't take the chance of another Chang debacle. If she let Bryn go home and the girl got arrested again, especially for something more violent, Jackie could kiss her job goodbye. On the other hand, could she lock the child up to cover her own ass and still be able to look Lou in the eye? If she were writing a law school exam question on conflict of interest she couldn't make this one up, the facts were so absurd. Of course, she should recuse herself immediately. But she had a window into Lou's life and she couldn't give it up yet. And maybe she could make things better for Bryn. For Lou. For herself.

"Ms. Donohue. If I release Bryn to your custody today, I expect you to keep her to a strict schedule. She goes to school, she comes home, she does her homework, eats dinner, goes to bed. Can you do that? Can you pick her up after school and bring her home so there's no possibility of her getting sidetracked?" As Jackie spoke, Tara looked furtively at Lou and Jackie saw him nod once. Tara reached over Bryn and said something to Ms. Reynolds, who answered Jackie.

"Yes, Judge. Ms. Donohue says her friend can help by picking up Bryn at school while she's at work."

What did that mean? What was going on between them?

"Okay, we're on for next Tuesday."

Mike led the parties and attorneys from the courtroom. Lou didn't wait for Tara or Bryn. He walked out without looking back.

Jackie picked up her phone from where she kept it behind the bench.

"Meet me (alone) in twenty minutes. You know where."

When Jackie arrived, Lou was sitting in the exact spot where she'd been eating her tuna sandwich the day she met him back in March. It seemed like a lifetime ago.

She walked past him and sat two steps above and a little to his left. Close enough to allow them to talk but far enough away that a passerby wouldn't know they were together. For a few moments they sat silently, both gazing at the flower seller, his offerings sparse in the crisp autumn air. Jackie had rehearsed so many times what she'd say to Lou if she saw him again. Now everything was different.

"How could you?"

"Oh, Jackie—" Lou rested his elbows on the step behind him and looked up at the sky. "That question covers too much ground."

"Okay. I'll break it down for you. How could you not tell me you have a child?"

"Would it have changed anything?"

"It would have changed everything." Jackie raised her voice as a group of Japanese tourists passed on the steps between them. "You lied to me about something so fundamental. You didn't have a marriage that fell apart, you had a *family*. A whole life. Why didn't you tell me about Bryn, Lou?"

"I was afraid. I tried to tell you a couple of times. I know what you think about fathers who don't live up to their responsibilities and you're right. I thought you'd put me in that category. But it isn't true. I was a good father while Tara and I were married, but I couldn't force it after a while. Bryn had other things she wanted to do more than hang with me. I didn't know if you'd understand."

"Are you back together with Tara?"

"Not exactly."

"Don't play games with me. I deserve to know what's going on. Have you gone back to your ex-wife?"

"No." Lou chanced a glance backward, but Jackie avoided his eyes. It was so much easier to speak to the back of his head. She was

156

furious and blown away by what she'd learned when he landed in her courtroom. Yet being this near to him made Jackie's heart hurt.

"Is she a good mother?"

"Tara's a wonderful mother. Attentive and loving. But Bryn's at a tough age and Tara has been doing it on her own. It's been hard for both of them."

Lou ran his hands through his hair, his telltale sign of anxiety. Jackie realized that he was frazzled by her questioning; she felt for him, but she pressed on. There were things she needed to find out.

"Does Tara know who I am?" Jackie hated the pathos in her voice.

"No. I don't kiss and tell." She could feel Lou smiling slightly. It was a flippant response, but she knew he was telling the truth.

"What a mess," Jackie said.

"It's a mess you can't get involved in. Hand Bryn's case over to one of your colleagues. That must be what you're required to do. Pretend none of this ever happened."

Of course, Lou was right. She couldn't possibly adjudicate Bryn's case. It wasn't only emotionally dangerous but ethically improper as well. But fate, in the guise of the judicial assignment system, had brought Lou back to her. Jackie wouldn't give him up so easily again. She had a chance to prove to Lou and to herself that she was a different person now, flexible and compassionate. She could bend the rules, if not outright break them. And maybe she could rescue Bryn, for Lou's sake.

"I'll see you next Tuesday. I'm not making any promises, but I'll see what I can do. Make sure Bryn stays out of trouble." Jackie walked down the steps and touched Lou's shoulder as she passed.

As Jackie strode briskly to the courthouse, Judge Pearl was in her head again, his booming baritone declaring, "Justice that is not blind is not Justice." She remembered the day in class when he said it, how she'd believed in the principle from the depths of her being.

Now she wasn't so sure. Where did love fit in?

157

Lou

Friday afternoon arrived and Lou watched from Tara's car as the kids spilled out of the high school. The scene reminded him of when he was a little boy playing in his parents' driveway and he'd kick over an anthill to see the tiny bugs scurrying in all directions. Even back then he sensed that while he'd set the ants free, he'd simultaneously destroyed the whole system and rendered them homeless. That's how the kids looked to Lou emerging from Bryn's school. Free, but wild. Unmoored. They stood in clumps, the boys hooting and slapping each other on the back, the girls giggling and pointing. The initial impression was of unadulterated joy, but Lou felt an underlying menace.

Maybe, though, he was reacting more to the fact that Bryn seemed so utterly disconnected from it all. She stood alone off to the side, her whole being concentrated into her cell phone, typing furiously. At least she's communicating with someone, Lou thought. He pulled the car around the circular driveway in front of the entrance and stopped next to her. Bryn barely looked up as she got in.

"Hey. Put your seatbelt on, please," Lou said. Jackie's requirement, an order, really, that Bryn be picked up at school each afternoon and escorted back to the house had sounded like a small price to pay to keep her at home until the next court date. And yet, three days in, these twenty minutes had fast become the worst part of Lou's schedule. Bryn hadn't spoken a word to him. Today, she went so far as to put her earbuds in and tune him out entirely. When Bryn failed to buckle up, Lou reached over and carefully pulled the seatbelt across her.

Bryn didn't register Lou's presence.

158

They drove in silence out of the school parking lot. Lou recalled how his own father had taken advantage of car rides to lecture him about unpleasant matters. He'd always prefaced his remarks with, "I know this isn't fair since you're a captive audience . . ." The strategy seemed worth a shot.

"Could you turn that off, please, for a couple of minutes?" Lou projected his voice over the din, though Bryn was barely eighteen inches away. She glanced at him and then pressed a button on her cell. She left the earbuds firmly in place. Clearly this was not going to be a lengthy interaction. Lou was secretly a little relieved.

"I know my being back in the house has been confusing for you." Bryn rolled her eyes dramatically and turned her face toward the window. Lou wondered if she was afraid she might cry and he wasn't sure how to continue.

"I want you to know that your mother and I are going to help you through this court case together. It's going to be fine. We didn't always agree on everything when we were married, obviously, but—"

Bryn swiveled around so quickly that Lou reflexively hit the brakes. They both lurched forward and then slammed back into their seats. Lou checked the rearview mirror to make sure no one was about to crash into them. He didn't dare look at Bryn, but he could feel her eyes on him before she spoke.

"So now that I'm a screw-up, you think you get to come here and save the day? Rescue poor Tara and Bryn? Who do you think you are? Superhero Lou. I should've pulled that blade on you instead of on that bitch at the bowling alley."

She hit the button on her phone and the noise started up again.

Lou shook his head slowly. He hoped against hope that Bryn's "confession" about the boxcutter was nothing more than a show of youthful bravado. A few minutes later he pulled into Tara's driveway. Bryn opened the door while the car was still in motion and practically flung herself out and away from him. In her haste to escape, she got her arm caught in the retracting seat belt. It threw her off balance and she stumbled out of the car, landing on her hands and knees in the gravel.

"Shit!" Her elbow was bleeding slightly and her cell had skidded under the car.

Lou leaned toward the open passenger door. "Brynny, you okay?"

She lay flat on her stomach, retrieved her phone, and then pushed herself up from the ground.

"Fuck you."

He watched as she unlocked the front door, went into the house, and slammed it shut.

Lou rested his forehead on the steering wheel. He had an almost irresistible urge to take Tara's car and drive far away from the neat suburban house with curb appeal where life was spinning out of control. But he'd given his word to both Jackie and Tara that he'd be a responsible adult and it felt important—crucial—to keep that promise. With so little of his life progressing in any comprehensible direction, they'd given Lou a role to live up to. He was determined not to let these two women down like he had in the past.

He went into the house and put a pot of water on to boil. It was an evening that cried out for spaghetti.

"Why isn't Bryn eating dinner?" Tara asked when she got home from work, twirling her pasta on her fork. "Did you two have a fight?"

"I don't even know how to answer that question."

Lou hadn't been surprised when Bryn didn't come out of her room when he announced that dinner was ready. He wasn't that keen on sharing a meal with her either, truth be told. Intellectually he understood that her hostility was only partly aimed at him. Still, it was painful to be the target. Lou knew that it was unrealistic to expect Bryn to understand that he wasn't living his best life either. That his disappointment in himself was corrosive to his soul.

160

Tara put down her fork and wiped some pesto from her lips with her napkin.

"Lou, I know it probably doesn't look like it, but we've managed okay without you. We'll get through this too. If you stay, stay for the right reasons."

Lou studied his ex-wife from across the table. She was so different than when he'd met her ten years earlier. Then, she'd been soft, naive, but impetuous. Ditching the rock & roll boyfriend Froggy and raising a child on her own when still practically a child herself. Lou had been drawn to her, had wanted to protect her. Now she seemed stronger, determined, the fragility still there but trapped underneath a gritty exterior. Had the divorce transformed her into the woman who sat before him? Or had she simply grown up? Lou had an urge to reach out and caress Tara's face. But he wasn't sure what the gesture would mean and he didn't want to send any more mixed signals than his presence had already.

"What would be the right reasons?" Lou asked.

"I can't answer that for you. I know what some of the wrong reasons would be. Pity. Obligation. Inertia."

Lou got up earlier than usual the next morning for his Saturday bike ride, desperate for space and serenity. Somehow, though, as far and as hard as he pushed himself, he didn't feel the endorphins take hold as they normally did when he rode. Maybe his agitated state of mind was so extreme that even the natural releases of sweat and strain couldn't provide relief.

Seeing Jackie had surprised and confused Lou. In his muddled emotional state, it was hard to remember what he'd hoped to achieve by leaving her, and now she was front and center in his world again. Jackie hadn't overtly proposed restarting their relationship, but he'd sensed an undercurrent of longing during their conversation. He wondered how she'd possibly balance the personal and the professional, knowing how seriously Jackie took her job. But he also believed she'd help Bryn if she possibly could. Lou felt a tremendous pressure to keep everything and everyone in play to rescue Bryn from this fiasco.

He rode for an hour in big looping circles around the neighborhood, unable to formulate a goal or figure out a destination. After he'd passed Tara's house for the third time, muscle memory, both leg and heart, took over. He took back roads for six or seven miles, the sun cutting through the bare branches of the trees and lighting up the piles of leaves on the ground. He dismounted in front of The Brotherhood Synagogue, the small congregation in Mount Vernon where he'd been bar mitzvahed thirty years earlier. Like most of his friends, Lou had stopped going to the prayer services after that religious coming of age milestone, preferring to play ball or hang around with his crew. His father, on the other hand, had been a regular until his health deteriorated and he couldn't travel even the short distance to attend. Lou hadn't been inside the building since his father died. Yet here he was, standing in front on a Saturday morning, straddling his bicycle and watching the people arrive for prayers.

An older woman with stiff gray curls sporting a powder blue suit and matching hat approached the building. She looked Lou up and down.

"Nice outfit," the yenta muttered. Lou's red Spandex riding gear, though easier on the eyes than it had been weeks ago when he was flabbier, was still not appropriate worship attire. Embarrassed, he mounted his bicycle.

"Well, you're here for a reason. Come on." She motioned him toward the entrance.

Lou leaned his bike against the side of the building and followed the woman, donning a black nylon yarmulke from the box inside the door and wrapping himself modestly in the largest prayer shawl he could find.

Lou sat down in the back row, the wooden bench hard beneath him even through the padding of his shorts. The room looked dustier and more formal than he remembered from the days when he ran up and down the aisles collecting strawberry sucking candies from old Mr. Picker or being reprimanded by the shush-ers (the self-appointed men who roamed the sanctuary maintaining decorum among the congregants.) These days the members looked as fusty as the thick burgundy curtains and almost as inanimate. No self-respecting child would be caught dead there.

Lou didn't open the prayer book, unwilling to pretend he'd come to speak to God when in fact he had no idea why he was there. Instead, he sat quietly and let the text and melodies of the prayers, so ingrained in his subconscious, gently wash over him. He'd never actually understood much of the Hebrew. The prayers had been drilled into him at an early age by his teachers, a pedagogy of another era. Memorize, memorize, memorize and the feeling and the belief will eventually follow. Lou didn't think he'd ever achieved the end envisioned by his teachers, but he was a good memorizer. As he sat in the pew, he had to concentrate on not belting out the tunes and the liturgy, word for word.

He was so engrossed in the service that he didn't notice when an older gentleman sat down beside him until he touched Lou lightly on the elbow.

"I feel bad for the new young rabbi. Stuck here in this dying congregation. The average age of the members must be 80. There's no future here." The man assessed Lou and apparently determined he was too spry to be a congregant. "Are you visiting someone?"

"You could say that." Lou pictured his father and his own younger self sitting a few rows ahead.

The rabbi pronounced the prayer for the new month of Kislev, invoking God's blessing for gladness and joy, salvation and consolation, livelihood and sustenance, life and peace.

"You chose an auspicious day. Chanukah is coming at the end of this month." The man ignored the shush-er who had passed down the aisle with his finger pressed to his lips, glaring. "The holiday of miracles."

"I could use a miracle." Lou shifted uncomfortably in his seat as his shorts, not meant to be worn inside, became too warm.

"Miracles are everywhere. You have to open your eyes."

Lou was about to ask the man to tell him more, to convince him that some act of divine intervention might set everything right.

But when he turned, the man was gone.

Jackie

The Tuesday before Thanksgiving and Bryn was due back in court. At the pretrial hearing, Jackie would determine whether or not the police legally seized the boxcutter when they confronted the girl in the bowling alley. If the cops had acted within their authority, the weapon would be admissible as evidence against Bryn in her upcoming fact-finding. An open-and-shut case of weapon possession. If Jackie found that the cops had violated Bryn's constitutional rights, screwed up somehow, the weapon would be inadmissible. Jackie would be required to dismiss the charges.

Jackie hadn't made any move to have the case reassigned to another judge. She figured she'd either decide the case as any other judge would, regardless of her connection to Lou, or she'd go out on a limb for Bryn and put herself in a better position with Lou if it seemed like she still had a shot of reconciling. Jackie had managed to convince herself that both options were viable.

She was anxious to get to the courthouse. Anxious to see Lou again. But first she had a stop to make.

Mindy always hosted Thanksgiving for the whole family. Sam's father had recuperated nicely from his hip surgery and was out of rehab, and Jackie was looking forward to seeing her own parents who'd come up from Florida. They'd be surprised at Lou's absence at the dining room table, unless Mindy had filled them in. As hopeful as Jackie was that she'd be able to right the ship with Lou now that he was back in her orbit, there was no way he'd be spending the holiday at Mindy's in a couple of days' time.

"Are you humming?" Mindy led her sister into her apartment and took the bags of wine and bakery-bought pies that Mindy insisted be dropped off well before Thanksgiving day, "just in case." Jackie chose not to be insulted that Mindy planned to continue to drink Bordeaux and eat dessert no matter what calamity had befallen her older sister.

"I didn't realize I was humming, but I suppose so. Do you have a problem with that?" Jackie hadn't had a chance to fill Mindy in on the wild events of the prior week. Or, more truthfully, she hadn't quite known how to broach the topic with her sister, who'd been quite vocal in her opinion that it was time for Jackie to get over Lou.

"You're more upbeat than I've seen you in a while. What's going on?" Mindy inspected the pies as she put them in the fridge—pecan, apple, lemon cream—and nodded her approval.

"I saw Lou yesterday."

"What? Where? You're not stalking him, are you? You could get arrested for that."

Jackie gave Mindy the abridged version. She included the salient facts of Lou's materialization out-of-the-blue in her courtroom, Tara's chic and teary-eyed appearance, and Bryn's existence. Mindy stopped puttering around her small kitchen to fix Jackie with the same benevolent but searching look that she used on her daughters when she tried to ferret out who'd left chewed gum in her sister's bed.

"Let me get this straight. You're humming happily because you found out that Lou lied to you about his past the entire time you two were together. On top of that, all indications are that he's reunited with his ex-wife and juvenile delinquent step-daughter. This somehow makes you feel good about your chances of getting back together?" Mindy sat down heavily on the closest kitchen chair as if the effort of posing these questions had drained her and waited for Jackie's response.

"You can put that negative spin on things if you want, but don't expect me to. I'm optimistic because Lou is back in my life. He cares about what happens to Bryn and Tara and it's going down in my courtroom. He needs me. I plan to make this work out for everyone." Jackie looked away from Mindy, unwilling to subject herself to the disapproval she thought she'd see on her sister's face.

Instead, she heard genuine concern, bordering on fear, in Mindy's voice.

"Oh, Jackie, I'm worried about you. This would be a huge step backwards for you. Instead of less controlling, you're stepping in to orchestrate everything. You're not thinking straight and you're talking crazy. You can't get in the middle of this. You'll lose this judicial appointment on top of losing Lou. Is he worth it?"

"I know how it must sound to you. I don't know how it will play out, whether I'll be able to help Bryn or salvage my relationship with Lou. I promise I'll be careful. But I have to give it a try. A wise young woman once told me that love was being willing to give up everything that means something to you to get a second chance. I love Lou and I want him back. And I'm running out of time."

Jackie spent an extra few minutes in her robing room before she took the bench, primping in a way she normally eschewed. She let down her hair, brushed it out carefully, and reapplied her mascara and lipstick. She stowed her glasses in her purse and put in her contact lenses. And although her robe covered her dress, her push-up bra gave her bust and her confidence a little boost.

Lou would be in the courtroom and she wanted to look her best. She'd read enough of the feature articles that appeared alongside his column online in the *Balabusta* to know that this preening was meant to impress Tara, not Lou. Lou had denied he was involved with his ex, but Jackie couldn't be sure. She had to operate as though Tara was an actual rival and not a theoretical one. Jackie would make sure that Tara saw her for the accomplished, attractive, and together woman she was.

Bryn and Tara were already in their appointed spots at the defense table. The girl was no longer dressed in the typical teenage clothes she'd appeared in the morning after her arrest. Then, she'd looked slightly ratty and bedraggled from a night of little sleep in the juvenile lock-up. Now, Bryn was wearing neat navy jeans, a pastel pink crew-neck sweater, and shoes with a pretty gold buckle that looked like they pinched her feet. Her wild red hair was tamed and pulled back from her face and she wasn't sporting the heavy, smudged black kohl around her eyes that had made her look defiant and a little skanky a couple of days before. She was the picture of sweet and compliant, innocent. Jackie had to give it to Tara. She understood the importance of making an impression, even if this was the second one rather than the first.

Lou sat in the same seat in the back row as though glued there from Bryn's first court date. He was freshly shaven and Jackie speculated that Tara had brought his outfit for him from Banana Republic. His khakis were pressed and his light blue button-down Oxford shirt looked new and stiff. He glanced up for a second when Jackie entered the room, but otherwise betrayed nothing.

When the attorneys were in place, Mike approached the bench. "You ready to go, Judge?"

"Yes. Let's begin." Jackie absentmindedly ran her fingers through her hair.

Mike grinned. "I'm probably not supposed to say this—all that sexual harassment training they make us take—but you look terrific." Jackie blushed at the unexpected compliment, but Mike didn't see as he'd turned abruptly to announce in his deep court officer voice, "Matter of Bryn D." The attorneys and the parties stated their appearances for the record.

Jackie took charge. "Okay, everyone may be seated. We're on for the suppression hearing today. Having received no further motions from the City, I'll take testimony regarding only the question of the legality of the recovery of the boxcutter. Mr. Lane, can you confirm that you do not intend to offer any identification procedures into evidence and no incriminating statements at the fact-finding?"

"That's correct, Your Honor." Mr. Lane shuffled the papers on the table in front of him, conferring quietly with the police officer sitting next to him at the Petitioner's table.

"Good. Please call your first witness."

Officer Jenkins was in uniform, his gun in its holster at his hip. He was tall and slender with a youthful face, smooth skin and wide-set eyes that made him look not much older than Bryn and nearly as frightened. When he sat in the witness chair he seemed to bend in an unnaturally pliant way. He reminded Jackie of the plastic Gumby figurine she used to play with as a child. Even his complexion was a little green. But as harmless as he looked, Jackie knew he held the key to the case against Bryn.

After he swore to tell the truth, Mr. Lane asked the officer to describe why he'd responded to the bowling alley that night.

"The call came over the police radio. The dispatcher called a 10-34, a possible assault in progress. I had to look it up on my cheat sheet, because it was only my third time out in the squad car. I graduated from the police academy a few weeks ago." Jackie pondered whether the officer's inexperience would work to Bryn's benefit. Maybe he'd been careless or failed to dot every i and cross every t. "But my partner knew what it was right away, and we were on routine patrol only a few blocks from there."

In answer to Mr. Lane's questions, the officer described the part of Greenwich Village where the bowling alley was located. It was a neighborhood that Jackie didn't know all that well. The details weren't important as long as the location was in Manhattan and she had jurisdiction. What mattered was that this was downtown New York City and Bryn was a Westchester kid who should've been home sleeping in her bed. Jackie watched Tara while the cop testified that they got the call after eleven p.m. and the people on the streets at that hour were a mix of yuppies, homeless, and mentally ill. Tara seemed to be holding back tears; Jackie thought Tara was probably asking herself when she'd lost control of her daughter.

"And were you the first officer to respond to the scene?" Lane asked.

"Yes, sir. My partner was securing the patrol car outside and I ran in." Jenkins glanced at Bryn and winced, as though remembering the scene was painful to him. Jackie thought the cop would like to be anywhere else other than sitting on the witness stand.

"Officer, is this your first time testifying in court?" Jackie asked.

"Yes, Judge."

"Okay. Relax. Tell the truth and you'll be fine." Her words were encouraging but she fixed him with a stern look and leaned toward him as imposingly as her petite body would allow. If he panicked and messed up his testimony, she had a better chance of finding some justification to keep the boxcutter out of evidence. A cop wet behind the ears was better for the accused than a calm and seasoned one. Jenkins fidgeted with the police badge hanging on a chain around his neck.

"Tell us please what you saw when you entered the bowling alley," Lane said.

"The guy behind the desk, you know, who gives the lane assignments and rents out the shoes? He pointed to the far end and said, 'lane 2, lane 2.' So, I ran over there."

"And what did you see?"

"There was a bunch of kids. They had their jackets and backpacks and stuff spread out on the benches a few feet away from the lane itself. The kids were standing up. There were maybe seven or eight?"

"Are you asking us or telling us, Officer?" Jackie liked to keep the witnesses in line. This one was putty in her hands.

"I'm sorry, Judge. I'm telling you. There were seven or eight boys and girls. Two girls were in the middle, kind of standing opposite each other. I couldn't make out what they were saying because the bowling alley was so noisy. But I could tell they were yelling. Definitely in each other's faces, if you know what I mean."

"Your Honor, may I confirm with the officer that the Respondent was one of the girls in the center of the group he is referencing?" Mr. Lane asked.

"Yes," Jackie said. She knew it was absurd, but Jackie wished that Jenkins would look over and say that Bryn was not one of the girls he saw that night.

"Yeah, that's one of them." Jenkins gestured toward Bryn with his head and whole upper body, almost emerging from his seat. Bryn flinched. Then the officer took a tissue from his front pants pocket and wiped his forehead. Jackie wondered what had him quite this rattled and made a mental note of his discomfort.

"Okay, Officer. What happened when you approached?"

"The girl, this one, was facing in my direction. She was wearing one of those crossbody bags—a black one, across her chest. She had something in her hand and she was holding it out toward the other girl. I couldn't tell what it was. When I got closer it seemed like she saw me, or saw the uniform, because she stopped yelling and put whatever she'd been holding inside the bag and zipped it up. Then she backed a few feet away from the other girl. It happened fast, but that's what I saw."

Jenkins seemed to be picking up steam as he testified, gaining confidence in his own recollection. Jackie decided this was a good time for a break. Maybe it would throw him off his game.

"Mike, I need a short recess," she said.

Angela looked up from the law secretary's desk. "Do you want to let Mr. Lane finish up with the direct examination, Judge? I don't think it will be much longer. You could take a break before the cross-examination," she suggested.

"No. I'd like to take a recess now." Jackie stood and went into her robing room, leaving Angela staring after her. Out of the corner of her eye, Jackie saw her law secretary shrug. Jackie figured everyone probably thought she needed to use the bathroom urgently. So be it.

She sat down at her desk and counted to sixty. Then she pulled out her cell.

She read Lou's text. "This is going badly, isn't it?"

"It's going entirely predictably. Sit tight." There might not be much she could do, but for this moment, Lou was counting on her. Jackie felt a surge of adrenaline. She gave herself an encouraging thumbs up and sat for another moment thinking about where the holes in the cop's testimony might be.

When Jackie was back on the bench, Mike reminded the officer that he was still under oath. Jenkins continued. "At that point, my partner, Officer Ruiz, had come into the bowling alley and he ran over to where I was. We both approached the group of kids and separated the girls. I mean, they weren't actually on top of each other or anything, but we were trying to defuse the situation." Jackie smiled, despite herself, at the rookie officer's use of the academy jargon. "I took the Respondent and my partner had the victim."

"Officer Jenkins, I prefer that you not call anyone the victim because that's precisely the factual determination that I have to make. I have no idea yet if the other girl is a victim or not. So, you can call her the Complainant or use her name." Jackie's speech was mostly meant to rally Lou and she saw him sit up straighter when he heard her words. But the spillover effect on Jenkins was clear. His brow was furrowed and he looked confused.

"What is the Complainant's name?" Mr. Lane asked.

"I don't remember it offhand. Can I check my memo book?" Jenkins shifted in his seat, feeling for his small spiral notebook and flipped the pages, scanning for the entry. "Yeah, here it is. Paloma. I remember thinking it was a cool name."

"Okay, Officer. What happened after you separated the girls?" Mr. Lane was almost as inexperienced as his witness, but even he seemed to sense that the officer was getting off track, the story losing momentum.

"Right. So, Paloma said that she and the Respondent had been talking about one of the other kids that was there with them. A boy named Cal."

Just as Jackie figured. She wondered how often the boy at the center of these disputes was worth the trouble.

"It started as them exchanging some words about who Cal liked better and so forth. But Paloma said the Respondent got angry and started cursing at her. Then she pulled some sort of blade out of her pocket and sort of stuck it out at the Complainant." At Lane's request, the officer demonstrated. He gestured with his arm outstretched, indicating that Bryn had held the blade somewhere in the vicinity of Paloma's midsection. The motion looked more awkward than menacing and Paloma told Jenkins that Bryn hadn't verbally threatened to hurt her with the boxcutter or lunged at her.

Bryn bowed her head and focused on the table while Tara put her hand lightly on the girl's shoulder. Jackie wondered. Was this incident the tip of the iceberg, portending a serious escalation into violent behavior? Or a momentary lashing out, totally out of character for the girl? There was no way for her to know. The prudent course would be for her to assume the worst and nip the problem in the bud by coming down hard on Bryn. But Jackie had too much at stake here to make prudence her only consideration. Extra-judicial emotions of regret and longing and jealousy and love were all at play.

"What happened next?" Mr. Lane asked.

"I frisked the Respondent in case she had other weapons on her, but I didn't find anything. Then I opened the bag she was wearing and I found the boxcutter."

"Officer Jenkins, is this the bag that you searched?" Mr. Lane gave the bag to Mike, who walked over to the witness stand and handed it to the officer. It was made of a fashionable black leather, approximately six inches by nine inches, with three silver zippers dividing it into compartments. Tara's eyes narrowed as she looked at it from the distance of the defense table and Jackie realized it must be a Banana Republic item. She wondered if it was last year's style.

"Yes, sir, that's the bag." Mr. Lane offered it into evidence at the hearing.

"Admitted."

Mr. Lane then took out a plastic evidence bag and gave it to Mike, who broke the seal on it and handed the bag to Jackie. She removed the boxcutter and looked it over. So small and ordinary. Yet it had gotten Bryn into so much trouble. Jenkins identified the boxcutter as the one he'd taken out of Bryn's bag.

"Okay. Are you offering this into evidence for the limited purpose of this hearing?" Jackie asked.

"Yes, your honor." Mr. Lane looked relieved to be finished. The assigned legal aid attorney asked a series of questions but didn't have a lot to work with given how straightforward the testimony had been. If this was going to go in Bryn's favor, Jackie would have to rely on her own creativity. It wasn't going to be easy to pull off.

"The City rests, your honor," Lane said. The attorneys looked expectantly at Jackie, waiting for her to render the decision that seemed so obvious. Jenkins had done everything by the book. Bryn pulled at the barrette restraining her hair and it came undone, her red mane springing out in all directions, a moment of wild release. She looked up at Jackie, a challenging glare that seemed to say, "do what you have to do."

Jackie felt a prickle of cold sweat on the back of her neck. She wasn't ready to decide Bryn's fate or her own. She'd buy herself some more time.

"All right. Thank you, Officer Jenkins. I'm going to take advantage of these next few days that the court is not in session to consider the testimony and do some research on the applicable law. Please be back in court on Monday morning at 9 sharp for my decision. Have a good Thanksgiving."

At once, Angela sidled up to Jackie and spoke in a low tone so the others couldn't hear.

"Judge, do you need to reserve decision and drag this out over Thanksgiving? There was no conflicting evidence to cast any doubt on the officer's testimony. How could that boxcutter not be admissible?" If Angela had a wedge of lemon stuck in her mouth, she couldn't have looked more sour. Jackie had sensed Angela turn against her, unofficially joining forces with Ms. Lopez the day she'd held Darlene Clark in contempt of court. If the near miss with Patricia Chang hadn't been enough of a transgression to push Jackie off the bench, she knew Angela would bide her time until Jackie's next blunder. Jackie had to be so careful here, even as she felt the constraints slipping away.

"I appreciate your observation, Angela. This is a serious Fourth Amendment issue. You know better than anyone that I'm still getting up to speed on criminal law and procedure and this hearing has Constitutional implications. I need to make sure I do my job carefully and methodically. A young woman's liberty is at stake."

With an effort she turned from her traitorous law secretary and back to her loyal court officer. "What's next on the calendar, Mike?"

At the lunch break, she texted Lou. "Come for dinner tonight at 7. I've learned a thing or two about the kitchen in your absence."

"Isn't that against the rules?" Lou responded.

"We're so far past that question."

Lou

Lou had contemplated bringing Jackie a single red rose, a sentimental tribute to the day they'd met. But Tara and the divorce had been a large part of that first encounter, albeit lurking in the background. Lou didn't think Jackie needed that reminder. He went with her favorite gladiolas this time instead.

"Hey, Mr. G! Long time no see!" Dennis opened the door to Jackie's building and let Lou into the lobby.

"Yes. It's nice to see you." Lou folded his umbrella. It'd been raining on and off all afternoon and he was glad to be inside. After he left the courthouse, he'd killed the afternoon aimlessly walking around his old neighborhood feeling disoriented and dispirited. Although he didn't need to account for his whereabouts, he'd told Tara he was having dinner with an old friend, which was more or less true.

"Should I ring up to the Judge's apartment? Let her know you're here?" Dennis raised his eyebrows higher with each question. He was no gossip, but he clearly enjoyed being privy to some inside scoop on the residents. Lou's appearance, especially bearing gifts and after such a long hiatus, was news.

"No, it's okay. She's expecting me." And then he added, "I'm here for dinner. I'll be back down shortly." As though Jackie's honor, or his, called for an explanation.

"Whatever you say, Mr. G." Lou meandered over to the elevator. He heard Dennis, ever the professional, call up to announce his arrival.

The door was ajar but he knocked, a strange sensation in and of itself, and walked in without waiting for an answer. The delicious aroma of pad Thai and coconut curry floated over him. "Wow. It

176

smells fantastic in here. You weren't kidding about learning how to cook." Lou breathed in deeply to show his appreciation for Jackie's culinary efforts and handed her the flowers.

"How thoughtful—these are beautiful. And I said I learned something about the kitchen, which is to stay out of it. I ordered in."

Lou watched Jackie, her back to him, as she arranged the flowers in a simple vase on the kitchen counter and filled it with water from the sink; she was in no rush and seemed totally relaxed, as though his being there were an ordinary occurrence. She was wearing an outfit he didn't recognize, a scooped-neck sweater dress in a tranquil aquamarine color. He could tell it was made of something soft, cashmere or angora, and it hugged her breasts, her hips, her rear. The urge to touch her was almost unbearable, but Lou reminded himself that wasn't why he'd come. Actually, he wasn't sure why he was there, except that Jackie had summoned him. And she was calling the shots.

Without much preamble—the whole situation was awkward already—they sat down at the table. Jackie had set it with her nicest dishes and the crystal wine glasses she saved for special occasions. Lou was touched, but thought the Martha Stewart display was misplaced. Was this a play for him to come back to her? Jackie couldn't possibly believe he'd resume the relationship because she'd pulled out all the stops to make a nice presentation for dinner. He recalled a *Balabusta* column where he'd given this exact advice to his readers, women who often felt neglected, unappreciated, or underloved. Reignite your man's interest in the bedroom by showing off in the kitchen. He came close to telling Jackie that it wasn't often a winning strategy because most men couldn't care less how the table looked as long as there was food on the plate. But he had more important things to discuss.

"It's not looking good for Bryn, is it?" Lou asked, in between mouthfuls. "The cop's testimony seemed pretty reasonable. I believed him."

"I can't talk about the case. That would be inappropriate."

"You can't talk about the case, but you can be the judge deciding the case? You can have me over for dinner in the middle of the hearing? I'm not sure where you're drawing the lines."

Lou was out of his depth. He didn't like having to hold his own on Jackie's turf. Instead of playing along that first day in court, he should've followed his instincts and come clean with Tara about who Jackie was, had Bryn's lawyer ask for a different judge. He'd been so shocked that Bryn had landed in Jackie's courtroom that he'd convinced himself that her involvement was the only way Bryn stood a chance. Now they were too far in for him or Jackie to make a plausible retreat. She'd somehow taken the reins from him completely and it was unsettling. Jackie was holding all the cards.

And then there was the dress she was wearing. She looked so good. It had been so long.

Lou was called back to the moment when Jackie changed the subject. It wasn't a more welcome topic of conversation.

"What's going on with your writing? I read in your column that you left me so you could concentrate on working on a novel." Jackie took a long drink of wine as she studied him and Lou realized her interrogation style was just as he'd seen in court. Pointed and intelligent, potentially dangerous. There was no question she was still angry at him for his cowardly desertion and for the lies he'd told while they were together. He knew her fury was well-deserved and there was no point in making excuses for his abominable behavior. But Lou had told the truth about the writing. Jackie had been overbearing in her own way and Lou had felt too penned in to let his imagination blossom. What was his excuse for his failure since they'd been apart?

"I haven't written a word."

Jackie touched his left hand where it rested on the table next to his wine glass. He thought at first that she meant to be sympathetic. But the way her fingers lingered was closer to an invitation. It was electric.

"I'm sorry about that. Believe it or not, I want you to succeed. But maybe if you're still having trouble writing, it had nothing to do with me in the first place."

"You may be right." Lou wondered where that left them. Jackie's implication seemed to be that Lou would fail to realize his dreams with her or without her, so why not at least make her happy by being together? There was a warped logic to it. They ate in silence, the food filling in for the words they couldn't find. After a few minutes, Jackie seemed to locate her voice and her purpose again.

"When you walked out in September—" she began.

"Jackie, I want to explain—"

"Please, don't. There was so much time to explain before. Now I hope you'll listen. I think you owe me that much."

"Of course." Lou braced for the worst, but Jackie took a totally unexpected tack.

"When you left, I had a lot of time to think about our relationship, about you, about myself."

"Listen, Jackie, I was a bastard to end things the way I did, and I'm so sorry, but is there any point in—"

"It's not you I want to talk about. It's me. I've figured out things about myself that were obvious to everyone else, but not to me. I'm a perfectionist, bossy, driven. I understand now that the same character traits that made me successful professionally also made me hard to be with in a relationship. I don't show love easily, even when I feel it. That's what I regret the most about us—that I wasn't able to let you know how I felt about you."

Lou started to protest, but Jackie held up her hand. "I was stubborn, but you opened my eyes to the little pleasures of life that were always around me that I'd missed. The laughter, the fun. It's hard to go back once you've experienced it."

Jackie took another long drink of her wine before continuing and Lou did the same. "Losing you forced me to reflect and to change.

It's a steep learning curve and I don't always get everything right, but I'm turning things around. And I'm doing it for me, not for you."

Lou was relieved. Jackie had realized that she was better off without him. Then she turned everything on its head.

"I've also figured out that I don't want to be only an outsider looking in, telling families how to live and how to love. I want a life filled with love and a family of my own. A life with you."

Lou felt ashamed, but his plate was so full with Tara and Bryn he had no ability to work through his dormant feelings for Jackie. There was only so much one man could handle. So, Lou said nothing and hoped Jackie would know he was sincere.

When they finished eating, Lou cleared the table and rinsed the dishes and the break gave him a chance to regroup. When he returned to the living room he felt more in control. Until Jackie asked him to join her where she was sitting on the couch.

She was curled in the corner, her legs tucked attractively under her, the supple dress now pulled even more tautly over her curves. When he sat down next to her, he could smell the hints of jasmine and vanilla of her perfume. Intimate moments from their time together came rushing into his head and it was a matter of seconds before she leaned into him. He kissed her tentatively at first, alarm bells blaring in his brain. Then he banished the danger signals and kissed her with the ardor of a man recently rescued from a desert island. The fabric of the dress accentuated the softness of her body and soon there was no daylight between them as they pressed the length of their bodies together.

"I need to know what you're thinking." Jackie pulled back, breathless but with her wits about her.

He didn't have the heart to tell her that at that moment he was thinking with only one part of his body.

"I need to know what you want," she persisted.

"I want us to stop talking." Lou reached to draw Jackie close to him again and she settled back into his arms. His desire was so strong he felt he might weep.

She continued to kiss him and her words were all the more shocking being wet and warm near his ear.

"We both want to help Bryn."

Now it was Lou's turn to pull away. He sat up abruptly on the couch. What was Jackie proposing?

"I'm not looking for one night, Lou. I want you back."

"Are you blackmailing me? You'll make Bryn's case go away in return for me?"

"No! Of course not. That's not what I said and not what I meant. I'm not making any promises about Bryn. But I want us to go back to the way we were."

The moment had clearly passed. Jackie stood up and primly smoothed out her dress, the passion extinguished but the cards laid bare.

Sitting on the MetroNorth train back to Tara's house in New Rochelle, Lou went over the evening again and again. He hadn't rejected Jackie. He'd said he needed some time to think, and some things were clear now that he could consider them more calmly, away from that perfume and that infernal dress. Lou wanted Jackie to make Bryn's case go away, although he couldn't fathom how that would happen. And he'd desperately wanted to have sex with her, but that was neither surprising nor a meaningful metric of anything. She was a beautiful woman and he'd been celibate for nearly three months.

It was also clear that the "new" less controlling Jackie was still calling the shots.

What baffled Lou the most was the 180-degree turnaround Jackie seemed to have done about settling down and having a family. Unlike other women he knew, she'd been adamant that she didn't need a piece of paper to prove how they felt about each other. And the role she played with her nieces seemed to satisfy whatever maternal instincts lay dormant. Jackie had maintained that seeing the dark side of family life play out in her courtroom daily had cured her of any romantic vision of marriage and parenthood.

What had changed? Why did she want Lou, the man who'd abandoned her and lied to her, to be her husband and the father of her children? Lou turned each piece of the puzzle over in his mind. And then he reached the conclusion he'd been avoiding. It was as simple as his father had said in the dream.

Jackie was in love.

Jackie

Normally punctual to a fault, Jackie arrived at Mindy's apartment for the Thanksgiving festivities fashionably late after a truly awful night's sleep. Her evening with Lou hadn't gone as she planned. The meal had been lovely, the food delicious, her table setting impeccable. Even the initial conversation, which, given the months of silence, could have been painfully awkward at best and unbearable at worst, had been cordial. And the romantic interlude had started just as she'd dreamed of for months. There was no question that the chemistry was still there. That gave Jackie hope.

No, it was the part about Bryn that had come out all wrong.

Jackie had told Lou she wanted to help Bryn and she meant it. Months earlier, Lou had reminded Jackie that her school firesetter, Moshe, was just a kid who made a stupid mistake. Jackie thought the same was true of Bryn. And despite herself, Jackie admired what she'd seen of Lou's ex. Tara was contrite and respectful in court, a hardworking and basically responsible parent who wanted to do better.

Still, Jackie's position as the judge on the case remained untenable, to put it mildly. Intimately involved in Bryn's legal woes, she was simultaneously longing to be intimate with Lou. It was a convoluted mess that she hadn't totally engineered but she hadn't extricated herself from either. Jackie cringed replaying her quid pro quo—*I'll get Bryn out of this mess if you promise a future with me*—in the midst of hot and heavy foreplay. She was afraid that her clumsy tactics had backfired, that Lou would be repulsed by her. She'd have to find a way to rescue the situation. But her planning would have to wait.

"Aunt Jackie's here!" Dara threw her pudgy 4-year-old arms around Jackie's hips. Mindy's kids were always giddy at family gatherings, especially the two younger ones, who boomeranged from grandparent to grandparent in a relentless game of show and tell. Since their recent sleepover at Jackie's apartment, the girls had been more physically demonstrable in their affection for their only aunt. She squeezed Dara in return, gave Caroline a hug, and returned Nicole's "too cool for school" fist bump.

"Put your coat in Dara's room on the bed. The hall closet is full," Mindy called from the kitchen where she was tinkering with the gravy.

"I'll take you," Dara said. Jackie shook off the vision that had kept her up most of the night, herself and Lou on the cusp of a memorable reunion, shattered by the mention of Bryn's legal problems. She let her little niece lead her by the hand to her frilly pink bedroom.

Her mother was lying so still on the bed that Jackie almost threw her navy wool peacoat right on top of her.

"Mom! Are you okay? What's going on? Why are you lying down?" Jackie was about to scream for help when her mother sat up and put a reassuring hand on her arm.

"You ask so many questions. I'm fine. My sciatica is acting up. The pain goes all the way down my left leg and up into my lower back. When did I get so old?"

Linda sat on the edge of the bed and reached past Jackie for her sneakers, wincing as she put her feet into them.

"Wait, Mom. Don't bend over like that. I'll do it."

"I can put on my own shoes, Jackie. I'm not ready to be put out to pasture yet."

"I know you can. But you can also accept some help once in a while." The only person more stubborn than Jackie was her mother; she'd learned from the best. Jackie knelt down on the floor and did

Linda's laces as Dara looked on in awe, shoe-tying a major accomplishment that she'd yet to master.

"Thank you."

"No worries. Let's go out and join the others. Mindy has outdone herself. And you're not old."

Jackie took her mother's elbow and gently helped her up from the bed. Linda's back had been an issue for some time now, but she was otherwise hale for her 75 years. At 79, Jackie and Mindy's dad, Henry, was not in quite as good physical shape, knees and hips both cranky with age. But he was mentally sharp and more accepting of the effects of the passage of time.

"Did you see the chocolate turkeys? I helped Mommy pick those!" Dara ran out ahead of them back into the living room.

"Where's Lou?" Linda asked as she scanned the assembled guests. So, Mindy hadn't said anything. All the better. Jackie could claim that Lou had another commitment and not have to expose his more extended absence. If she convinced him to give their relationship another try, Jackie's parents would be none the wiser and not ill-disposed toward him. A white lie for a good cause.

"He was invited to spend the holiday with an elderly aunt and uncle out on Long Island and he felt he should go."

"Oh, that's nice. I'm sorry we won't see him."

Jackie had never sought her mother's approval of the men she dated because she was so unduly critical. Hardly anyone made the grade in Linda's world because who could be good enough for Jackie, her perfect daughter? Their mother's wholehearted acceptance of all of Mindy's boyfriends and eventually her husband Sam irked Jackie, but she bit her tongue. For the sake of family peace, Jackie chose to believe that Linda was sincere when she said she missed Lou at the table.

Jackie looked around the room for her father and spotted him reclined in the brown leather chair in the corner, watching the football game on mute with one eye and scanning the sports section of the *New York Post* with the other. His whole face lit up when he saw his older daughter. He moved his feet to one side, patting the ottoman in front of him.

"Aha! My favorite jurist! Come sit with your old dad for a few minutes before this whole hullabaloo gets going."

"I think it's already begun." Jackie gave her father a kiss on the cheek and sat down. Dara and Caroline were playing tag and racing around the apartment oblivious to Mindy's entreaties to cease and desist. And Nicole had decided that now was a good time to introduce the adults to the latest Nicki Minaj rap song at full volume, explicit lyrics included.

"How do the kids listen to that junk?" Her father was old school. Tony Bennett, Frank Sinatra, Shirley Bassey. Jackie had been raised on the crooners, listening along with her parents in the evenings as she did her homework sprawled out on the living room floor.

"Nicole's got it going on. She understands that the music is one thing and the way you live your life is something else." Jackie smiled at her niece, who was now chanting obscenities with total abandon and minimal understanding. "It's the beat and the vibe she's responding to, not the words," Jackie explained to her father. She thought of Bryn and wondered whether the abundant violence in the lyrics of popular music had infiltrated her teenage brain and made it seem acceptable to carry that blade. What would protect Nicole, only three years younger, from the same influences?

"If you say so. You're the expert." Henry was the best kind of proud father. He supported and encouraged both his daughters in the paths they had chosen. He never made them feel that he favored either Jackie's choice to focus on her career, or Mindy's decision to devote herself to husband and children. And, if her father felt it, he never overtly showed any disappointment that neither woman "had it all." Jackie knew how crazy tickled her dad was that she'd achieved so much. She felt almost sick when she contemplated what her father would make of her compromising her professional integrity to help

Bryn and advance her personal objectives with Lou. But maybe in this instance the end would justify the means. And if she pulled it off, no one would ever know.

"Hey, watch, watch." Her father pointed excitedly to the screen. Mindy was her dad's football buddy growing up, not Jackie, but she followed her father's gaze to the television. The quarterback reared back and threw a bullet the whole way down the field with no one in sight to catch it. Out of nowhere, another guy appeared, gathering the football into his chest and running like hell into the endzone.

"Yaaaaaah!!! Atta boy!!" her father yelled.

"That was nuts! Why did he take that chance?"

"The Hail Mary pass. A desperation play when there's nothing left to lose. Hardly ever works, but when it does, it's a thing of beauty." Her father watched the slow-motion replay with almost as much delight as the first time around.

"Let's sit down and get started," Mindy said. "Otherwise we'll be here all night." Jackie knew the comment was directed at their mother. Linda was an early-to-bed and early-to-rise kind of gal and she liked the evening to wrap up no later than 10:00 p.m. Every year she started vacuuming at the moment she felt the guests were in danger of overstaying their welcome.

"Where do you want us?" Sam's mother, Ann, was a stickler for etiquette. No way would she have set the table without place cards and now she stood, lost.

"Anywhere is fine. It's family," Mindy answered.

Jackie watched her father get up slowly and make his way toward the dining room table.

"Soon you'll need a crane to get me out of that chair," he said. Jackie admired how her father tried to keep his sense of humor in the face of his advancing frailty. It was hard for Jackie to watch her parents age. She was grateful that they had each other.

187

Jackie picked a seat at the end of the table next to the kitchen so she could help Mindy. As soon as she sat down, Dara climbed onto her lap with Caroline following close behind.

"I want to sit on Aunt Jackie's lap," Caroline said.

"I got here first," Dara countered. Caroline grabbed her little sister's arm and pulled hard, trying to dislodge her. Dara wailed at the top of her lungs as though Caroline had managed to rip her arm out of its socket and wrapped her legs around Jackie's calves.

"You always get everything you want because you're the *baby*," Caroline whined. She made as though to kick Dara's foot, but seemed to think better of it when she caught her grandmother's eye.

"I wish Uncle Lou was here. Then there would be two laps," Dara said. Jackie held her breath, wondering if her nieces would spill the beans on Lou. She rushed to fill the empty moment.

"Okay, girls, listen. No one is sitting on my lap during dinner. How would I eat the beautiful meal your mother made? Or help her in the kitchen? Sit in the chairs on either side of me." The girls reluctantly pulled away from each other and took their appointed seats. Dara threw her left leg across Jackie's lap and Caroline leaned her head on Jackie's shoulder.

"Leave Aunt Jackie alone. This is supposed to be her day off from dealing with troublemakers like you," Mindy said. But she smiled and Jackie could tell she was pleased that the girls were showering her with attention.

"It's fine," Jackie said, putting a hand gently on each girl's head. "If this is as delinquent as they get, you're in great shape."

Mindy walked carefully out of the kitchen with the first course, a steaming tureen of curried pumpkin soup. She ladled it out at the table, her gleaming white china dramatically setting off the burnt orange. The others immediately dove in, but Jackie was distracted by the richly spiced aroma that potently called Lou to mind. It was the sort of dish he would've made and then lovingly shared the next week with the readers of his column. Jackie wondered if that's where Mindy had gotten the recipe. She didn't ask.

"It looks good on you," her father said in a low voice. He leaned toward Jackie from across the table and motioned to the two little girls splayed over her.

"What? Oh. Yes, they're very sweet." She picked at a non-existent piece of lint on her sleeve, knowing full well what her father was getting at.

"Lou may yet make an honest woman out of you and I think he'd be a great dad." It was the kind of ridiculously old-fashioned sexist statement only a kind-hearted father of a certain vintage could get away with. He took a spoonful of soup and blew on it several times. "Delicious, Mindy."

They made it through the rest of the dinner without any more mention of Lou. Jackie and Mindy served and cleared, with a little bit of begrudging assistance every now and again from Nicole. "Let's take a break before dessert," Henry said and everyone nodded, patting their bellies and declaring how stuffed they were from Mindy's wonderful food. Caroline and Dara scattered to opposite corners of the living room, perhaps grateful for a brief reprieve from the good table manners that their parents demanded.

"I want to try something new this year," Sam said. "Let's go around the table. Instead of saying what we're thankful for at this moment in time, let's say what we hope to be thankful for next year when we gather here again."

"I don't get it," Nicole said. She pulled out her cell and tuned out her father.

"Hey, no phones at the table," Mindy said. Nicole rolled her eyes and put her cell back in her pocket.

"I don't like it. I'm superstitious. If I say what I want to be thankful for next year, it won't happen," Linda said.

"That's silly, Mom. It's a riff on what we do every year, but this time it's forward looking. I'm asking you to think about what would make you happy in the year to come, what you'd be grateful for." Sam was relentlessly positive. In that way, he reminded Jackie of Lou, whose upbeat attitude had been contagious.

"Ok. I'll start," Sam's dad said. "Next year I hope to be thankful that both my hips are in working order and that I can get around on my own steam." Everyone applauded and he took a little bow from the waist.

"What about you, Mom?" Sam asked.

"I told you, this game's not for me. Does anyone want tea?" Linda escaped into the kitchen.

"Okay, I'll go then. I hope next year to be thankful that I've gotten a promotion and a raise." Sam worked incredibly hard. Jackie thought he deserved both.

"Next year I hope to be thankful that we've taken a nice family vacation somewhere, shown the girls a little bit of the world," Mindy said. Jackie knew that sometimes her sister felt trapped in their apartment, taking care of the girls 24/7. Still, she wondered whether it was sensitive for Mindy to make a comment like that in front of the whole family when Sam was working so hard.

Jackie's dad proclaimed that he'd be grateful to be alive to play another round of this game, which elicited a host of "don't be ridiculous," and "stop that" responses from the guests.

All eyes turned to Jackie.

"Next year I hope to be thankful that I'm not here by myself."

Jackie fought off the food coma that threatened to force her straight to bed when she got home. She knew that she had work to do on Bryn's case and not much time. She opened her laptop, pulled up WestLaw, and typed in a query.

"Search of closed containers outside of a subject's grabbable area."

It was a narrow aspect of the Fourth Amendment law on search and seizure regarding what was permissible conduct by the police. Jackie remembered the basic concept from law school, but she hadn't had an occasion to revisit the subject since the bar exam. For an hour, Jackie researched. Can the police open and search a closed backpack or handbag when the bag isn't within reach of the person and therefore poses no immediate danger to the police or others?

Not without a warrant.

Jackie was satisfied. It wouldn't be easy, but she could fashion an opinion in Bryn's favor. The cop was inexperienced and nervous on the stand. His testimony was vulnerable to some "finessing."

The ball was in Lou's court. Would Jackie have the guts to pull the trigger if Lou gave her the green light?

Lou

Lou started down the stairs in a t-shirt and boxers, momentarily forgetting it was a holiday and Bryn and Tara might be home. He hurried back to his room to get dressed when he spotted Tara in the living room.

"Sorry, I didn't mean to scare you." Tara fiddled with the toggle buttons on her duffle coat, a Banana Republic classic, but didn't take it off.

"It's your house. You don't have to apologize for being here."

"Right. Can I talk to you about something?"

"Sure. Why do you have your coat on?" Lou sat down on the steps.

"I only have a couple of minutes. I have to be at work at 9 to set up for the sale. The mall opens at midnight for the crazy Black Friday shoppers. It's going to be mayhem."

She perched tentatively against the back of the couch. Lou thought "mayhem" was a good word to describe what was going on at her home too, but he didn't say so. Tara looked wan and depleted and Lou fought the urge to go into the kitchen and make her a protein smoothie.

"So, normally, I mean, you know this obviously, I would've taken Bryn out to Vegas to see my parents for the holiday."

Lou nodded.

"I couldn't take Bryn this year because I had no idea where this hearing was going. Anyway, we have to be in court Monday morning so it wouldn't have worked." Tara bounded off the couch and started to pace, a clear indication that she was getting up to the difficult part of the conversation. It was a habit that Lou had relied on when they were together, a little heads-up that he better focus on what came next. "So, I was hoping that maybe we could have Thanksgiving together tonight, just the three of us?"

As distracted as Lou was by his own predicament with Jackie, he heard the ache in Tara's voice and understood that her question was not about turkey. Banking on the reservoir of trust they'd built over the years they were together, she was asking if he'd be there for her now. Like any couple, they'd leaned on each other in big and small ways to get through the difficult times. Lou was Tara's support when her parents' move to Nevada left her feeling abandoned. Tara had tenderly sewed the missing buttons on Lou's overcoat before the funeral on the freezing day he buried his father. They had history. Lou could give her Thanksgiving.

"Look, I have nowhere else I need to be. Honestly, the thing is—" He gestured toward the kitchen and shook his head. Lou usually found cooking therapeutic, but somehow he couldn't bring himself to stuffing a bird or roasting Brussel sprouts. "I've got so much on my mind."

Tara stopped pacing and studied him, asking without words, "What could you possibly have on your mind that I don't have on my mind?" Lou wasn't about to tell her that Bryn's liberty might depend upon his decision whether or not to commit himself to the family court judge deciding her case. The whole thing was so surreal.

"That's totally fine. It doesn't have to be home-cooked. I meant we shouldn't let the holiday pass. I think that would send the wrong message to Bryn. Like she's ruined everything or normal life has stopped. Maybe we could go to a restaurant?"

Lou made a reservation at The Monkey's Tavern in New Rochelle, a nice but not extravagant watering hole with surprisingly good food that he and Tara had stumbled upon years earlier. On Thursday nights they had live music. Once in a blue moon before Tara's parents had left town they'd left Bryn and gone to listen to some local band with a strung-out guitarist and an earnest singer, unwinding over a burger and onion rings. Those had been happy times. When Lou saw the place had a traditional Thanksgiving menu for a reasonable fixed price, it seemed like the way to go.

"Bryn, honey, we're going to be late." Tara already had her car keys in her hand. She'd put aside her Banana Republic attire in favor of a pumpkin-colored cable-knit sweater and a shortish black velvet skirt. It wasn't an outfit meant to seduce so much as a gentle tribute to a time when Lou couldn't keep his hands off her. He hadn't forgotten.

"You look lovely," he said.

She smiled. "You clean up nice, too."

When Bryn finally emerged, she'd ditched the "innocent girl" clothes she'd worn in court a couple of days before in favor of one of her usual, "I'm playing with you, but don't mess with me," outfits. Her red spandex shirt exposed both her shoulders and her midriff, her low-rise jeans were tight. She'd gelled her hair in a frenetic and aggressive way that gave her an almost electrified look. The whole ensemble was vaguely comical given her childish face and figure. If Lou still had any say, he would've told her to go back to her room and start over. But he was powerless. He stood next to Tara, who bit her lip, held her tongue, and picked up her purse.

Lou had made the reservation for 6:00. Maybe the place would have been less depressing either earlier or later. It was a Thursday, but there was no music and the lights were too bright. The tables were mostly empty except for one elderly couple in the corner eating but not talking to each other and a single guy near the bar picking at his fingernails and staring into space. Even though Lou had zero interest in sports and even less in television, he was glad the football game was on, for the noise. The waitress was a woman of no fixed age but past her prime, with a spare tire around her middle that would've made the Michelin Man proud. She was in no rush to take their order despite the paucity of other patrons.

194

"What can I get you?" she croaked out when she finally sauntered over to their table. Her voice was breathy but not sexy and Lou wondered if she had emphysema.

"Isn't there a set menu for Thanksgiving?" Lou was sure he'd read that on the website.

"Yeah, there is." The waitress shifted her considerable weight from her right leg to her left and tapped her pen against her order pad.

Tara and Lou exchanged a quick look. "We'll have three of the Thanksgiving specials, please."

"Suit yourself." The waitress meandered away toward the kitchen to deliver the news of their surprising selection.

Lou took a sip of water and contemplated the beyond surreal circumstance of sitting with his ex-wife and ex-stepdaughter in a dismal restaurant in dismal New Rochelle on Thanksgiving. It was the stuff that novels were made of, but it wasn't the story he wanted to write. Tara sat next to him, rubbing the base of her neck as though searching in vain for the lustrous hair she'd lobbed off after the divorce. Had she been trying to transform herself into someone new? Had she succeeded? Lou thought maybe all three of them would've been better off if they'd stuck with who they were before everything fell apart. But it was too late for that.

Lou figured he might as well give small talk a try.

"So, do you have to go back to open the store at midnight?"

"No, thank God. I was there all day. My assistant is doing the nut job shift. What normal people feel compelled to shop for Christmas when the turkey is barely cold?"

"You got me. Not having to buy gifts for Christmas is a big perk of being Jewish. And my parents never went in for that eight days of Chanukah—a gift for every night thing either."

"Anyway, setting up the store was chaos. Do you remember Jack? Short guy, chipped front tooth? You used to say he'd be better off working in a hardware store than Banana."

"Nope." Lou buttered a roll and passed the basket to Bryn, who didn't touch the bread, setting it down in the empty place next to her.

"He decided today was the day to demand a raise and reduced hours. Right before the Thanksgiving Day sale! He starts ranting and raving, waving his arms right by the new-sweater display, saying that I treat him like a dog and no one could pay rent on the shit salary he's making."

"What did you do?" Lou had frankly thought Tara's talents were wasted at the mall, even though she'd risen up through the ranks over the years. She was a good manager who actually relished handling the meltdowns of her subordinates, mostly kids half her age whose sole credential was that they were good looking (Jack apparently notwithstanding). And Tara was addicted to the employee discount.

"I told him to shut his mouth or I'd fire him on the spot, sale or no sale."

Bryn had sat through her mother's story without so much as a word or a change in the scowl she wore on her face. Lou remembered when Bryn was a little girl and her high-pitched chatter was constant and adorable, laced with laughter and malapropisms that they intended to write down and never did. Since his return in September, Bryn hadn't strung together more than ten words and most were expletives. Nonetheless, Lou was undeterred.

"Reading any good books in English class?" he asked.

"No."

"Who do you have for English?"

"Would you know the name if I told you?" Bryn glared at Lou. She took a breadstick and broke it in half and Lou had the sensation that if she could snap his head off the same way, she might. He wondered if all kids went through phases like this, or whether some were more even-keeled. Lou had the fleeting alarming thought that maybe Bryn could use a little time in juvenile detention to realize how good she had it at home.

The waitress ambled over and unceremoniously set down their food in front of them with a heavy hand. She left the table without waiting to see if they needed anything else. Lou was ravenous and dug in, but Tara and Bryn picked at the turkey and fixings. He regretted not cooking the meal at Tara's, which would have cost him a lot less money and at least they'd have had leftovers. When the check came, Tara offered to split it.

"Don't be silly. Let's get out of here."

Lou noticed Tara check her watch several times on the way home. What difference did it make what time it was? Maybe a nervous habit she'd picked up since they split.

"That was the worst Thanksgiving ever," Bryn tossed out over her shoulder as she headed for her room.

She didn't sound angry, just resigned. Lou wasn't sure his assessment was any different. He was grateful when Bryn didn't slam the door. That seemed like progress.

Tara went to the kitchen and put up a pot of decaf French Vanilla.

"None for me, thanks. When did you switch to that sickeningly sweet coffee anyway?" Lou had eaten everything on his plate and most of Tara's too at the restaurant. He didn't think he could even stomach a decent coffee and definitely not this sad excuse for one.

"It's not for you. I invited Harrison over for dessert." She busied herself in the refrigerator with her back to Lou, pulling out the half & half and a store-bought pumpkin pie he hadn't noticed on the shelf.

"Why would you possibly do that?"

"I figured with the kids staying with Anastasia for the holiday, he'd probably be by himself. I thought he could hang out with us for a little while, have some pie." She set three plates at the dining room table and went back into the kitchen for mugs from the cabinet. As she was taking out the cutlery, the doorbell rang.

"Can you get that, Lou? I'll finish setting up here."

Lou opened his mouth, but no sound came out. He hadn't seen Harrison since he left him sitting by his bicycle on the grass months ago and he hadn't planned on seeing him again. Yet here was the big lug outside his ex-wife's door, honing in on their family Thanksgiving celebration.

Or whatever tonight had been.

Lou felt confused, the only coherent thought in his head that he didn't want Harrison to see how great Tara looked in that skirt.

He opened the door in a daze, blocking the entrance like he used to do when the Jehova's Witnesses came around.

"Hey, buddy! Howya doin? Happy Thanksgiving!" Harrison was clean shaven and the smell of Paco Rabanne cologne nearly felled Lou. Harrison's shoulders were even broader than Lou remembered, and off the bike, he seemed a good six inches taller. He looked hale and hearty and Lou felt scrawny in comparison. Still, Lou was the man of the house, kind of, and he stood his ground. "Tara invited me over. Can I come in?"

Lou recovered his senses. "Of course. It's her house," he said for the second time that day. He stepped aside and let the giant enter. Lou was on the third step up to his attic hideaway when Tara called him back.

"Lou, please sit with us. We didn't have dessert, remember?" Lou thought that was hardly the point. But if Tara was giving him the opportunity to chaperone, he'd better take it.

They sat around the small table and tried to make chit chat, avoiding all sensitive topics such as children, ex-spouses, careers, living arrangements. They were left with politics and religion— Harrison's support of the border wall, Lou's dislike of the new Supreme Court justices, and Tara's position that the Pope should embrace same-sex marriage. After they'd exhausted these weighty topics in under ten minutes, Tara and Harrison ate their pie in silence. Lou had no appetite.

"This is really good, Tara. Did you bake it?" Harrison asked.

"No. Lou does most of the cooking and baking around here these days. I bought this at Rococo's on Main Street."

"Delicious," Harrison said. "Hey, do you ever make a fire in that fireplace in the living room?"

"I don't think the flue's been cleaned since I left," Lou said.

"Do you like a fire, Tara?" Harrison's voice had taken on a new tone, smooth like the pumpkin pie and nearly as nauseating.

"Sure," Tara said.

"I like a fire," Harrison said, his voice even deeper than a moment before. "It doesn't take a lot to heat me up. I'm always ready."

Then Lou heard a sound he couldn't identify at first, a light, clear ringing that felt like a cool wet cloth on his now sweaty brow. After a few seconds, he recognized the sound as Tara's laughter, a musical giggle he hadn't elicited in years. He pushed his chair abruptly away from the table.

"I need to get some air." Lou practically ran out of the dining room and into the kitchen. He opened the top cabinet and pulled down a shot glass and the bottle of single malt scotch he'd stowed there. Opening the back door, he stepped out into the night and let the screen door swing shut behind him. He sank into one of the rocking chairs and threw back a shot, watching the fireflies and wondering why they were still out frolicking this late in the season. More creatures that didn't know where they belonged or how to behave. He considered getting plastered, but couldn't work up the energy.

The night had gone from bad to worse. Lou realized with a start that he hadn't come to any resolution about whether to accept Jackie's proposition/proposal, although he knew time was running out. Monday morning she'd decide Bryn's case. He felt the pressure like a heavy stone on his chest, crushing his lungs.

No, tonight had been all about Tara, a woman he'd securely relegated to his past. It had been over between them for a long time, years before the final divorce decree. Harrison's arrival had clarified all of that, hadn't it? She'd giggled, for God's sake, at the stupid oaf's disgusting innuendo. And now, here he was, sitting outside alone. Lou was pouring himself a second drink when the screen door slammed again.

Bryn sat down in the opposite rocker. She'd changed into jeans and a sweatshirt, washed the crap out of her hair and pulled it back in a ponytail. She looked sweet and fourteen again. Lou reminded himself not to be fooled. It didn't take long to be brought back to reality.

"It's fucked up to drink alone."

"Watch your language, young lady. And what would you know about it, anyway?"

"Pour me one. We can drink together and I'll fill you in," Bryn suggested with a straight face. Lou prayed it was a bluff.

"No way. Your mother would kill me. Although she probably wouldn't notice as long as that Neanderthal is in there."

"Guess it worked," Bryn said, sighing.

"What are you talking about?" Lou had only had one drink, but his addled brain has trouble following.

"You are so clueless. C - LOU - less."

"That's clever. Harsh, but clever. So, clue me in."

"She invited that asshole over here to make you jealous. Can't you see that?" Bryn delivered the news directly, and it belted Lou in the heart.

"I don't think so. Your mother doesn't want me back. Every kid whose parents get divorced has that fantasy, but it isn't true." Lou felt sorry for Bryn and for himself.

"You're not my parent. And don't blame me because you're too stupid to see what's going on." She got up from the rocker and drained the glass Lou had poured for himself.

"Do you want me back?" Lou asked.

"I couldn't give a flying fuck." Bryn turned away and wiped her eyes on the sleeve of her sweatshirt. When she walked back into the house she yelled over her shoulder, "He's leaving."

Lou got up unsteadily from the rocker, emotion rather than alcohol causing his knees to wobble. He raced into the house, careful to close the screen door quietly. He stood in the entryway to the living room, watching as Tara saw Harrison to the door.

"Thanks for coming over, Harrison. Have a good weekend," Tara said. She smiled, and he kissed her on the cheek but didn't try for anything more.

Lou had come up silently behind her. When Tara turned from the door, they were inches apart.

"Tara, I—"

"What?"

"I don't know. I'm not sure—"

Tara stepped toward him, closing the small space between them. She brushed her fingertips on his chest and kissed his lips. Then she took Lou by the hand and led him to her bedroom. Their bedroom.

She closed the door and locked it.

"Are you sure?"

"I'm sure."

Lou woke early the next morning. He couldn't talk yet, didn't have the words to make sense of what had happened. Maybe Tara couldn't either. She kept her eyes closed and her breathing even, although he was pretty sure she was pretending to sleep as he tiptoed out of the bedroom. Upstairs, he stretched out on his back on the futon.

His mind was clearer after making love to Tara, but his feelings were astronomically more confused. Lou needed to slow things down while he figured it all out. But Jackie was working on her own timetable, not his. He was desperate that Bryn not suffer because of his paralysis. He picked up his cell to call her.

"Jackie?"

"Yes, Lou."

"I'm not ready." Jackie said nothing, but Lou thought he heard the sound of her drinking her coffee. "Please, I'm begging you, don't take it out on Bryn."

Jackie

"Here you go, Judge." Mike handed Jackie the evidence bags containing the exhibits admitted at Bryn's suppression hearing.

"Thanks." Jackie waited for Mike to leave her robing room and pulled out the black crossbody bag. She ran her fingers over the leather and turned it around in her hands. She unzipped each of the compartments and peered inside. What was she looking for? The bag was empty now, of course. The personal belongings that weren't relevant to the case—maybe a lip gloss, some money, a return train ticket to New Rochelle—had been given to Tara after Bryn's arrest. There was no question that the boxcutter could fit inside the large section of the bag as Jenkins had testified. No, Jackie was looking for something more intangible. A vibe. About Bryn. About Lou.

She wasn't sure what to make of Lou's indecision. On the telephone he'd said simply that he wasn't ready. But Lou wasn't a man to deliberate. He was impulsive. Their relationship had started with his impromptu approach on the steps of the State Courthouse and ended as abruptly with his spontaneous departure. Jackie had no idea whether to be encouraged or deflated that he was conflicted now. She wondered if anything had become clearer for him over the Thanksgiving weekend.

"Guess who I met?" Mike's voice startled her and Jackie jumped a little in her chair.

"You shouldn't sneak up on me like that."

"Sorry. I forget that freaks people out. I'm just quiet. I don't do it on purpose."

"Okay. So, who'd you meet? I don't play guessing games."

"Your sister!"

"What? Where?" Jackie shoved Bryn's purse back into the evidence bag and ripped the plastic down one side. Mindy had never visited Jackie at work and she couldn't imagine why she had shown up today of all days.

"Hey, hey, let me do that." Mike took the bag gently from Jackie. "She's here in the courtroom. Should I bring her back?"

"Do you have to?" She adored Mindy, but Jackie didn't need her here in the middle of all this craziness. "No, of course. Please bring her in."

Mike gave Jackie a quizzical look before he turned and went to retrieve her sister.

A moment later, Mindy plopped her oversized purse on Jackie's desk and sat down in a chair across from her. "Your court officer is hot. I mean, in a middle-aged, ex-cop, receding-hairline sort of way. Courteous, but manly. Is he single?"

"Keep your pants on, Min. I'm his boss."

"Wouldn't be the first time." Mindy looked around the small room. "I thought your robing room would be, I don't know, grander or something. Stuff on the walls, like a big mural of an American Bald Eagle or the Scales of Justice. The Seal of the State of New York? At least your framed law school diploma."

"Sorry to disappoint you. What are you doing here, Mindy? Lou's case is on in fifteen minutes. You can't cross paths."

"Lou is exactly why I'm here. I'm doing an intervention. I have to stop you from ruining your life."

"You watch way too much TV."

Mindy was not to be deterred. "My God, Jackie. Are you that desperate to get him back? There are other men in the world. I'm afraid you're going to do something rash and throw away everything you've worked so hard to achieve." She stepped around the desk closer to Jackie, reaching out her arms to embrace her. Jackie scooted her rolling chair to her left and came dangerously close to crashing into the American flag that stood behind her desk.

"I don't do rash and I don't hug at work. Besides, I haven't made up my mind yet which way I'm deciding. I'm keeping my options open." Jackie held up two typewritten sheets, one in each hand, snatching the papers back when her sister tried to read them. "Look, Mindy, here's the deal. I'm sure Bryn's a good kid who got in over her head. But every judge in this courthouse would find her guilty of weapon possession in the blink of an eye."

"I don't understand what you're saying. What's there for you to decide then?"

"What I'm saying is that Bryn's at no disadvantage with me being the judge on her case. I can only help her. Either her case comes out the same as it would with another judge or it comes out better. I can play it by the books and let Bryn deal with the consequences of her behavior," Jackie said, holding up the decision in her right hand, "or I can give her a pass and a second chance, for Lou's sake," holding up the one in her left. "And for mine."

Jackie lifted her robe off the hook behind her chair and put it on. She smoothed it over her dress and checked herself in the mirror. She took a lipstick out of her purse and reapplied.

"So how will you figure out which way to go?"

"When I see Lou, I'll know if there's still a chance for us. He's got no poker face at all. That's why the guys played cards with him—he's an open book. And he served good snacks."

Jackie allowed Mike a few minutes to get the parties in place. Then she took a page from her court officer's playbook and stole into the courtroom, surveying the scene unnoticed before Mike called the case.

She could feel the difference immediately, a shift in the kinetic energy. Instead of taking a seat in the back as he had before, Lou stood in the row directly behind Bryn and Tara. Jackie saw him point to his stomach with one hand and mime to Bryn with a closed fist to punch him in the abs. Bryn didn't smile in response, but her eyes no longer shot daggers at Lou. When Tara shook her head at Lou and his antics, Jackie read connection, not exasperation. They were a unit. Not the three disparate individuals who had landed in her courtroom ten days earlier.

"In the Matter of Bryn D." Mike asked the attorneys to state their names and directed everyone to be seated.

Taking it all in, Jackie was ninety-nine percent convinced of Lou's second and final desertion. She picked up the decision she was obligated to render as an impartial judge who'd sworn a solemn oath to uphold the Constitution and the laws of the State of New York. The lawful decision. Jenkins' testimony had been straightforward and the law was clear. The officer's search of Bryn's bag and the recovery of the boxcutter had been totally legit. If she'd lost Lou, Jackie would at least decide the case with her judicial integrity intact.

"Are you ready, Judge?" In four words, Jackie gathered from Angela's tone that she was annoyed. Her law secretary was unaccustomed to Jackie issuing a decision without so much as a consultation. But Angela was the least of her worries right now.

"Yes, I'm all set."

Jackie cleared her throat and was about to read her decision out loud. Then she glanced over at the defense table.

Bryn sat very still, staring straight ahead, her hands folded in front of her on the table. Tara held her head high, dignified and respectful, one arm loosely wrapped around her daughter's waist. And Lou? Seated several feet behind them, Lou was still on the outside. It might not be over yet.

Jackie remembered her father on Thanksgiving and the Hail Mary pass. He'd called it a thing of beauty, when it worked. It was Jackie's last chance, a desperate play for Lou's love. If it didn't work, it would be over and she'd find a way to move on. Jackie pulled out the alternate version of the decision.

"The police are permitted to search a person who is legally under arrest without a search warrant. The police are also permitted to search the area within that person's immediate control, sometimes called the 'grabbable' area, which includes containers such as backpacks, handbags, suitcases, etc. The issue here is whether the Respondent's crossbody bag was within her grabbable area at the time that Officer Jenkins searched it and recovered the boxcutter. If the court credits Officer Jenkins that the Respondent was wearing the bag, then the search was legal. If the court does not believe that the Respondent was wearing the bag, then the search was illegal."

Bryn's brow was furrowed as she tried to follow what Jackie was saying despite the legal jargon. Lou and Tara looked almost as befuddled.

"The court makes the following observations about the officer's demeanor on the witness stand. Officer Jenkins was nervous. He was fidgeting with his badge and also broke out in a sweat. At one point he winced and looked uncomfortable. The court also observed the officer repeatedly looking to Mr. Lane, the attorney for the City, as if seeking approval of his testimony. Jenkins was unable, at times, to maintain eye contact with the court. The court further notes that Jenkins was inexperienced. He'd only recently graduated from the academy. This was his first patrol and he didn't even know what type of incident he was responding to when the police code came over the radio."

Jackie glanced briefly at Lou. He looked concerned, a small frown playing on his lips, but his shoulders had relaxed a little and he'd leaned back slightly on the bench. Jackie thought he might have figured out where she was going with this, even if he was wary of her motives.

"Jenkins testified that when he got to the bowling alley, the Respondent was part of a group of seven or eight kids. They had their backpacks, bags, shoes, jackets and other belongings on the benches surrounding the bowling Lane. The officer claimed, however, that the Respondent was wearing her bag over her chest.

"The court does not credit the officer's testimony that Respondent was wearing her bag across her chest at the time that she was seen arguing with the complainant. The court finds it more credible that the Respondent's bag was on the bench with the other property. The officer's anxiety was an indication to the court that aspects of his testimony were false. The officer's inexperience may have led him to conduct an unlawful search and then lie about it on the stand.

"Because the court believes, contrary to the testimony of Officer Jenkins, that the bag was not within the Respondent's grabbable area, the court finds that the police were required to obtain a warrant before searching the bag. Therefore, the recovery of the boxcutter was illegal and the evidence will not be admissible at the fact-finding."

Jackie's decision was met with silence from the attorneys on both sides as well as the parties. Angela was the only one not left speechless by the unusual turn of events.

"Judge, may I speak with you for one moment in your robing room before the proceedings continue?" It was less of a request than a directive and Jackie told Mike she needed a five-minute break.

Out of earshot of the others, Angela didn't hold back. "With all due respect, Judge, you misconstrued the facts to justify suppressing the weapon. There was absolutely no basis to conclude that the girl wasn't wearing that bag."

Jackie did her best to look incredulous. "It's my job to determine the credibility of the witness. That's the whole point of the hearing. I can't rubber stamp anything the prosecutor offers. I have to make my own judgement based on all of the facts and circumstances in front of me, including the demeanor of the witness on the stand. Officer Jenkins was a nervous wreck."

"The officer was nervous because it was his first time testifying. I'm not sure what's going on here, but I know it isn't right. This decision won't hold up if the City appeals it." Angela was so enraged that she stomped her feet on the ground like a toddler and Jackie knew she'd report on her to Judge Spinelli before the day was done.

"There's nothing going on, Angela. And I'm not worried about being reversed. The Appellate Division gives great deference on questions of credibility to the judge who saw and heard the witness. But I appreciate your input. Let's finish this up." Jackie walked back into the courtroom, her trembling hands stuffed into her pockets under the robe.

"Ms. Reynolds, I will entertain your motion now."

The Legal Aid attorney's nose twitched and Jackie was afraid she might burst into tears. The decision had gone her client's way, but it was so bizarre that the lawyer looked like she wished she'd lost instead of won.

"Yes, Judge. I move to dismiss the petition. The suppression of the weapon means that there is insufficient evidence of weapon possession, especially here, since there is no other corroborating evidence. The officer couldn't describe a weapon in my client's hand and there was no evidence that the Respondent threatened to cut or stab or slash the complainant, which might have suggested that she had a sharp object."

"Mr. Lane, would you like to respond?"

"Yes, Judge." Mr. Lane looked around the courtroom as though he expected salvation to appear, perhaps in the form of a supervisor. But none did.

"Your Honor, I oppose dismissal of the petition. Respectfully, I will discuss with my office taking an appeal to the Appellate Division."

"Of course. You're certainly free to discuss whatever you'd like and to take whatever appeal you'd like. The Respondent's motion is granted and the petition is dismissed."

Jackie turned to the court reporter. "Off the record please, Judy."

She sat forward and leaned toward Bryn and Tara.

"Young lady, you caught a break here today. Because the case is over, I can't order you to do anything. But I strongly suggest, Ms. Donohue, that you immediately put some psychological counseling in place for Bryn. This incident could have ended in real violence. I don't know what else is going on in your life, Bryn, but the fact that you've been running around in Manhattan without your mother knowing makes me suspect that you could benefit from some help. Don't screw up this second chance."

Jackie prayed that Lou had caught her Hail Mary pass. That she'd get a second chance too.

"Mike, what's on next?"

Jackie walked toward their special spot during the lunch break, not at all confident that Lou would be there. She didn't see him on the steps of the State Courthouse and she was about to turn around and go back when she noticed him sitting on a bench on the plaza, close to the flower seller. She walked over and sat down next to him.

"Why are you sitting here instead of over there?"

"I don't know. Change of pace?" Lou shrugged.

But Jackie understood. He wasn't sitting in "their" spot anymore because they weren't "them" anymore. It was over.

"You did something really special in there," Lou said.

"I did something crazy and stupid and illegal."

"I didn't ask you to do it."

"No? No. I guess you didn't." Jackie shifted a little closer and Lou put his arm around her shoulders.

"Why did you?"

She thought about telling him that letting Bryn off was a Hail Mary pass that he hadn't caught. It was true, but she had more important things to say.

"I wanted a future with you. Seeing you in court with Tara and Bryn, I realized you already have what I want, with them. You've gone back to her, haven't you?"

"I don't know if it will work, but I have to try. They need me and I need them."

"I'm not going to pretend to be happy for you. But I like them. Don't let them down."

Lou was quiet for a moment. "Are you going to lose your job over this? Or get disbarred?"

Jackie rested her head on Lou's shoulder and breathed in the smell of him. She wanted to stay in this moment when Lou understood what she'd sacrificed for him.

Then Angela walked up the block toward them, Estella Lopez at her side hanging on her every word. Jackie sat up straight and moved down the bench from Lou, but it was too late. Angela nodded once.

June

Lou

Lou caught Tara as she was heading out the front door.

"Whoa," he said, reaching out his arm and touching her shoulder. "Why are you sneaking out of here?"

"I'm not sneaking. I can't sit still. I'm nervous."

"Don't be. It's going to be fantastic," Lou said, pulling her into a hug, pressing his face against her neck so he could smell her perfume.

"Here's my ride," she said, pulling gently away. "I'm leaving you the car. You won't forget to pick up Bryn from school and come straight to the store, right?"

"How could you even ask me that?"

Tara walked down the driveway to the waiting Uber, looking a little more confident with each stride. She turned and waved as she ducked into the car.

"Amazing," Lou said, his voice joyful in the warm June air.

Bryn was sitting on the front steps of the high school with Tariq and Isabella, two of her new friends, when Lou pulled up. She wasn't ever going to be that popular girl who was elected homecoming queen—if they still had such a thing—but Bryn had definitely distanced herself from the mall and bowling alley crowds. Lou thought these two were good kids. A little fringe too, maybe, but respectful when they came over to the house and serious students. The three of them seemed to be having a conversation, although they had their cells out, so it was hard for Lou to tell. The phones were a sad extension of their bodies, a limb like their arms or legs but not nearly as useful. Lou tapped the horn lightly to get Bryn's attention.

"Hey," she said, climbing into the car.

"Hey, to you. Big afternoon ahead." Lou pulled away from the curb slowly and Bryn waved to her crew.

"Tariq and Izzy are coming to the party later," she said.

"Great!" This celebration was almost as much about Bryn as it was about Tara, and Lou was thrilled for them both.

"FYI, I got a B on that English paper you helped me write."

"Huh. Well, a B isn't so bad. I got plenty of B's in ninth grade." Lou glanced over at Bryn, who was focused on trying to get some gum off the bottom of one sneaker with the toe of her other.

"I could've gotten a B without you. Maybe you need to work on your writing." She turned toward him, a benevolent smirk on her lips.

"Maybe I do." As much as Bryn loved to rib him, Lou could feel her approval. He'd worked on his novel steadily and productively since everything settled down after her case was dismissed in November. Then in March, with a good draft in hand, he'd leveraged his reputation and readership from the *Balabusta* to sign with an agent. Lou almost fainted when the book sold to a decent mid-sized publisher for a respectable advance for a debut author just after Memorial Day. Revising would be even harder than what he'd already accomplished, but he had a new sense of purpose.

They drove along in silence for a little while. Bryn looked out at the cars whizzing by on the parkway and Lou wondered what it would be like teaching her to drive in a couple of years.

"I'm so proud of your mother. She's wanted this for so long."

"Yeah."

"You know, I'm proud of you too," Lou said.

"For what?" The edge was back in Bryn's voice and for a second Lou was sorry he'd said anything. But it was true, he was proud of her. He was no child psychiatrist, but he felt like it was important for her to know it. Especially today, when most of the focus would be on Tara.

"For the way you've moved on from all that stuff."

Bryn ignored Lou's comment and turned on the car radio, which was set to Tara's classic rock station. "Bennie and the Jets" filled the space between them and she turned up the volume. When Elton had finished, Bryn turned the radio off.

"Why did she do it? Why did she let me off?" Her swagger gone, Bryn was a little girl again.

"She didn't believe the cop."

"That's bullshit and you know it."

Lou took a deep breath and kept his eyes straight ahead, on the highway. "I guess she thought you deserved a second chance."

The store wasn't large, but the location was fantastic. Tara had decided that her money was better spent by renting in swanky Bronxville rather than in downtrodden New Rochelle. She'd taken a chunk of her savings and then borrowed most of Lou's advance. For the rest, she hit up her three older brothers, who were more than happy to help her realize her dream.

Tara had festooned the entrance with pink and silver mylar balloons and an enormous "Grand Opening" banner. She'd rigged the speakers so music could be heard inside and out on the sidewalk and ditched the classic rock in favor of a station that teens would listen to and parents could stomach. That was the whole zeitgeist of the store. A trendy boutique for young adults with clothes their mothers would never wear themselves, but would still be willing to pay for.

"I want the vibe to be funky, but not risqué," Tara explained. Lou and Bryn had to talk her down from actually calling the store "Funky, Not Risqué." Once her first choice was vetoed, she'd refused to tell them the real name, planning to surprise everyone on opening day. But that was about the only aspect of the project on which Bryn and

Lou weren't consulted. Bryn was Tara's go-to teen, helping her decide which items to stock, how to display them, and putting together outfits that she and her friends would wear to school or to parties. Lou did the books, but also helped with the advertising: writing the copy, and figuring out which print and internet sites to use for the marketing and publicity. The store was Tara's baby, but Bryn and Lou were the supporting cast.

"Ready?" Lou held the door open.

"Bring it." Bryn gave her hair a scrunch and bounced through the portal.

The store was packed. Local teens and their moms were gathered around display tables and racks, examining the merchandise, while friends and former colleagues of Tara's dipped crudites into hummus and sipped champagne from rented flutes. (Lou had vetoed Tara on serving the drinks in plastic cups.) Tara stood in the middle of it all, talking and laughing, and waving as new people came in. Lou's impulse was to rush over and take her in his arms, but she looked like she was having so much fun he didn't want to disturb her. He saluted from the entryway and she flashed a smile just for him.

Lou meandered around the room. He nodded at the moms he knew from the years when he'd been the working-from-home step-dad, balancing the books between driving carpool, arranging playdates, and making dinner. Not much had changed, yet everything had changed. He went to check on the refreshments and signaled for a waiter to top off the babaganoush.

In the corner, Lou spotted the brothers, three tall men wearing nearly matching flannel shirts. They'd come to support their sister and to check on their investment. Lou ambled over, trying to look nonchalant after his unlikely reappearance in Tara's life. Bill had traveled the furthest, from Albany. Lou offered his hand and Bill shook it with a perfunctory but polite, "Good to see you, Lou." Jack nodded and looked back down at his drink. Connor, the youngest, pulled him aside.

"You're not going to take off on her again, are you?"

It hadn't been like that, but Lou didn't see a point in getting into it. Not here.

"No. I'm here for as long as she'll have me."

In his hasty retreat from the brotherhood, Lou walked straight into Harrison. He was standing alone by the buffet table, loading his plate with carrots and looking quizzically at a spinach-feta dip.

"Oh, hey, Lou. This is great. Do you know if there's cilantro in this dip? I'm allergic to cilantro. Break out in hives all over."

"What are you doing here, Harrison?"

"Came to show my support, man. Chase and the kids were talking about the grand opening party during carpool."

Lou started to walk away when Harrison took hold of his arm with a little too much force and pulled him back.

"Tell me the truth, dude. I never stood a chance with her, did I?"

"No, bro, you didn't. And definitely cilantro. I made the dip myself."

Lou was grateful when their conversation was cut short by Bryn's voice rising above the din. "Quiet, quiet! My mom's going to speak!"

There were some chants of "Tara, Tara," and someone brought a crate over and directed her to stand on it so everyone could see her. She stepped up, wobbling a little on her high heels.

"Wow. This is totally crazy," she said, beaming at her guests. "Thank you all so much for coming out. I hope you'll all be here often."

Lou marveled at Tara's composure. His own knees felt a little weak.

"I want to take a minute to talk about the name of the store," Tara said.

"What is the name of the store?" Bryn blurted out. Several people laughed.

Tara smiled. "I wasn't trying to be mysterious, but I got some grief at home about my first choice," she said, looking pointedly from Lou to Bryn. The murmuring started up again and Lou shushed the guests.

"I'm calling the store 'TBD'. The initials stand for 'Tara and Bryn Donohue,' because Bryn is my partner in everything we're trying to accomplish here." Bryn blushed, something Lou wasn't sure he'd ever seen before. Everyone applauded and Tara had to raise her voice to be heard.

"But there's more to the name. TBD, as you all know, also stands for To Be Determined. TBD was my mantra in this whole project. I was determined to get this done, determined to succeed. And TBD has a third meaning. That the future is wide open, to be determined. You never know who'll come through for you, what's going to happen, or how things will pan out. Everything in life is TBD. So here's to the unfolding future and to sharing it with the ones you love." Tara looked at Lou then, and his heart soared.

He must have fallen asleep because when he opened his eyes, Tara was lying on her side in the bed, propped up on her elbow, staring at him.

"What? Is everything okay?"

"Everything's good. I just couldn't sleep."

"Still wired from this afternoon?" Lou asked, stretching his arms over his head and yawning widely. Three a.m. was not a civilized time to start the day. He'd set the alarm on his phone for 6:30 to go back upstairs. Lou was still sleeping up in the attic bedroom for part of each night, visiting Tara's bedroom after Bryn went to sleep and returning upstairs before she awoke. Bryn was no fool. She knew what was going on and Lou would have bet money she was happy about it. But Tara held on to some old-fashioned notion of propriety and if they weren't remarried, Lou was officially relegated to the upstairs bedroom. Lou understood Tara's caution. There was only so much upheaval a child should have to suffer. They'd been back together since Thanksgiving, nearly six months, and every day that

217

went in the right direction was a triumph for them all. But it was still TBD.

He reached under the covers and ran his hands along Tara's right hip and thigh, the cotton p.j.s gone and the cool feel of her silk nightie a reminder that she wanted him, expected him, in her bed. She lay down with her head on his chest. He ran his fingers through her hair, the short and trendy cut that so beautifully framed her face and defined her new persona. He felt the lump rise in his throat before the onslaught of emotion that it portended.

"Thanks for waiting for me," Lou said.

"I wasn't waiting for you. But I'm glad you came home."

With Tara's blessing, Lou had made himself a cozy office hideaway in the second bedroom upstairs. Although it was the middle of the night, he went there rather than tough out the remaining hours tossing and turning on the futon. He had a column due the next day and it was time to tell his readers what was going on.

It wasn't lost on Lou that the last time he'd written a revealing column about his personal life he was sitting in Cafe Zaz on the day he left Jackie, some nine months earlier. Nine months! Enough time to bring a new life into the world. And in a sense, that's how Lou felt, the rebirth his own. It wasn't a "new beginning" like he'd experienced when he and Tara had divorced or when he'd walked out of Jackie's life. Those times he'd been running with no clue where he was headed. This was a homecoming, a nod to his and Tara's past and a cautious leap into the future.

Lou opened his laptop, bathing the small room in an eerie glow. When he'd started working from the house, he hadn't wanted to spend money he didn't have on his office set-up, so he perched on an outdoor patio chair pulled up to an old card table. When he worked at his makeshift desk, he had to stretch his arms up and over to reach his keyboard, his posture like a dog begging for scraps at the kitchen table. But he was happy not to attempt either wit or profundity engulfed in the aroma of bialys and lo mein at the mall. And although Bryn was no longer allowed free rein to roam the shopping center, Lou still felt better that he wouldn't be the one to spy on her if she made a return appearance with her former friends against Tara's wishes.

For months he'd written his column with only the vaguest of allusions as to where he was and what progress he'd made on his novel. Initially, he'd been reticent to hint at where he was living because he didn't want to hurt Jackie further or give her the misimpression that he'd reunited with Tara when in fact, for the first three months, he was merely tolerated by his ex-wife. Besides, once Lou had decided to be coy about his personal life, his editor latched on to the idea. It was a gimmick, like "Where's Waldo," but it worked. Women read his column searching for clues. Now he was about to put an end to the mystery in the interest of honesty. He needed his readers. The journey didn't feel complete without them on board.

DOROTHY HAD IT RIGHT

There's no place like home. You can all picture Dorothy in her ruby slippers, chanting those words, over and over as she propelled herself out of her dream and back to the only reality she knew. Dorothy had to travel down the yellow brick road to realize that she had everything she needed from the beginning, intelligence and courage and love, if only she would open her eyes.

Do you believe in communication from the afterlife? I know this may sound strange, but some months ago, when I had hit an emotional rock bottom, my dead father came to me in a dream. He told me that the greatest rewards would come to me if I looked past my own individual desires and figured out where I was needed the most. Because when you give love with generosity, it comes back to you.

219

That's what I'm trying to do. I've come home to my family. There's a long road ahead. There are hurts to be healed, and there is trust to be regained. But I need them and they need me.

Lou pressed send and closed his laptop, gratitude filling him both for the unexpected opportunity to love and be loved by the woman he had fallen for so many years earlier, and the chance to parent the child he adored. Even his dream of being a published author was on the verge of being realized. When Lou had left Jackie, he'd been convinced the project would be a legal thriller or a political suspense novel, something escapist. He didn't want to escape anymore. A different genre called to him now. He opened the laptop again to the title page.

Second Chances
 (a love story)
By Lou Greenberg
Everything in life is TBD . . .

After several hours of working, Lou crawled back into Tara's bed feeling energized but sleep-deprived. It was 5:30 and he had a little time to rest before Bryn awoke. He'd come clean with his readers, removed a burden he hadn't fully realized he carried. He was about to fill Tara in when he found her sitting up and reading the online edition of the Post, frowning.

"Look at this," she said, handing the iPad to him.

There on the screen was a small article under a classic Post headline, "She's Not in A Family Way," accompanied by a one-inch square color photograph of Jackie. Lou's heart sank.

Family Court Judge Jackie Martin and the State of New York have agreed to part ways. According to the announcement by Supervising Judge Jane Spinelli, 'Judge Martin has decided that she does not wish to seek a ten-year appointment as a judge on the Family Court. We thank her for her service and wish her well in her future endeavors.' Judge Martin could not be reached for comment. Although there did not appear to be any official finding of misconduct, the Post has uncovered in its own investigation several instances of questionable judicial temperament, one lapse that almost led to a casualty in the courthouse, as well as one case when Martin may have been required to recuse herself because of a link to a litigant. But the official line is that Jackie Martin is simply moving on to new opportunities.

Lou closed the iPad and shut his eyes.

Jackie

Jackie threw her good shoes into her tote and sat down on the couch in her living room. She strapped on the new Velcro sneakers she'd picked out with her youngest niece the day before.

"Choose the ones with the Little Mermaid on them. She's my favorite," Dara had advised.

"I don't think they make those in my size. Otherwise, I definitely would." Jackie had gone with the fuschia pair with Dara's approval.

"Here, you can have this," Jackie handed Dara the helium balloon the store clerk had given her.

"Really? Don't you want it?"

"I'd rather you have it." It turned out that sometimes it wasn't that hard to please a five-year-old.

Mindy was proving more difficult to make happy than her daughter. She'd reluctantly agreed to meet Jackie on the East Side for her appointment. Even though it was hot, Jackie looked forward to the walk across town and breaking in her new sneakers. One of the many lessons she'd learned from her time with Lou was that wandering around New York City in high heels was a mistake. There was always time to change.

Jackie entered Central Park at 67th Street and landed unintentionally at the Adventure playground. When she realized where she was, she sat on a bench outside the fenced in perimeter. No one liked a lone adult without children in tow sitting inside a playground, even someone as seemingly unthreatening as diminutive Jackie in her pink Velcro sneaks.

Jackie loved this playground. She'd been half a dozen times to help Mindy when Sam worked weekends and Nicole and Caroline were small, before Dara was born. She'd pushed the girls on the swings and stood at the bottom of the slide to catch them when they came careening down, laughing or crying. She'd watched Nicole while Mindy whisked Caroline off to the toilet during those messy potty-training days. Sitting outside now, Jackie remembered how intrigued she'd been back then with the imaginative climbing structures, the sprinklers and wading pool, and the sand. So much sand! Like you weren't in the middle of Manhattan at all.

Jackie was still an onlooker, but she viewed the scene with more comprehending eyes. In this little oasis in what could be the harshest of cities, these strangers had formed a kind of community. Where years earlier she'd perceived a collection of individuals, now she recognized families. Sometimes unlikely combinations of people, trying to figure it out. Jackie knew from her time as a judge that, in all families, sometimes uncertainty and even anguish lurked below the surface. But there was also so much love.

The young mom rifling through her backpack for a tissue to wipe her son's nose could be Mindy, enjoying a sunny June afternoon and dealing with the normal stresses of daily life. Or she could be Darlene Clark, suffering in silence, trying desperately to hold it together but sometimes failing in dangerous ways. That dad in the Mets cap watching his daughter play on the jungle gym might have his suitcase packed by the door, ready to abandon his family as soon as he gets home. Or he could be Moshe's dad, tenderly placing a velvet yarmulke on the boy's head to remind him who he is in the midst of all the chaos.

And the kids? The children were all Bryn, still a work in progress, on the brink of greatness or disaster.

Jackie had carefully negotiated her departure with Judge Spinelli, scripting the announcement to ensure that she left on the best terms possible. Since then, she'd gone over and over in her mind the cases that had tripped her up, looking for the thread that linked them together. She felt certain that there were lessons to be learned from the good work she'd done and from her mistakes. Maybe most of all from her mistakes.

She'd always remember Darlene Clark's case, the first time she'd watched a mother lose custody of her children. The gut-wrenching moment was seared into Jackie's soul, a warning to wield power sparingly and with the utmost care. It had taken an encounter outside of the courtroom to allow Jackie to see past Clark's rage to the woman in real distress underneath. Jackie was proud she'd put the wheels in motion to get Clark the psychiatric treatment she needed to reunite with her children. And she'd immediately recused herself after the *ex parte* encounter, preserving her own integrity.

There were other cases that left Jackie feeling less sanguine. Visions of Patricia Chang, her husband's hands around her neck, still haunted her. Although tragedy had been averted by Mike's quick actions and she'd be forever grateful to him, it was Jackie's lowest moment. She'd been so wrapped up in her own despondency over Lou that she'd missed the signs of real physical danger. She'd envisioned only the loneliness Ms. Chang faced. It could have cost Chang her life, either that day outside the courtroom or some other time in her own home.

And Bryn's case? That was in a category all its own. Her decision on Bryn's motion to suppress the boxcutter was legally indefensible, a breach of Jackie's oath to uphold the Constitution. It would be a black mark on her legal career and her soul forever. On the flip side, she'd given Bryn a second chance, with two parents to guide her through life's inevitable minefields. Jackie had acted out of love and she wouldn't look back.

Jackie glanced at her watch. She had a few more minutes before she needed to cross the park and meet Mindy. She watched a young woman, perhaps an au pair, hand a little boy a small Ziplock bag of Cheerios. The child's polite acceptance of the snack, the way he sat obediently on the bench and ate the Cheerios one by one with a mysterious twinkle in his eye, reminded her of Moshe F. and the visit she'd paid him earlier in the week at the residential facility.

Inexplicably, out of all of the litigants she'd encountered, Moshe remained an enigma and left her feeling unsettled. She'd considered his case dispassionately and acted well within her authority. Yet she still wondered. Had she been too lenient, as Angela contended, influenced as she'd been by Lou's vision of mercy? Or was there a way, within the rules or outside of them, that she could have done more for the boy? It wasn't logical, but Jackie felt that a part of her wouldn't be able to move on without some resolution on Moshe. She couldn't have said whether she sought atonement, understanding, or inspiration. But if he was willing to talk to her, she needed to see him.

Jackie had called Moshe's parents to ask their permission. His father seemed hesitant at first, questioning her motives as well as why she was no longer a judge. She'd tried to explain why she hoped to see Moshe, sidestepping as much as possible the reasons for her leaving the bench.

"I felt badly having to place Moshe in the residential facility, especially for so many months, although I gave him the least amount of time permitted under the statute. I imagine he was angry and scared. Maybe he still is. I've felt those emotions myself lately. I thought visiting with him might be cathartic for both of us."

Moshe's dad said he'd check with his son and get back to her. Jackie didn't think she'd hear from him, but a few days later, he called.

"Moshe said he'd be happy for you to come. Not too many kids get visits from their judges." Jackie could hear a note of amusement in the father's voice, and pride in his son as well. She was happy for Moshe that his father had stayed true to him.

"I hope you told him that I'm not his judge anymore or anyone else's."

"I did. But I think you'll always be his judge to him." Moshe's dad filled Jackie in on the protocol of visiting at the facility and gave her directions by public transportation. He suggested she go on a Saturday afternoon, as Moshe observed the Sabbath and would be free to visit without other obligations.

When she got there, she was directed to the library, where Moshe was one of several boys doing homework or reading. The irony of seeing Moshe surrounded by books was not lost on Jackie, but he looked comfortable and relaxed, his yarmulke perched at a jaunty angle on his head. He stood up when she entered the room and Jackie motioned for him to sit.

"I know your dad told you I'm not a judge anymore. You don't have to stand."

"I stand whenever an adult comes into a room, Judge. That's what we do in my school. It's a sign of respect."

"So it is. Very impressive. Please call me Ms. Martin, ok?"

"OK." Moshe settled down in his chair and Jackie sat across the table from him.

"This place doesn't look too terrible, but I know it isn't home. I'm sorry you have to be here."

"You put me here," he said. Not belligerent, just matter-of-fact.

"Well, you played a part in that, didn't you?" Jackie didn't want to fight with the boy. She tried to start over.

"The school here must be different from what you're used to. I guess you have the regular subjects, like history, English, math—but in your old school you also had a lot of Jewish studies, right?" In her mind's eye, Jackie saw the metal trash can, the sacred texts going up in smoke and then the water drowning the rest. What was wrong with her? She wasn't here to torment him.

"Everything is different here. Except that it's still only boys, not coed. That was one change I would've liked." Moshe smiled shyly at Jackie and she laughed.

"Plenty of time for girls later, Moshe. What are you reading?" She gestured toward a thin volume on the table, open but unintelligible to her, the words in Hebrew.

"My father wants me to keep up with my learning while I'm here."

"Is that what you want?" It hadn't been relevant to Moshe's case, so she hadn't asked him in court whether it was significant that the fire destroyed the religious texts, or whether that had been an unfortunate but unintended consequence of starting the fire.

He spoke softly then, and Jackie had to lean across the table to make out what he said.

"I told you during the case that I didn't mean to hurt the people in the school. I didn't want to hurt the books either. In my religion, words are nearly as precious as human life."

Jackie clamped her mouth shut so that she wouldn't ask the follow-up question, why did he set a fire in the Yeshiva's library? Maybe he didn't know the reason himself.

"So, tell me what you're reading. Perhaps you could share something with me."

Jackie felt Moshe assessing, trying to determine whether she was serious or not. She nodded, hoping to encourage him. Now that she'd asked, she needed to know.

"It's called Pirkei Avot, The Sayings of the Fathers. I don't understand a lot of it. It's like one-liners of the great rabbis. Usually people study it in the summer, on long Saturday afternoons in the park." He looked around as if suddenly surprised that there was no grass, no sunshine, and no other pious people enjoying the Sabbath afternoon learning from the sages.

"Could you share something? Maybe one line that made sense to you?"

"Okay." He flipped around for a moment, and then pointed at the words with his finger, translating as he went. "Hillel would say: Do not judge your fellow until you have stood in his place."

Jackie nodded. She didn't want to judge anymore. She wanted to live.

"Let's walk around the block one more time," Mindy said. They'd already circled twice -- down Park from 68th Street to 67th, up 67th to Madison, up Madison from 67th to 68th, and back down 68th to Park. Jackie's feet ached, even in her comfy sneakers. She looked at her watch. They stood in front of the white brick building with the private entrance to the side, its discreet green awning announcing the "New Beginnings Clinic" in a dainty script. Jackie gave Mindy a few more minutes by slowly pulling her heels out of her bag and leaning against the side of the building to change out of her sneakers.

"Are you coming in with me or not?"

Jackie didn't mean to sound impatient; she needed Mindy's support. And while her sister's hesitation gave Jackie pause, she couldn't let it stop her from at least exploring the possibilities.

"Well, it looks clean. And mom would like that the office has its own entrance, separate from the apartment building. Mom always says that's classy. She picked her dentist because he has his own door," Mindy said.

"You don't have to do this if you're too uncomfortable. But here's the thing. If I decide to go forward, I need you to be with me 100%. I can physically have a baby on my own, but I can't have a baby alone."

"You've already decided?"

"I've decided to investigate my options. I would think you, out of everyone, would understand. Being a mother is the most important thing in the world to you."

"It is, of course. And I know there are all sorts of routes to motherhood. I just personally can't imagine doing it without Sam. I'm worried about you going it alone." Mindy looked out at the passing traffic on Park Avenue and Jackie thought she might be considering hailing a cab.

Jackie had her doubts too. But she wasn't going to give up before she'd even begun.

"I'm going in now. I hope you'll come with me." Jackie opened the door and walked into the foyer. Mindy followed.

Dr. Sonia Perlmutter's office was decorated in sandy hues of peach and beige, as though it had been magically transported from Miami Beach to the Upper East Side. Jackie and Mindy sat on a plush couch opposite the doctor's comfy upholstered chair. There was no paper-covered table with cool metal stirrups in sight. Jackie guessed there'd be time for examinations and sterile medical procedures later, if she took the plunge. On the website she'd read that the initial visit was for the doctor to help the woman assess whether artificial insemination was the right course for her.

"I'm nervous," Mindy said.

"I am too. Remember, it's just a conversation."

Jackie suspected that, more likely, this appointment was an opportunity for the doctor to size up the potential patient, to see if she'd be an acceptable liability risk for the clinic before going any further. She figured most of the women came here with their husbands or partners after long bouts of infertility. And then there were the women like her, deciding whether to forge ahead with motherhood on their own. Jackie thought of the many single moms she'd presided over in her courtroom who hadn't made a conscious decision to raise a child alone. Would she pay the same emotional price? Jackie had no way of knowing.

"Good morning, ladies. I'm Dr. Perlmutter. Which one of you is Jackie?" Her voice was as calming as the decor, a woman not easily rattled. Jackie thought *she* would have made a good family court judge.

"I'm Jackie. This is my sister, Mindy."

"Welcome. Good thing the air conditioning is working in here— nice and cool." Jackie hoped Dr. Perlmutter would give up trying to make small talk. She didn't have to wait long.

"So, Jackie. You're here to have an initial conversation about artificial insemination, correct?"

"Yes." Jackie made the mistake of glancing at Mindy, who had forced her mouth into a tight smile that was thoroughly unconvincing.

Bringing her might have been a mistake. Jackie thought it would be all right as long as she didn't look at her. She shifted slightly away from Mindy on the couch and focused all her attention on the doctor.

"Great. I always meet with the potential patients first, to get acquainted a bit. I know you've filled out some of this information on the intake form, but I prefer to have a conversation, if that's okay."

"Sure," Jackie said. She was good, this doctor. Her voice was almost hypnotic. Jackie thought she'd tell her anything.

"Let's start with the easy stuff. What do you do professionally?" Dr. Perlmutter smiled sweetly at her. Jackie wondered if it was a trick question, but was glad she had an answer.

"I'm between jobs right now. I'm an attorney and I've accepted a position teaching at N.Y.U. Law School, my alma mater. I'm quite excited to be going back."

"You did? Why didn't you tell me? She used to be a judge." Mindy sounded proud and sad.

"Well, that's impressive. So, you won't find the costs associated with this procedure burdensome? Many insurance plans don't cover it entirely. And of course, there's the financial responsibility of having a child if we are successful."

"I'm prepared for the financial responsibility," Jackie assured the doctor. "I own my apartment, I have some savings, and I'll have a steady income."

"Wonderful. There will be plenty of time to discuss the medical procedure itself, but in its simplest form, sperm from a donor is placed into your reproductive tract to impregnate you. If it works, it's as easy as that."

"Not terribly romantic," Mindy said.

Jackie glared at her.

Dr. Perlmutter looked quizzically at Mindy and addressed Jackie more directly.

"Of course, you're 40, which is a slightly advanced maternal age for a first child. It's possible that more specialized procedures may be required to achieve a viable pregnancy. We'll conduct a full medical evaluation if you decide to go forward. Do you have any history of major physical or mental illness or any significant surgeries?"

"No. I've been fortunate," Jackie said.

Mindy nearly jumped out of her seat.

"What about that emergency appendectomy you had ten years ago? Remember how scary that was?" She turned toward Dr. Perlmutter. "She called me in the middle of the night, screaming in pain into the phone. I had to wake Sam, my husband, and tell him I was leaving to go with Jackie to the hospital and that he should watch Nicole—she was a baby then—and make sure to feed her in the morning in case I didn't get home in time."

Jackie shook her head. "I'm sorry, Doctor. My sister was supposed to be an extra pair of ears not an extra dose of hysteria."

"Actually, can I ask another question?" Mindy said. Jackie almost said "no," but then she remembered this was Mindy. She was capable of stumbling onto something crucial, even if she didn't realize it.

"Yes, go ahead, Mindy," Dr. Perlmutter said.

"I may get the facts wrong, but I read an article in the *Balabusta*—" Jackie cast her sister a warning look, but Mindy kept talking, "and it was about this woman who did the 23 and me kit and found out her father wasn't her biological father. Then her mom admitted she'd had artificial insemination. The craziest part was that it turned out the sperm wasn't anonymous but was actually from the doctor who ran the clinic." Mindy looked triumphant, as if she'd exposed the whole enterprise as a sham.

Dr. Perlmutter cleared her throat, and Jackie wondered whether her sister had succeeded in shattering the uber-smooth facade of the woman.

"Well, certainly you won't have that issue with me," she said. "Seriously, there were abuses of the system in the past. I'm familiar with that case you're describing. As you'll remember, that woman is now in her mid-fifties, so it was at the inception of this whole field. Science has come a long way, as has the attitude of the public generally. I think you can rest assured that the sperm donor will be anonymous and chosen from the list of screened donors."

Mindy was still shaking her head, seemingly unconvinced, and Jackie wondered which fancy law firm had written up the clinic's undoubtedly mile-long clinic waiver form. Dr. P moved the conversation on. "Okay, that brings me to my next question. Do you have a support network that will be there for you, Jackie, both during the pregnancy and afterwards?"

"You're looking at her," Jackie said, motioning toward Mindy. "And my parents will help. They don't know I'm thinking about going this route yet, but they will love their grandchild, no matter what."

"Having support is critical. You may want to think some more on who else might be there for you," the doctor said, her eyebrows raised as she looked at Mindy.

Mindy's upper lip started to tremble.

"Sorry, that was a poor attempt at humor, Mindy. You're going to be great. You're clearly emotionally invested." The doctor reached over and gave Mindy an encouraging pat on the knee. Mindy took a tissue from the box on the side table.

Dr. Perlmutter got up from her chair, sauntered over to a credenza in the back of her office, and poured two glasses of water with lemon. She handed one to Jackie and one to Mindy. Jackie sensed a change in the doctor's body language. What was coming next?

"Have you always wanted to have a family, Jackie?"

"Wow. That's a pretty personal question."

"This is some pretty personal stuff we're doing here," the doctor said. "And I need to make sure this is something you have thought through."

Jackie paused. It was the first rule of cross-examination: never ask a question to which you don't already know the answer. She figured that Dr. Perlmutter expected her to say that yes, she'd been longing for a child since she herself was a little girl playing with baby dolls and imagining herself as a mother. She thought about giving that answer, for simplicity's sake, but then remembered truth-teller Mindy sat beside her.

"I was focused in my 20s and 30s on establishing myself professionally. I worked very hard and it didn't leave a lot of time for a personal life. I love my nieces and I think I'm a good aunt, but until recently I hadn't considered having a family of my own."

"And what has changed?" Dr. Perlmutter asked.

"I fell in love." Jackie chanced a sidelong glance at Mindy, who reached over and squeezed her hand.

A look of confusion passed over the doctor's face and she flipped through the paperwork. Jackie had indicated that she was on her own and interested in an anonymous sperm donor.

"Then you have a partner?" Dr. Perlmutter asked.

"No. He wasn't the right one for me. But I learned how much love I have to give, and I realized I have the courage to move forward on my own."

Mindy blew her nose loudly into the tissue. "His name was Lou. I guess you don't need to know that."

Jackie emerged from the station into the plaza a week after her appointment with Dr. Perlmutter, her t-shirt damp and sticking to her back. She was way too hot for coffee, but she could feel Roger's eyes on her as she passed his cart. "Good luck, Judge," he called out, just like the old days. She waved, choosing to believe he meant it sincerely.

She went through the separate side entrance of the courthouse, designed so the judges could avoid mixing with the litigants and jurors, but mostly useful to bypass the metal detectors installed after

9/11. Jackie marveled, as always, at the implicit belief underlying this lax security that there could never be a disgruntled judge or ex-judge who might come to the courthouse packing heat. Personally, she didn't feel an urge toward violence. At least not until she stepped into the judges' elevator and Angela followed in on her heels.

"Good morning, Judge."

"Officially for a few more minutes, Angela. I'm going to my robing room to get my things together. Is that where you're headed?" Jackie had hoped for some time to sit in her courtroom alone.

"No."

"Where are you going?"

"I'm going to 7. To my new courtroom."

"Wow. Judge Spinelli already assigned you to a new judge? That was fast. Is it Judge Hopkins? I'm sure you'll keep him in line."

"Actually, it's *my* new courtroom. I've been appointed as an interim judge to fill your vacancy."

Jackie noticed for the first time how stale the air was in the small space, as though the oxygen had been sucked out by a holier-than-thou attitude that often came with the gavel and the power to judge other people. Angela would fit right in.

"Well. Good for you. That's what you've always wanted." The doors opened on the fourth floor and Jackie stepped out. "Make sure your own ambition doesn't bite you in the ass."

There wasn't all that much to pack up. Jackie carefully folded the letters she'd received from Judge Spinelli—the first one that extended her evaluation period and the second one urging her to discuss a graceful exit—and put them in an envelope. She thought about lighting them on fire for the momentary satisfaction it would give her to see them burn, but she pictured Moshe and didn't want to set off the alarms or sprinklers. She unplugged the Keurig and put the extra pods into the box.

"Knock, knock. Can I come in, Judge?" Mike stood in the middle of Jackie's robing room.

"You already are in. You must have been phenomenal at Capture the Flag when you were a kid. So sneaky! And it's just Jackie, now."

"I prefer stealthy," Mike said. "Sounds more clandestine, like a foreign agent or something. And it's just Mike, too. Same as always."

Jackie picked up the mug he'd given her and started to wrap it in newspaper. Her hands were trembling. Mike took the cup gently from her.

"Here, let me do that," he said.

"Sorry. I don't know what's wrong with me." Jackie sat down in the chair behind her desk. "I feel kind of jittery."

"Totally understandable. This stinks." He finished with the mug and placed it carefully in the box. He looked around the empty room. "What else goes?"

"I'm almost done and it only filled one box." Jackie looked around and saw that, in fact, she was completely done. "Sit down and cool off for a few minutes?"

"Sure. You know, Jackie, if it's okay for me to say so, this is a damn shame. You would've made a hell of a judge in time."

Jackie bridled. "Do you want to add in your critique of my performance?"

Mike smiled at her and shook his head. "Don't be that way. I meant that you were only starting out. You were bound to have some missteps along the way while you got your footing. The important thing was that your heart was in the right place and you were learning how to fit compassion into your judgements. A lot of judges never come close to that."

Jackie looked at Mike and realized he was sincere. "Thanks, Mike. I appreciate that vote of confidence."

"I have to say, having seen you in action, I was a little surprised you didn't fight it. Tell Judge Spinelli to shove it."

Jackie realized how it must look. Like she'd caved. But Mike didn't know the whole story. There was no way she could take the chance that Judge Spinelli and Angela would expose her connection to Lou, maybe even get Bryn's case reinstated. They had made it clear to Jackie they would've done just that if she had defied them and tried to win the appointment for the full term.

"It's okay. I've learned a lot about myself. Things have changed."

"Like what?"

"You're awfully bold, now that I'm not your boss anymore, aren't you?" Jackie picked up some loose paper clips on her desk and noisily opened the drawer to deposit them inside, hoping to avoid more conversation. She wasn't sure she was ready to tell anyone what she was thinking. As much as she liked and trusted Mike, he seemed an unlikely confidante. But here he was, the only person who was sorry to see her leaving, patiently waiting for her to say what was on her mind.

"Remember my sister Mindy? She once asked me how someone with no children could judge other people when I had no concept of the pressures these families face trying to keep everything from imploding. I thought I could, that it was a matter of enforcing the law and being tough and imposing order. But I was wrong. It's so much more complicated than that. I wasn't the right person for this job."

"I don't think that's true. You were doing fine. I'm not a parent either, and I think I have a good sense of what people are going through after all this time working here. You were getting your feet wet." Mike got up and walked over to the window. "Speaking of wet, it's pouring," he said.

Jackie had the sense that Mike was a little embarrassed, maybe felt that he might have said too much. But his kindness opened her up.

"It's not just my feeling about the job that's changed. I realized I want something different now, something in addition to a career. I want a family."

Mike turned away from the window and pulled the guest chair over to Jackie's side of the desk.

"If that's what you want, that's what you'll have. You'll be a great mom. And I envy the person who gets to share life with you. Are you serious with someone?"

"I have a list of potential biodads."

Mike opened his mouth, but no sound came out.

"Ha! You're speechless. That's a first."

"What do you mean, you have a list?" Mike sounded wounded and Jackie immediately regretted making light of the situation. It was so hard to talk about.

"I'm 40 years old. If I'm going to have a baby, I have to get started as soon as possible. I'm willing to go it alone. I'm considering working with a clinic to have a baby through artificial insemination. I'm narrowing down a list from the potential sperm donors."

Mike sat back in the chair, as if Jackie's confession had physically pushed him away. "Don't say that, Jackie."

Jackie knew that Mike meant well, but she felt a little ping of frustration sounding at the back of her throat.

"It's okay. I don't expect you to understand. I don't know why I'm even telling you this. You caught me off guard." Jackie leapt up from her chair and took her black robe off the hanger, folding it carefully before sticking it in with the Keurig, although she couldn't fathom what she'd do with it. She moved as far away from Mike as she could get in the small room and turned her back to him.

"Who's on the list?" he asked.

"I'm not sure we should talk about this."

"I'm sorry, Jackie. I was just surprised. Please. I'm listening."

Jackie thought back on her conversation with Dr. Perlmutter. She'd need the support of people she trusted, and she trusted Mike.

"I don't know the actual men. It's anonymous. But I can choose things like height, for example. I only picked tall men because I'm so short—that way the kid stands a chance of being somewhere in the middle. You can also select for 'profession'—they call it 'doctorate.' It doesn't mean that the guy has a PhD, necessarily, but he's a professional with hopefully a certain level of intelligence."

"I knew a hell of a lot of brilliant cops when I was on the force. Could run circles around these lawyers and judges. Anyway, you can't control for the things that really matter, right? Loyalty, kindness, sense of humor."

"No, I guess not." Jackie felt like Mike had burst her bubble and she didn't know whether to be grateful or deflated.

"I don't want to see you give up on love, Jackie. You're too special for that."

"I'm not giving up on anything."

Mike walked silently to where Jackie stood and put his hand lightly on the small of her back.

"I would be honored if you would put me on your list to be a potential donor."

"Oh, Mike. That's so sweet but—"

"I'm completely serious. I'm way taller than you. But there's a condition."

"What's that?"

"Don't rule out that you might also find love."

One Year Later

Lou

"It's too hot for the boats! Let's go see the polar bears in the zoo instead," Tara said.

"No way. There's a breeze on the water. It's fine." Lou pulled Tara along. Bryn hung back a few steps.

Lou spoke to the guy in charge and soon had a row boat at the dock.

"Let's go, ladies. The clock is running."

"You two lovebirds go without me. You make me want to puke." Bryn sounded disgusted, but she was smiling. "I'll sit here. I brought a book."

"Okay, but don't move," Tara said.

Lou rowed Tara out to the middle of the lake. They sat in silence for a bit, enjoying the stillness. There weren't a lot of people crazy enough to be out there in the heat, but Lou felt the time was right.

He went down on one knee in the center of the boat, causing it to rock precariously.

"What are you doing? I don't want to end up in the water. I just had my nails done."

"Shh. Give me a chance here." Lou pulled out a ring from his jacket pocket. "Let's make this official, again," he said.

"Oh, Lou!" Tara took the ring and held it in her hand. "Hey, this is my old ring from the first time around."

"I know. I found it buried in your dresser drawer. You liked it then, I figured you'd like it now."

"You're such a romantic." Tara kissed him and then slipped the ring on her finger.

As they rowed back to the shore, Tara pointed with her chin to two people walking on the path near the pond. "Isn't that Bryn's judge?"

The woman was obviously pregnant, maybe six months. The man was tall and burly in a dark leather bomber jacket. They walked close together, not touching, engaged in conversation. The man, who looked vaguely familiar, said something that made the woman laugh.

"Nah, I don't think so."

As the two got closer to the lake, Lou almost called out, "Don't bother, buddy, she doesn't do boats," but he knew Jackie could take care of herself.

They returned the rental and sat down on the grass with Bryn.

They told her the news.

Another Year Later

Jackie

Jackie sat on the dais and shifted around, pulling her dress a little further down over her legs. Eight months after having Amanda and her pre-maternity clothes were still a little tight. She'd thought about buying a new outfit for today but it didn't seem worth the expense. Jackie smiled when she recalled the conversation with Dr. Perlmutter about her finances. She'd had absolutely no clue how much it cost to have a baby. They came with so much paraphernalia.

The banner overhead declared in gigantic purple letters:

"NYU LAW WOMEN—HAVING IT ALL"

Jackie had nearly declined the invitation to be the junior faculty speaker for the luncheon.

"Maybe if the theme were 'Been Through it All' or 'Seen it All,'" she'd said to Mindy. "Who am I to talk about having it all?"

Yet here she was and it was her turn to speak. Jackie took her place at the podium. The room was filled with students, faculty, alumnae. Several hundred accomplished, strong, confident women, seated at round tables enjoying their first course and each other's company. She was proud to be among them, just as she had been when she was a law student nearly 20 years earlier. And right in front, at the table of honor, were the three most important women in Jackie's life. Her mother, Mindy, and next to Mindy, reclining in her stroller, Amanda. Jackie mouthed "I love you," to the baby, who yawned in response. Then she took a last sip of her water and began to speak.

"I have to admit that when NYU Law Women first approached me about speaking at a program about Having It All as a woman and as an attorney in this moment in history, I was reluctant. As you heard in that generous introduction, I've been fortunate to have practiced law in the private sector in support of the previous Mayor of New York City, and in the public sector as a Family Court Judge before turning to academia. As you also know, I've been blessed with a daughter, Amanda, who has the best seat in the house and is sleeping through my remarks."

There was a general chuckle from the audience and a number of women shifted in their seats to get a glimpse of the baby.

"Is that what having it all means in this context? Juggling, more or less successfully, professional and personal life? Does it mean making as much money as your male counterparts? Does it mean having the most prestigious title? Is it a requirement of having it all that you find love? Have children? Is the idea of having it all real, or another hoop to jump through that women have imposed on themselves and that we will judge ourselves harshly for if we fail?"

Jackie took a few steps out from behind the podium to feel closer to the audience. They watched her so expectantly. She hoped that what she had to say, what she felt she'd learned, would resonate with them.

"I want to share three thoughts with you about having it all that I hope you'll consider as you go forward, whether you're a law student starting out or an established attorney, a young woman or a woman in her prime.

"The first is that having it all is a purely subjective notion. There's no magical combination of personal and professional accomplishments that fits every woman. Having it all is as unique as each of you sitting here. And the corollary to this first observation is that measuring yourself up against someone else's 'all' isn't only a meaningless comparison. It's destructive.

"The second thing I've learned is that having it all is a lifetime endeavor. At one point you may have a job where you earn real money, and at another point you may commit yourself to serving those less fortunate and struggle to make your own rent. At one time you may be in a serious relationship, and at another point you may choose to travel the world with only yourself to answer to. The key is to view all of these aspects of yourself as the pieces of the mosaic that make up your life. You can and do have it all, just not at one moment in time.

"The last thing I'd ask you to think about is this. What does it mean to have it all? I think what it means is to be grateful for what you have. Each and every woman in this room has it all already. With gratitude as the foundation, we can move forward to define the goals we hope to achieve over our lifetimes."

Jackie returned to her table with the sound of applause ringing in her ears. Only when she sat down and her heart stopped racing did she realize that Amanda was no longer sleeping in her stroller, but was cooing softly in her father's arms.

"Hey, how did you sneak in here? This is a women's only lunch!" She smiled at Mike and reached for Amanda, her warm weight so solid in her arms.

"The uniform and the gun helped. I told them I was your private security detail."

Jackie leaned over toward Mike, Amanda snuggly between them, and spoke softly in his ear.

BOTH ARE TRUE

BOOK DISCUSSION GUIDE

1. When the novel opens, Jackie is both anxious and over-confident about her new role as a Family Court judge. How do we see these conflicting emotions play out in her interaction with Lou, and her encounters with Ms. Clark on the subway and in the courtroom? How would you describe Jackie's character at the beginning of the story?

2. Jackie's New York is very different from Lou's. Although she appreciates the vibrancy of the city, she's often overwhelmed by the sheer mass of humanity on the streets, in the subway, and in her courtroom. Lou is the exact opposite, reveling in every experience. What do their differing reactions say about their personalities, and are they predictive of what goes wrong in their relationship?

3. Was the description of Family Court, including the range of cases, the interactions among court personnel, and the intensity of emotions, what you would have expected? Does it differ from other types of court experiences with which you're familiar?

4. Is Lou genuinely a sensitive guy at heart, or is his writing persona and his column just an act? Did his stay at home role during his marriage, where he was the caretaking parent to Bryn, help form him? Or is he a freeloader, living off two strong women, Tara and Jackie? How does his character develop over the course of the story?

5. Jackie's sister Mindy is her best friend. How are the two women similar and how are they different? Is Jackie able to hear Mindy's advice about the need to change? Is it really possible to change one's basic personality for the sake of love, and is that too much to ask?

6. Jackie struggles to balance her desire to control the families that come before her with her growing sense of compassion for them. Is she successful? How would you rate her interaction with Ms. Clark when she shows up at Jackie's home? Or Moshe and his family in the arson sentencing and later at the juvenile facility? What goes wrong in the Chang domestic violence case and what does Jackie learn from that experience?

7. Why did Tara let Lou back into her home when he arrived on her doorstep? And why did she allow a brief stint crashing on the couch turn into an extended stay? What would you have done in this situation? How would you explain Bryn's trajectory after Lou left? Is her behavior directly attributable to the divorce or are there other factors at play?

8. What is Jackie's view on motherhood? Does she want what Mindy has, or is she striving for something else? What makes her so angry when she sees the teen with the fake baby on the subway? And how did you feel about her desire to have a child at the end of the novel?

9. What was Lou's experience with his friends after he and Tara divorced? Is it typical for couples to divide up their friends? Why was Lou left with no one? Did his attempt to reconnect with Harrison make things better or worse? Did Lou's column compensate for his lack of human connection? Do men and

women, in your experience, have a different need for intimate friendship?

10. When Bryn ends up in her courtroom, Jackie knows that the only ethically and legally permissible course is to recuse herself from the case. Can her decision to stay on the case be justified as a way to help Bryn outside the strict legal framework? Or does she let her longing for Lou hold sway over everything else? Does Jackie get off too easy in the end?

11. Jackie's handling of Bryn's case, especially her stretching of the law, was clearly improper. Some judges are corrupt and take bribes to influence their decisions; do you think there are instances where judges act out of compassion or other not strictly legal concerns short of outright illegality? When considering Jackie's actions, does it matter to you that Paloma, the other girl at the bowling alley, was not hurt in the incident?

12. Was Jackie's attempt to seduce Lou an act of desperation? of love? Was her offer to help Bryn a quid pro quo or a genuine expression of her desire to help the child? Were you surprised at Lou's reaction?

13. Both Jackie and Lou find love by the end of the novel. Did you think they would end up together? Were you satisfied as a reader by the paths their lives took? What did they learn from their own romance that allowed Jackie to let Mike into her life, and Lou to rekindle his relationship with Tara? How important were the children, Amanda and Bryn, in the equation?